Toe Tags & TNT

Rolland Love

Copyright © 2001 Rolland Love

All Rights Reserved

ISBN 0-941520-03-X

Published 2003

Published by Dog Days Publishing Company in 2002
P.O. Box 2138 Shawnee Mission, Kansas 66201.
©2001 Rolland Love. All rights reserved.
No part of this publication may be reproduced, stored
in a retrieval system, or transmitted in any form or by any
means, electronic, mechanical, recording or otherwise,
without the prior written permission of the author.

Manufactured in the United States of America.

The characters and events in this book are fictitious. Any
similarity to real persons, living or dead, is coincidental
and not intended by the author.

Cover illustration.: T. L. Palmer
Cover art used with permission,
All Rights Reserved.
Dog Days Publishing Company ™
Shawnee Mission, Kansas USA
www.ozarkauction.net

Chapter One

Randall pulled our motor home off the main highway and stopped in front of a run-down building with a hand-painted sign that read, Best Food Any Where Restaurant. Eat All You Can.

"What do you think about this place?" Randall asked. I leaned forward to get a better view.

"No," I said, when I saw the peeling gray paint and a swarm of flies buzzing around the screen door. "I'm not hungry. You go ahead an eat."

Randall sat back in the seat and drummed on the steering wheel with the tips of his fingers, an irritating habit he had gotten into when things did not go his way.

"Nothing else until Kingman," he said sharply. "That's sixty miles down the road, you know."

Randall's criteria when it came time to choose a place to eat was simple: Is food being served, and if so, is it plentiful and cheap? Cleanliness, taste, and the possibility of food poisoning were not a concern.

It was hard to believe a guy who was such a jock in high school could get so badly out of condition. At college he joined a fraternity where the primary goal was to drink beer and play cards—by graduation day he had gained a hundred pounds.

"Tell you what," I said, as I looked at a gut the size of a basketball hanging over the top of his faded Levis, "You go on in and eat. Breakfast is not a big deal to me."

"Are you sure?" Randall looked at me with vacant, unfocused eyes. He had played blackjack until dawn this morning at a Las Vegas casino.

"Go on ahead. I need to lie down for a while. My back hurts. I need a rest."

Randall gave me a crooked little smile. "Okay, Mark, I certainly will."

Six weeks on the road together had taken its toll on our friendship. That was to bad because we had been friends since we were five. I even wished I had not picked him to be the best man at my upcoming wedding.

Randall parked the big rig by a lone pine tree. It was the only vegetation in the sand-covered parking lot. I rolled down the window to get some fresh air. As he opened the door to step outside, someone inside the building screamed. An old man wearing jeans, a faded red shirt and a blue baseball cap stumbled out the front door. He was muttering something to himself as he shuffled along beside the building until he reached the corner and disappeared from our view.

"He looks familiar," Randall said, "like someone I saw on that most wanted criminals TV show."

Seconds later the front door banged open and a tall, thin cowboy wearing a black, wide-brimmed hat ran outside. "I'll get even!" he shouted back over his shoulder as he stomped away toward a rusted old pickup truck with an empty horse trailer in tow. "Nobody pulls crap like that on the Duke."

For some stupid reason, Randall burst out laughing. That stopped the raging cowboy cold. The bowlegged creature cocked his head to one side and looked at us in disbelief.

"Makin' fun are ya', Mister?" the cowboy yelled, as he pulled a knife from a sheath on his belt. "We'll have some real fun now."

I could not believe what was happening. The cowboys I had known in the past were as friendly as could be. Randall did it again, only this time he set us up to get killed.

"Tell him you're sorry!" I screamed at Randall. "Do it now, damn it. Do it now."

"I'm sorry!" Randall yelled, his voice quivering as he fumbled with the ignition key and dropped it on the floorboard. We grabbed for it at the same time. I smashed my mouth into the back of his head. My eyes filled with tears and I tasted blood.

"What now?" Randall gasped, rubbing the back of his head. "What are we going to do?"

The cowboy hunkered down like a scared rabbit when the restaurant door banged against the side of the building and a third man, with a shotgun cradled under his arm, lumbered out into the parking lot. "Where are you, Duke?" he bellowed, as he squinted his eyes against the glare of the early morning sun.

It was easy to see why anyone might be afraid of the giant standing less than a hundred yards away from our motor home. He was easily seven feet tall, broad in the shoulders and his stomach was huge. A thick, red beard hung to the top of his silky, black pajama bottoms. His chest was bare and what we could see of it was covered with tattoos.

"My God, what is it?" I asked, leaning across Randall's chest for a better look.

"Steroids gone wild," Randall said solemnly. "Probably another government experiment got screwed up."

He could be right, I thought as I stared at arms the size of telephone poles and remembered some of the tales about research projects that had gone wrong. I shivered, picked up the key from the floorboard and jammed it into the ignition.

"Let's get out of here, fast. Come on, let's go."

"Yeah, right," Randall moaned. "We're driving a thirty-five-foot motor home powered by a steam engine, remember? Just stay low. Maybe they'll kill each other."

The big guy pumped a shell into the chamber of the shotgun when he spotted his quivering prey. "I'm blowin' your head off, Duke! I told you not to ever come back."

A puff of dust boiled out from under the big guy's feet each time he took a lumbering step forward.

"I'll never do it again," Duke said, as he walked backwards until he reached the truck. "Please don't shoot," he begged, as he climbed inside.

I leaned into the seat and grunted when a pain that felt as if someone hit me in the back with a hammer shot up my spine. Adrenaline caused my heart to pound.

In addition to my fear that I might not live long enough to leave the parking lot, I worried about my fiancée, Ann, and how terrible it would be for her when she found out I got myself crippled-up again. What if I needed to be rolled down the aisle on a stretcher? Would I have the strength to perform on our wedding night?

"That skinny cowboy might make it." Randall loosened his grip on the steering wheel. "Oh no," he groaned, "is the giant gonna shoot?"

I leaned forward just in time to see the big guy shoulder the shotgun and pull the trigger. Boom! The shot wad exploded the back window in the pickup truck and filled the air with a shower of sparkling glass.

Duke lucked out. The main force of the pellets hit the passenger side and seemed to miss him completely.

"Look at the feisty little bastard go," Randall said, as we watched the truck peel out onto the pavement with the trailer swaying from side to side. He headed down Highway 93 lickety-split.

Leaning out the window, his shaggy, blond hair whipping in the wind, Duke shook a fist and yelled, "I'll get even you pug faced prick! Nobody alive cheats me!"

Randall tried to hide his 260-pound, five-foot-ten-inch frame from the big guy's view by slumping down in the seat. He looked at me wide-eyed. "God help us. I hope we're not next."

The big guy watched the beat-up old Chevy pickup truck until it faded away into the shimmering heat waves that danced up off the road. He pumped his shotgun and an empty red hull fell onto the ground as he stomped back toward the restaurant. He didn't so much as glance in our direction before he disappeared through the open door.

"My Lordy. We must have become invisible."

"Come on, let's go." I clasped my quivering hands together to stop them from shaking. "What was that noise?"

It sounded as if the back door of the motor home was slammed shut.

I looked at Randall and we listened carefully. Silence. Randall started up the engine and recklessly pulled out onto the highway. The big rig swayed back and forth as we left the parking lot headed for Kingman, Arizona, in a cloud of dust.

Surely we've paid all our dues, I thought, as I took a deep breath and sighed, so thankful to be out of the potentially fatal situation. Little did I know what we just witnessed in the parking lot was only a small taste of what was yet to come.

"Spooky characters." Randall wiped the sweat from his forehead with the back of his hand. The high-backed, red leather captain's seat squeaked loudly when he settled into the command post from which he would drive us home.

"Pretty bad boys all right." I looked into the side mirror and frowned when I saw Randall was dragging along the pine tree. In his reckless haste to leave the parking lot, he ran over the scruffy little thing and jerked it out of the ground. It was caught under the rear of the motor home and looked like a plume of green exhaust. I thought about all the pine trees I had planted as a kid when I was a Boy Scout. The dark green branches bounced up and down on the asphalt pavement.

"How much longer to Kansas City?" I asked, figuring nothing short of an explosion and a fire would get me outside the motor home again until Randall dropped me off at my fiancée Ann's front door.

Randall looked at his watch and considered my question for a good long while before coming up with an estimated time.

"Twenty hours, more or less, if I can stay awake." Randall chuckled. "Yeah. With the new faster speed limit, we should hit KC around ten o'clock tomorrow night. There's plenty of time for you to get ready for the big wedding next Saturday."

"That's not funny," I said, remembering the time he really did fall asleep at the wheel and totaled my car.

Randall raised his voice. "I know you're thinking about the one lousy wreck. Does that mean I'm branded for life?" After a long silence, in a much more civilized tone, he said, "Don't worry. I'll pull over if I get sleepy."

"I still can't believe the size of that big guy," I said, changing the subject. "He could have wiped us out with one swipe of a meaty hand."

"What I can't believe is the size of this lump." Randall rubbed the back of his head. "How's your mouth?"

"My mouth is okay. But my back is starting to bother me some. I think the painkiller is about to wear off."

Randall rattled the pill bottle in his shirt pocket and gave me a wicked smile. "I've got your Percodan right here. Do you want one now?"

"I will before I lay down," I said, thinking it seemed as if everything he had done for the past week caused me misery and pain.

"You must not be in too bad of shape then." He sounded as if he thought I was just looking for sympathy.

"Give me a break, man!"

Randall had put the metal tool chest by the side door of the motor home with the handle sticking straight up. I caught my foot on the handle and hurt my back as I fell. "It hurts like hell." I watched the badly crippled pine tree break loose from under the wheel well and come to rest on the shoulder of the lonesome desert road. "I actually passed out, you know." I looked out the window and wished once again I were home with Ann so she could take care of me.

"Yeah, I know. I was there, remember? You lucked out with us only five minutes from the hospital. You'll be okay. Take a pill if it hurts. That's what drugs are for."

"It could have been a lot worse, I guess."

"Probably will be, if you don't take care of yourself. Remember what the ER doc said when he gave you a shot of Demerol? Stay flat on your back until you get to Kansas City."

"I'm headed for bed right now. I'm out of your life." I grabbed the back of the seat and eased myself up slowly to avoid more pain.

"You're doing the right thing, my friend. If you take care of yourself, I may not have to roll you down the aisle in a wheelchair come next Saturday."

Randall clicked on the radio and began to bang on the steering wheel with the flat of his hand when the beat of a Doors song poured from the speakers, and Jim Morrison wailed, "come on baby, take a chance on love."

Bad luck continued to hover over me every step of the way. As I started for the back bedroom, I caught my toe on the corner of a throw rug and fell down. I landed on a mop bucket Randall should have emptied and put away after he cleaned the floor. As I lay on the carpet with soapy water soaking the front of my T-shirt, I thought about asking Randall to take me to the station when we got to Kingman so I could catch a train to Kansas City.

"What happened? Do you need any help?"

"I need the Percodan." I grabbed the handle on the bathroom door, pulled myself to my feet and started back toward the front.

Randall scolded me. "You're determined to hurt yourself, aren't you, Mark? Here, take one of these and go to bed."

"You won't need those, you little peckerhead!" a gravelly-voiced old man yelled, jerking the bottle from my hand. I stared in disbelief. It was the same stoop-shouldered character that ran out of the restaurant and disappeared behind the building.

"My God!" I shouted, as I slapped my chest.

"What the hell!" Randall yelled. He jerked the steering wheel to one side and pulled off onto the shoulder of the road.

"Sit down, you little rat," the old man said and shoved me back into the seat. I whimpered when he placed the barrel of a revolver beside my head. Smoke from a cigarette, which dangled from his ashen gray lips, curled up into deep-set, dark eyes that looked as cold as steel.

"Please don't shoot me, sir," I begged. "I'm getting married next Saturday."

When he looked at me and smiled, I thought I might have stirred up some emotion that would cause him to cut me a little slack.

The old man winked, exhaled a puff of smoke through his nose and said, "hells bells, son, I'm not doing anything special Saturday. I can be your Best Man." Laughing at himself, he managed to stir up a coughing fit, which caused spittle to run from the corner of his mouth onto his bearded chin. "With your bad back and all, you may need some help on the honeymoon too."

In a feeble attempt to come up with an answer that would keep him from being my Best Man, and having been caught completely off-guard, I stuttered around until Randall finally jumped in and tried to save me. "Get over it, Mark." He looked over his shoulder at the old geezer, then back at me. "You know your fiancée called off the wedding. Poor Mark took it really hard. I'm afraid he may need professional counseling."

"I'll be all right," I said humbly, trying to support Randall's feeble attempt to put on a good show. "Ann and I...we had been together for so long. I just don't know what to do."

It was easy to see why Randall thought the old man might be a wanted criminal. In addition to having a bloody gash over his right eye, he was wearing tattered clothing and had matted, gray hair that looked as if it belonged on a goat. He had a shifty look and carried a large caliber revolver with a hole in the end of the barrel the size of a dime.

There was a long silence before the old man said anything. When he finally spoke, he made it clear trying to fool him ever again was not a healthy idea.

"Called off the wedding, did she?" He grabbed Randall by the arm and stuck the raised front sight of the barrel up inside one nostril. He and the barrel of the revolver lifted Randall off the seat with ease. After he had Randall's neck stretched out like a snail's, the old man leaned over close to his ear and growled, "Bullcrap, Randy Boy." After a short silence he calmly said, "You try to fool me again you'll be on ice, like a dead player dropped out of the game."

"I'm sorry," Randall blubbered, as he jerked his head to one side, freeing himself from the business end of the weapon. "Please sir, I'll never try it again."

"Hey," the old man muttered, "I've been fooled enough for one lifetime. Turn the damn radio off too. I can't half think with rock-n-roll blastin'."

"I'm sorry it bothered you," I said, as I clicked off the power switch.

"What's up ahead?" he asked, as he pointed at a deserted rest stop.

"It's a place to stop and rest," I said. "Go take a leak. Get a drink of water or whatever."

"I know that already. I mean the blue box. That's a telephone, right?"

"Looks like it. Why, do you need to make a call?"

"No I don't," the old man said with a smile, "but you do. You're going to call Ann. Pull this big machine into the parking lot, Randall. Me and Mark have got some sweet stuff to say."

"Oh please, sir," I begged, as my stomach tightened, "she's worried enough about the wedding. I don't want to upset her even more."

"So the wedding's still on," the old man said with a smirk, playing mind games with me.

"It's still on all right. Please don't make me call her. I'll do whatever you say."

When Randall drove the motor home beside the pay phone, the old man leaned forward and looked deep into my eyes. "I nearly got married once myself. I was standing on the top of a mountain when I fell in love. I might tell you about it sometime, if you live long enough."

"Thank you, sir," I said in anticipation of him aborting the plan to have me make the phone call.

"I'll let it go this time. You boys ever cross me again, you're buzzard meat."

"Is it okay to go on now?" Randall asked. He pulled back out onto the highway when the old man gave him a nod.

Once we were headed toward Kingman again, the old man seemed to slip away into a trance. It was as if a switch had been turned off inside his head to stop the insanity of his mind from further ravaging his soul.

He leaned back in the yellow director's chair he had dragged in from the combination living room and kitchen area. He strategically placed it just far enough behind the high-backed, red leather front seats to be outside of our peripheral view. For the next thirty minutes, the three of us sat like mummies and stared down the road through a bluish-gray haze of cigarette smoke that burned my eyes.

As I looked out across sand-covered wasteland, dotted with cactus and scrub brush, I thought about Ann. I saw her face as if she were sitting before me. I remembered how I used to run my fingers through her thick reddish brown hair. I wanted to kiss the lips that had given me so many smiles, hold her in my arms and tell her everything would be all right.

I looked at the old man out the corner of my eye and decided what I must do—even though it would be like something out of a bad dream. Even if it meant I must become a killer, I was determined to get free.

Chapter Two

A loud thud, which sounded as if someone had smacked the side of the big rig with a baseball bat, startled me. The old man jerked his head around and looked out the side window. The wind had blown a tumbleweed into the side of the motor home.

"Know what scares me more than anything?" the old man said, as he lit up another Camel and scratched his head.

"No," I said with some reservation. "What?"

"It's the way I used to be," the old man said with a smile. "I was bad dangerous back in the old days. Sometimes I even got scared of myself."

"Are you still that way?" Randall asked. "Dangerous?"

"No. No, I'm not," the old man said solemnly. He leaned back in the director's chair and looked out the window. "Now that I know I'm about to die, I'm not scared of anything. You know what I mean?"

"You're about to die?" Randall said, giving me a grim look.

"Yeah," the old man said soberly. "Probably be dead and gone in two or three months."

"What's wrong?" I asked.

He coughed. "Got me some breathing troubles. But don't you get depressed over it though. I mean, what the hell, people can only live so long."

"Why did you used to be so dangerous you even scared yourself?" Randall asked.

Much to my dismay, the old man smiled. "'Cause I liked to blow things up. I blew tons of stuff up during the war. That was my job when I was a Marine. I saved lots of lives during the biggest battle of all—even got me a medal."

"Oh, that's great," I said to myself, thinking how dangerous he could be if he got hold of some explosives. I looked out the window and watched a coyote zigzag through the scrub brush until it jumped down into a ravine and disappeared. I started to ask the old man which big war he was talking about, then decided not to chance getting him any more stirred up.

Hoping to direct him away from any further talk about blowing things up, I asked the old man what he did after he got out of the service. My diversionary tactic didn't work. He was too far-gone, recalling the good old blasting-things-apart days, to pay me any mind.

"I know more about explosives than even the DuPonts. They made a nice living off gunpowder, you know." The old man sounded a little too cocky about such a serious subject to suit me. "Look at this, if you don't believe me." He pulled up his pant leg to demonstrate. There were two sticks of dynamite stuffed down inside his black leather boot.

The old man pointed at a red wire attached to the top of an oily, brown bundle that ran up the inside of his pant leg. After giving me a squint-eyed smile that curled up the corners of his lips, he opened his shirt and showed us a detonator taped down over his belly button. "Anybody messes with me—I push the button."

"Oh my God," Randall moaned when he looked over and saw the device that could easily turn us into dog meat before we could blink an eye.

"No problem," I said. "We'll do whatever you say." I thought this situation looked very dangerous since all he had to do was accidentally bump into something and boom!

"That's good. Talk about a dog-lickin' mess! If I push this button, that's all she wrote. Like I said earlier, I don't give a hoot for damn. I'm a goner anyway."

How in the world could such a terrible thing be happening to me? I swallowed a couple of times to dislodge the lump in my throat. Just when I was on the verge of becoming a happily married man, too.

"We won't cause any trouble. Will we, Randall?" I was thinking about how well off we were when we thought the only thing we had to contend with was a deranged old man with a revolver.

"No sir," Randall said, "we sure won't. I can promise you that."

"You push me, I'll do it in an instant," the old man said, leaning forward as he looked at Randall, then quickly turning his head and glaring at me.

"Please, Mister," I begged. "We won't do anything to mess with you. Okay?"

"Mister!" the old man shouted. "Don't ever call me 'Mister'! Name's Harley. Just like the motorcycle. Mister! That's what I had to call them sons-a-bitchin' guards. Can I do this, Mister Roberts? Can I do that? I wish one of them were here right now. I'd poke this barrel where the sun don't shine. We'd see who called who 'Mister'."

Harley had gotten himself so upset his hands were shaking. He muttered to himself about how he hated the guards, and he called the warden a politically appointed retard. He lit another Camel, took a long drag of the cigarette and let the smoke drift slowly out through his nose. Sounding cranky and running right along the edge, he said, "Do we understand each other now, boys?"

"We sure do," Randall was quick to say. "We'll never call you anything but Harley again, will we, Mark?" Randall tried to ease the tension by introducing us. "My name is Randall and this is my friend Mark."

I did not know what set him off. It seemed as if we had reached an understanding about coexisting peacefully. Before I could answer, out of the clear blue, the sadistic bastard pulled back the hammer on the revolver and squeezed the trigger. Boom! For a second, I thought he had detonated the dynamite. Pieces of headliner drifted down all around us, the cab filled with dust, and the smell of gunpowder permeated the air.

Randall slammed on the brakes and pulled onto the shoulder of the road, coughing violently. We rolled down the windows and gasped for air. My heart was beating so hard I could feel it pounding in the back of my throat. I looked down when I felt something warm and saw a dark blue spot on the front of my jeans.

Poking the barrel of the revolver into my ribs, Harley leaned across my chest and sucked in a deep breath of fresh air. "Didn't mean to scare you, boys. Just wanted to make sure my weapon worked." He stuck the end of the barrel under his nose and took a big whiff. "Lordy, there's nothin' much better than the sweet smell of gunpowder. You know what I mean, Mark?"

"Why did you do that, Harley?" I asked.

He chuckled. "Didn't think you boys was takin' me serious."

"We sure the hell are now," Randall said, as he coughed again and cleared his throat.

"That's fine then. My mistake. By the way, I don't want to hear no cussin'. I heard enough ugly words while I was in the joint to last me a lifetime. I mean it, boys. I won't put up with one lick of foul language. I for sure don't want the F word used. Bad words plant bad seeds, and you know what can happen when those kind of things start to grow."

"Okay," I said, not having any idea what kind of things starting to grow he was talking about and not wanting to ask. "We don't like cussin' either, do we, Randall?"

"No, we don't," Randall, said. "There was never any cussin' took place in my house. Especially the F word, that's for darn sure. Or the MF word either for that matter."

"Mine neither," I said, glad we were getting on the good side of Harley with something. "It doesn't take any talent to cuss," I added for good measure.

Harley cocked his head back and glared at me as if I had done something wrong.

"What is it? Did I say something I shouldn't have or something?"

"No, not really. But all this kind of talk does bring one very important thing to mind."

"What's that?" I asked, wishing I did not have to know.

"It has to do with murder. I don't really want to kill you boys unless you force me. But hey, like I said, I've got nothing left to lose."

After gently patting both of us on the shoulder, Harley leaned back in the director's chair. "You know why I don't want to kill you? 'Cause murder can be such a bloody mess."

"We won't force you to do anything," I said. "Whatever you want, that's what we'll do."

"That's good. 'Cause I'll just blast you boys and drive this big eighteen-wheeler away all by myself."

"Have you driven a rig like this before?" I asked, wondering how anyone could confuse our motor home with an over-the-road eighteen-wheeler truck.

Harley scratched his head and seemed to be giving my question a lot of serious thought. "No. No, I haven't. I drove a tractor once, when I was a kid about twelve. How much difference can there be?"

"Did your dad own a farm?"

"A farm? Hell no! He never owned nothin' in his whole life. The tractor was at a construction site. The workers had gone home for the day. Dad just started the damn thing up and turned me loose."

"What happened after you turned it over?"

"You mean after the accident an' it caught fire? We ran like hell and jumped in the truck. Dad was drunk as usual. Drove right through somebody's yard as we escaped. Wiped out an entire bed of roses. Yeah, the old man was a real doozy. He went out for cigarettes a week later and never came back."

"You never saw him again?" Randall said. "That's too bad."

When Harley lowered his head and looked up at me through hooded white brows with tears in his eyes, I almost felt sorry for him for a second. Then I looked down at the revolver and wondered how I could possibly think about such a thing as sympathy.

"Yeah, well, my old man was just one of a bunch of ugly things happened when I was a kid. He toughened me up for stuff a whole lot worse to come, I guess."

Harley went on to tell us about an older brother named Lewis, who not only beat him up on a regular basis when they were young, but also framed Harley for the murder of his business partner. To add insult to injury, after Harley was given a life sentence, his brother and Harley's wife, who was also named Ann, of all things, ran off to Mexico together.

"I'm really sorry," I said, as I pulled a road map out of the pocket on the back of my seat and fanned my face. "Nothing that cruel should ever happen to anybody."

"You got that right. Some people are just born to suffer hell on earth, I guess. Does the smoke bother you?" Harley sounded as if he were actually concerned about my well-being.

"I suffer from allergies. Dust and smoke sometimes cause me to have a bronchospasm."

Harley laid his hand on my shoulder and patted me gently. "You'll have to get used to it, son. I'm hooked on tobacco and I ain't never been able to kick the habit. Hell, that evil weed kills a lot more innocent people than illegal drugs they lock people up for havin'. Don't you wonder how them tobacco companies got by sellin' that killer for all these years?"

"You got that right," I said. "All I can say is politics and money are powerful."

"The tobacco company bastards are the ones that need to get locked up. Throw away the key." Harley coughed, pointed out the side window and shook his head. "You wouldn't know it by the looks of all that open space, but the world gets more crowded every day. Like my buddy Rodney King said, we've all got to try to an get along."

Randall looked at me and smiled with his teeth clamped together. He jerked his head slightly and rolled his eyes toward the back of the big rig. I knew he was trying to tell me something, but for the life of me I could not figure out what it was.

"Your buddy, huh?" Randall sounded a little too crusty for comfort.

The last thing in the world I wanted to do was have Harley get upset again. It did not take much to set him off, and it was a no-win situation.

"You must be some kind of celebrity if you know Rodney King," Randall said, barely able to keep from laughing.

"That's right, Mr. Randall. I sure the hell am a celebrity. Rodney and me, that black guy them cops beat up, you know who the hell I mean?"

"Yeah, I know. Language."

"What?"

"You said we weren't supposed to cuss so I said, language."

"That's right, you're not. I say what the hell I want."

Harley glared, Randall shrugged his shoulders and I swallowed deeply to clear my throat as Harley continued. "Me and Rodney were locked up in the same cell together for three days and nights. We got to know each other pretty damn well, Mr. Randall. Pretty damn well."

Harley leaned back in his chair, laid the revolver in his lap and began to sway from side to side while he hummed "Amazing Grace". Humming and wheezing, high and low, he sounded like an old-fashioned squeeze box.

Leaning forward, Harley put his mouth up close to my ear. "You ever see the movie Deliverance? The part where the redneck bent the fat guy over a log?"

"Yes, I saw it," I said, feeling like a bird that had just been swallowed by a cat when Harley laid his hand on my leg.

"He squealed like a pig, remember?" When I didn't say anything, he moved his hand up my thigh a couple of inches and smiled.

My God! Is there no end to this insanity? If he was serious about trying to rape me, and it seemed as if that might be the case, I had to try to kill him first. I thought about the .22-caliber pistol in my suitcase. I remembered we had used up all the shells shooting rats at the Las Vegas dump a couple of days before. I figured a .22-caliber bullet probably would not stop him anyway.

I looked back over my shoulder. The butcher knife was beside the toaster. I could use it to slit his throat. I remembered the demonstration I had seen of how to cut through a jugular vein when I watched a recap of the O.J. Simpson trial. My concern was he might still have enough strength left to get off a shot or detonate the TNT. If only my back was not hurt and I could move faster, I would do it.

"Why did you bring that up about Deliverance?" I asked, as I slid my shaking hands under my thighs.

"Don't play stupid, Mark. You're a nice-looking boy. So why the hell not?"

I felt sick to my stomach when the degenerate old bastard kissed me on the cheek. I rubbed his spittle away with my shoulder and groaned. When I raised my elbow, I thought about slamming it into his throat. I really might have done it, too, except he leaned back in the chair before I could make up my mind. Now he was too far away for me to get the full effect of a hard blow. I could see me screwing it up and Harley getting off a shot at point-blank range, blowing my brains all over the windshield. The only good part would be if Harley made Randall clean it up as punishment for leaving the back door of the motor home unlocked.

I started feeling bad because I had been down on Randall. Even though he really screwed up, he was still my closest friend.

"What's the matter, Son?" Harley asked when I turned my head away. "Afraid to try something new?"

My mind kicked into high gear as I tried to think of a killing plan I would actually have the guts to try.

I could grab the revolver quickly and try to jerk it out of his hand, try to overpower him and choke him to death, or be really original: light the newspaper lying on the floorboard by my feet and shove it in his face, catching his beard on fire. While he was screaming and flopping around like a landlocked carp, I could push him out the door and leave him alongside the road, burning to death.

"Relax, Son," Harley said. "Life's too short to get so upset. Look at that, you're trembling."

"What did you say?" I asked spastically, turning my head around to face him when I felt his breath on the back of my neck.

"I said relax. You've got yourself so worked up you're shaking all over. Hell, I was only kiddin'. I'm not really that way."

"I thought you were serious," I said, taking a deep breath as I eased my head back against the seat.

Harley reached over and gently touched the end of my nose with the tip of his finger. "I'm not tellin' you I've never done it before. I'm just sayin' I'm not some kind of a damned pervert."

"Oh," I said quickly, wondering what his definition of deviate behavior would be if I were stupid enough to ask.

Looking at himself in the rearview mirror, Harley frowned and wrinkled up his nose. "Lockup's a strange place to be. Makes a body do weird things. Twists people around so they don't even know who they used to be."

"I've heard it's terrible," I said, as I looked down and saw a dark, red spot on the inside of Harley's forearm. I did not even want to take a guess about what medical ailment might have caused the lesion. I swallowed the bitter-tasting bile in my throat. I felt sick to my stomach.

I thought about my fiancée, Ann, again. I wondered if she would marry Bill Gilbert if something happened to me. The thought of him crawling into bed with her after she had saved herself for me was almost as hard to take as the thought of being killed by a lunatic like Harley. Even worse, what if I got Harley's disease?

I looked over at Randall, who had been quiet for a long time, and cleared my throat loudly. Turning his head around, he smiled and I smiled back. Cocking my head sideways as I looked down at Harley's arm, I cleared my throat again and rapidly blinked my eyes. I wanted to make him aware of Harley's condition, but before I could get Randall's attention, Harley started talking again.

"The wind has come up a lot, hasn't it?" He sounded a little anxious as he hunkered down and looked out the side window. "I wonder if it's going to storm."

I pointed up the road at a whirlwind chasing its tail out across the desert. It looked like a baby tornado as it swirled around stirring up a good-sized cloud of sandy, brown dust. I thought my acknowledgment of a change in climatic condition would be enough to answer his question without me actually saying anything, but I was wrong.

"You know another thing bothers me about you boys?" Harley said, as he took a wooden kitchen match out of his shirt pocket and dug a big wad of wax out of his ear. "You don't pay close attention when I talk. That bothers me plenty. Know what I figure when people do that to me?"

"No," I said. "What do you figure?"

"I figure they're makin' fun of me inside their brain. I don't like being trapped inside someone's brain. I feel like I'm smotherin'. I was cooped up too long for any more of that crap."

"We'd never make fun of you, would we, Randall?" I said, trying to get him involved in the conversation to give me a break.

Randall shook his head, and Harley rambled on, talking about brains as if it were one of his favorite subjects. "Speakin' of brains, I've eaten about every kind of brain there is, except for buzzard. There was hog brains, calf brains, sheep brains, squirrel brains and brains from something I didn't even know what the hell it was. It was back during the war. I was drunk at the time. You city boys probably never ate brains once in your whole life, I bet. Am I right?"

Randall looked at me with weary eyes, and shook his head. I solemnly said, "No, sir. I don't think we ever have. Right, Randall?"

"Right," he said painfully. "Don't think I ever have, for sure."

"You should eat 'em for breakfast. Make you feel smarter the whole day long."

From the way Harley tilted his head back and looked at me with his cold, dark eyes, I figured he was trying to determine if I was making fun of him inside of my brain. Not wanting to be accused of thinking about trying to kill him or something, I said, "I know how you feel about tight places. Almost drowned when I was a kid myself. Been claustrophobic ever since. I can't hardly even ride in an elevator anymore without getting in a panic."

Harley patted me on the arm and smiled. "Well then, you know exactly where I'm comin' from."

Harley licked his lips and continued with the simple-minded rhetoric we had come to know and hate. "Even if you don't remember diddly-crap, remember this, boys. A man can climb the highest mountain. He can go where nobody's ever stood before. They'll call him a great mountain climber. That's until he goes down on some guy just one lousy time. Then guess what they'll call him for the rest of his damned life?"

Harley's voice had a bitter edge to it again. He seemed to be riding on the crest of another mood swing that would compel him to jerk us around like puppets on a string. He needed to be killed. Not only for our sake, but also for the sake of every living creature that might cross his path.

I never thought of killing anyone before. I wondered if I would have bad dreams and wake up in the middle of the night, screaming because Harley was chasing me down a dark tunnel or blowing me up or something. I remembered an old Alfred Hitchcock movie where a killer was never able to wash all the victim's blood off his hands. Would that happen to me?

I looked at Harley sitting there in the director's chair—old, gray and puffy, a revolver in his lap, wired with dynamite. He was a man about to die, who wouldn't give a second thought to blowing us away. There was no choice. He had to go. Surely in this case, it would feel more like I only killed a rabid animal—not another human being. It would be like I had performed a public service, done my civic duty, or made a citizen's arrest.

"I'm sure glad I hooked up with a couple of studs like you boys," Harley said. "Hell, you'll pick up enough good-lookin' women to keep me busy. I've got no doubt."

"We're pretty shy when it comes to picking up girls," Randall said, and I agreed wholeheartedly.

"Oh yeah," Harley growled, "we'll see when it comes time to make a move."

"Look at that," Randall said, pointing up the road at a car with a tire leaning up against the rear bumper. "Looks like an older couple's had a flat. Maybe we should stop."

"Are you crazy?" Harley shrieked. "That's probably the FBI just made up to look like old people."

"Are you serious?" I said, wondering if there was any limit to his paranoia. I had seen similar symptoms in my Uncle Pete before he was taken away and treated for severe manic depression. Only he was not waving a revolver around and threatening to kill everyone.

"Damn right I'm serious. I'm not takin' any chances. Slow down." Harley leaned across my chest, rolled down the window and as we passed the car, he shouted, "Stay put. Help's on the way." Settling back into the squeaky director's chair, he mumbled, "Stupid law. They'll never outsmart me."

Randall had a pained expression on his face; his skin looked pale and clammy. "How far are you riding with us?" he asked.

I knew the question had not been well-received when I saw Harley flinch and his right eye began to twitch again.

"Why do you ask?" he wanted to know. "Don't want me around, do you?" He sounded like a little kid whose feelings had been hurt.

"It's not that," I assured him. "Randall was just curious. So am I. You know why?" I cleared my throat as I groped for the answer. "It's because...because I'm in charge of cooking the meals."

The instant I said it I knew I had made a big mistake. Trying to trick Harley was as stupid as putting your hand in a cage with a rattlesnake.

Harley pecked me on the shoulder with the barrel of the revolver, opened his shirt and pointed to the detonator for the TNT. He belched loudly and calmly said, "So you're the cook are you, Mark? Don't worry, Son. You'll have plenty of time to cook. I'll be around for at least two or three days, maybe longer if you guys keep treating me as nice as you've been."

The pain in my back was killing me. I had to take a chance and ask for a Percodan. Just as I started to open my mouth, Harley said, "I'm hungry, Mr. Cook. How about gettin' back there in the kitchen and servin' me up some home-cooked food?"

"I don't have any groceries in the motor home right now, but when we get some I'll cook whatever you want." I looked at Harley and forced a smile, remembering my mother telling me one time I didn't know enough about cooking to boil a pot of water.

"It don't matter. We'll just pull in and eat at Kingman. I need to pick up some smokes. I been wantin' to get me a nice chain saw too—nothing big, just something with enough power to cut through a good-sized tree without getting bogged down. Kingman would be a good place for me to start driving, too."

My heart skipped a beat when I thought about what serious trouble we had gotten ourselves into, and how life would probably never be the same again.

Chapter Three

Even though my back pain had gotten worse, I decided to wait until we stopped in Kingman before I asked for a Percodan. I would butter Harley up with kindness, make him feel as good as possible, and hope he would take pity on my suffering and just offer to give me a pill. If all else failed, I would beg and even cry if I needed to. Whatever it took, I would do. I couldn't ride all the way to Kansas City in this pain.

What worried me most was the fact Harley, having come from a correctional institution where he had access to a variety of mind-altering substances, would have picked Percodan as his drug of choice. Hopefully he was not hooked on the painkiller and would hog it all for himself.

"I'm sure sorry I left the back door to the big rig open, Mark," Randall said. "I screwed up again. Seems like I've done that a lot lately."

"It's okay," I said, thinking how I would probably never trust him again.

Harley brushed a cigarette ash off his pant leg and leaned back in the chair. "Yeah, you could call leavin' the door open a screw up, big time. Far as I'm concerned though, it was fate. I'd probably be dead by now if it wasn't for you boys. Guess I owe you my life."

"Oh come on, Harley," I said when I looked over my shoulder and saw him pucker up.

"Well, you did." He sounded as if he were about to cry. "I'll never forget it either, unless you do something to upset me again."

"Where did you get the KU cap?" I asked, looking at the Jayhawk emblem on the front.

Harley gave me a puzzled look. "KU cap? What's a KU cap?"

"That funny-looking bird on the front of your cap. That's a University of Kansas Jayhawk; I've got a cap just like it at home. KU is where Randall and I went to college. We're mechanical engineers. We actually built the engine that's powering this motor home. We worked with the Environmental Protection Agency during our senior year after we received a grant from the federal government."

"Well, you boys are a lot smarter than I thought," Harley said, as he slapped his leg and laughed at his own joke.

"Yeah, we've been on a tour showing off our creation for the past six weeks," I said proudly. I was getting a little carried away thinking about how cool it was we were able to get the funding for such a major project, actually build the damn thing, make it run, and get to go on the road, where we were praised everywhere we went as if we were a couple of heroes.

"Well good, I'm glad to hear it," Harley said, sounding jealous and not at all impressed. "Don't talk to me about it anymore, unless I say so. I've got a lot of other stuff to think about besides what a hotshot you've been."

"Fine," I said, feeling a little bit offended he wasn't more impressed.

"You asked where I got the cap," Harley said, as he took it off his head and looked at the Jayhawk. "I shot some college kid to get it. Lucky it wasn't you."

Putting it back on his head, he pulled it down snugly until it touched the tops of his ears.

"Are you serious?" I said. "What in the world did you do that for?"

"Why, you say?" Harley threw his hands up in the air and acted as if I had said something to offend him. "Hell, college kids are a dime a dozen. Why the world not?"

Looking over his shoulder, Randall moaned and made a face. "You didn't really shoot a student, did you, Harley?"

Harley poked his finger down through a hole in the top of the cap and lifted it off his head. "Just look at this, if you don't believe me. See the hole in the cap? See the cap run?" Dancing it up and down in front of him, he laughed until he got choked and went into a coughing fit.

Randall looked over his shoulder again. "We've seen it Harley. Put it back on your head, please."

That response was all the encouragement Harley needed to start acting like a comic. He pushed the end of the revolver barrel through the hole and held the cap up over his head, moving it back and forth like a conductor waving a baton. What a sadistic bastard I thought when he said, "I was only kidding. I jerked it off of a nail by the front door when I ran out of the restaurant. Needed something to cover my noggin. Gets chilly once the sun goes down. My blood's a lot thinner than it used to be when I was young like you boys. You know what I mean?"

"You had the right to take it, Harley," I said. Another sharp pain jolted my back, and I thought seriously about a suicide mission if Harley would not give me any medication and the pain became unbearable.

"Do they have real good food back there at the restaurant?" Randall asked. "Is that why they call it The Best Food Anywhere?"

"I wouldn't know. All I did was go in to rob the place. That's why I got all wired up with the dynamite. I figured if someone got the drop on me all I had to do was show them the TNT. Nobody screws with a crazy man holding his finger on a dynamite button."

"What happened?" I asked.

"Got caught up in a drug deal gone wrong. Stupid cowboy tried to pass ragweed off as marijuana. The big guy with the pea-sized brain tried to pay for the dope with phony money. Everybody got crossways with everybody. Bunch of dumb bastards."

"How do you know it was phony money?" I asked, figuring Harley had to be making up a lot of stuff.

"I saw the big guy make it on a copy machine, plain as day. He ran off two or three sheets and cut them up."

"That's one of the craziest things I've ever heard," Randall said. "How would anyone in their right mind think they could get by with such a thing?"

"There you go," Harley said. "They weren't a bunch of mental giants."

"Did they know you had the dynamite?" I asked.

"No. Hell, no."

"You could have just blown the place up," I said. "Why didn't you?"

"Just as I started to make my move, you boys pulled up. Figured I'd hitch me a ride instead."

Harley waved the KU cap at a couple of teenage boys that passed us in a black pickup truck with steer horns mounted on the hood. "Look at 'em go!" he yelled. "I wish it were me, young again and acting crazy."

"Talk about something crazy, I sure thought the cowboy back in the parking lot was going to get shot," Randall said. He looked over at me and rolled his eyes. Putting his hand up to his throat, he stuck out his tongue. I knew he was trying to give me a sign, but like the rest of his signals, I didn't know what he wanted.

"I wish the skinny little prick had been shot," Harley said. "He called me an old man as I ran out the door. That's the second-worst thing to calling me 'Mister'. So I'm old. So is everybody, if they live long enough."

"Good point, Harley," I said. "Real good point. You've got a great head on your shoulders." More importantly, you have my bottle of Percodan in your shirt pocket, I thought.

I thought about Ann and how we laid in the hammock under the big oak tree in her front yard the Sunday afternoon before Randall and I hit the road. I laughed when she told me to be really careful and I said could possibly happen to me?

"I'm just glad I didn't know those guys personally," Harley said.

"Why?" I asked.

"People judge you by the company you keep. That's why I'm so glad I ran into the likes of you boys. A couple of real upstanding citizens."

"Who owns the place?" Randall asked. "The restaurant that you went in to rob?"

"How the hell would I know? I was only in there about thirty minutes. Tell you what, boys. I don't want to hear any more questions about the stupid restaurant. Nothing else about dope, phony money, cowboys, or big overgrown turd brains with shotguns. Nothing else, unless I say otherwise."

"I never meant to push you about it," Randall said. "I was just curious."

"Yeah, well, curiosity killed the cat, you know. Pass me that cup." Harley pointed to a big, forty-four ounce plastic travel mug with Lucky Lady Truck Stop written above a big red heart.

"What for?" I asked.

"I've got to piss. What do you think for?"

When I picked it up, he grabbed it out of my hand. Scooting forward in the director's chair, he unzipped his fly, whipped out his tool and was ready to cut loose.

"Why not just go back and use the bathroom?" I said, figuring with my luck he would fill the cup to the top and spill it on me.

Harley poked me on the shoulder real friendly-like with the barrel of the revolver and laughed. "Right on, Mark. So while I'm back there pissin', you lock me inside and drive to the sheriff's office. Don't be a dork dick. First you say how smart I am, act like you want to be my friend. Next thing I know, you're playin' me for a fool."

After he finished doing his business, Harley handed me the cup and told me to pour it out the window. Randall slowed down and I dumped it outside.

"Thanks, Mark. Let me know if I can ever do the same for you."

"I hope not," I said, as I rolled up the window and tossed the cup behind the seat.

"How far is it to Kingman?" Harley asked.

"About ten minutes," I said, dreading our making the stop, not only because Harley would begin to drive, but also because the insanity of his picking up a chain saw bothered me a lot.

Harley pointed at the map I put in the compartment on my side door. "Get that map out, Mark. Let me take a good look at where we're going."

He unfolded the map, and I watched him follow old Route 66 with his finger until he reached Peach Springs. Turning north on Highway 18, he fingered his way up to Supai, Arizona. He looked over at me with a smile as wide as the destination he was plotting out. "Hell, boys, we should take the back roads and go to the Grand Canyon. How long has it been since you've been on good old Route 66?"

"Come on, Harley," Randall said. "That's a hundred miles out of our way. Not only that, but once you leave Route 66 and head north on Highway 18, the going gets rough. I went that way once with my dad when we were on vacation. It was a big mistake."

"Okay," Harley said, giving up too easily for him not to have an ulterior motive.

"Why did you want to go?" I asked.

"I don't. I just wanted to see what you two would say."

I knew better. He had a reason, and it was only a matter of a few hours down the road before I would find out what it was.

"There's Kingman, dead ahead," I said, deciding to make my move for a Percodan since Harley seemed to be as happy as he had ever been. I folded up the map and put it away, leaned back in the seat, raised up the small of my back and groaned.

"What's the matter?" Harley asked, his raspy voice sounding as if he had a genuine concern for my well-being. "Is something wrong?"

"It's my back. It hurts so bad I can hardly sit here without screaming. It's the worst pain I've ever had in my life. I know what real pain is, too. I've had my nose broken twice. I was run over by a truck when I was six. A rabid dog bit me when I was eight and had to take those shots. When I was twelve, I fell two stories down an elevator shaft and broke both my arms and my foot."

"That bad, is it, Son? It must be awful."

"It's really, really bad. Could I please, please have just one of my Percodan pills?" I made an extra effort to distort my face, even to the point of making my right eye twitch a little, just like Harley's. "It's really bad," I said again, just for good measure.

Harley calmly unscrewed the cap, dumped a half dozen of the pale yellow pills out into the palm of his hand and examined them closely. Putting all but one back in the bottle, he picked it up and said, "Here you go, Mark." I reached for it, but he jerked his hand back and laughed.

"What's wrong?" I asked.

"Nothing's wrong. I just wanted to see how badly you wanted it," he said, as he popped it in his mouth. "You'll get one soon, Son. You'll get one soon, don't worry."

I could barely contain myself—he had the unthinkable gall to take my medicine. The bastard's going to take all of them and not give me any. For some cruel reason, he wants to see me suffer. Taking a couple of deep breaths, I forced myself to calm down by thinking about the fact he would be dead soon, one way or the other.

"Good guy one second, bad guy the next," I said to myself, thinking about my Uncle Pete who lived with us during my senior year in high school until the day he was hauled off. He had the same kind of mental problems as Harley, so I was not a stranger to the world of multiple personality. He had not been as mean as Harley, but he did have a nasty streak that would cause him to act up every once in awhile. Most of the time, though, he simply coexisted in peaceful harmony with his own varied personalities and caused a minimal amount of trouble.

Cocking his head to one side, Harley stared at the label on the pill bottle, looking as if he were deeply troubled. "What's the name that's written on here, Mark?"

"That's my name, Mark Jameson." I hoped he'd had a change of heart.

"Not your name, damn it! What's the name of the pills inside the bottle? Where does it say they're Percs?" he snapped at me, raising his voice.

"It doesn't."

"Then why the hell do people in prison keep calling them Percs?" he asked, shaking the bottle in my face. "What are you doing, tryin' to make me look stupid again?"

"No. No. Not at all." I pointed at the name of the drug on the label. "It says Percodan, right here. Perc is just a short name for Percodan."

When I looked at Harley with weary eyes, he grunted and put the bottle back in his pocket. Maybe after he got something to eat, and right before he started to drive, I would ask him for a pill once again.

As if we did not have enough trouble, Harley's not being able to read or not seeing very well, or both, was not conducive to the safe operation of a wide-bodied motor home.

Even though I knew I was taking a chance, I wanted to know the extent of his condition before he got behind the wheel.

"Harley," I said softly, not wanting to sound threatening in any way.

"What is it now? Do I have to be dead and gone before you leave me alone about the damned pills?"

"It's not the Percodan. It's something else. I was wondering if you usually wear glasses when you read?"

Before he could say anything, a magnificent-looking young girl with long, dark brown hair, driving a red corvette, pulled up beside us and honked the horn. Randall honked back and waved.

"Roll down the window," Harley said. "I want to hear what she's got to say for herself."

She must have read our bumper sign. Laughing, she yelled, "I went to KU too. I'm headed for Kansas City. Is that where you're going?"

"This girl looks good enough to be a model," Randall said. "She reminds me a lot of Ann."

In spite of the sharp pain that shot up my spine, I raised up and leaned toward the window for a quick look.

"Kansas City. Yeah, we're headed home," Randall shouted into the wind. "Where have you been? We've been to...."

Before Randall could finish the sentence, Harley lunged across Randall's chest, causing him to turn the wheel to the left and swerve over toward the car. As if that was not bad enough, Harley stuck his head out the window and howled like a wolf.

The expression on the girl's face changed from the friendly smile of a newfound friend to a look of panic. Stomping down on the gas pedal, her head flew back against the seat and the red sports car streaked down the highway as if she were fleeing for her life.

"What the hell happened to her?" Harley asked, stupidly.

"In a hurry to get back to Kansas City, I guess." Randall sounded disgusted.

"To hell with her. She was an uppity bitch anyway. We've got more important stuff to do than talk to her anyhow. You know what I mean, Mark?"

"Yeah? Like what, Harley?" I asked, but I was thinking, "like listening to your stupid talk, or not knowing from one minute to the next if we were going to be dead or alive." I wished there was something I could do to stop him without getting shot or blown up. Soon I would be able to add 'or get chain-sawed' to the list.

"Like what?" Harley said, as he leaned forward and stared into my eyes. "Like you thinking with your brain for a change instead of your dick. Like me gettin' something to eat. Like picking me up some smokes. Like me getting' behind the wheel so I can put the pedal to the metal, and the last like of all, for right now anyway, like I want to pick up a chain saw. I've got me some cuttin' to do."

Chapter Four

Harley lit up another Camel, took a drag off the cigarette and let the smoke slowly filter out through his nose.

"Look." He pointed at a billboard with big, golden arches that stuck up above the main body of the sign. "Is that an advertisement for McDonald's?"

"The one and only," I said, wondering why he seemed so smart about some things yet asked such stupid questions about something as obvious as the billboard. It was just one more spooky thing about Harley that did not make any sense. "Is McDonald's where you want to eat?"

"You bet. It must be really good. I saw on TV where billions of hamburgers have been sold. Where the hell do you think he raised all those cows? Maybe you better slow down, Randall. We don't want to miss the road."

"We won't miss it, Harley," Randall said. He pointed at a sign announcing we had arrived in Kingman, Arizona. "It's the first exit after we get on I-40. We're only five minutes away." Randall flipped on the turn signal, maneuvered the circle off the highway, merged with the busy eastbound traffic and headed toward Flagstaff. Another motor home passed us on the left, and the driver honked his horn. A nice-looking Spanish woman with long, black hair sitting in the passenger seat leaned forward and waved. Randall honked the horn and the three of us waved back.

"People around Kingman sure are friendly," Harley said, as if he were judging the entire city by someone who had waved and honked his horn. "Of course, they've got every reason to be."

"Why is that?" I asked.

"Kingman is the headquarters for the Historic Route 66 Association of Arizona. That's why." He gave me a disgusted look, and I felt as if it were information everyone in the world should know.

"So what's that got to do with anything?" I asked, defensively.

"I'm a member," Harley said proudly. "It would behoove you boys to join up too. Yeah, I know a lot about Kingman. Clark Gable and Carole Lombard were married in the old courthouse right over there about three miles." He pointed toward downtown as Randall turned off at the Cottonwood Falls exit and followed the street until he reached the drive-thru entrance at McDonald's.

Harley leaned forward to read the menu.

"May I take your order, please?" a pleasant-sounding young lady asked over the loudspeaker, catching Harley completely off-guard.

"Son of a bitch!" he yelled, jumping backwards. He jerked the revolver up and pointed it at the speaker that hung above the menu as if he were going to blow it away.

There was a burst of laughter from inside the restaurant. I heard someone ask, "Who is that idiot?" There was a loud crackle of static, and the speaker went dead.

"What's the matter, Harley?" Randall asked.

"Yeah, what's the matter?" I repeated, hardly able to keep from laughing when I saw Harley's mouth drop open.

"What the hell do you think? Stupid thing blastin' out at me like that. I'm a little nervous, you know. You would be too if this was your first time."

"First time?" I said, looking at Randall, wondering what kind of perverted story we were about to hear. "First time for what?"

Harley lowered his head. "A McDonald's," he said quietly. "What do you think?"

Seconds later, the voice of a man, speaking slowly and clearly, the way a person would if he were talking to a drunk, talked to us on the speaker. "May we take your order, Mister?" There was a long silence while Harley's deeply troubled mind digested the impact of being called 'Mister'.

"Please watch your language," the McDonald's man said. "There are children present."

I heard a kid crying in the background. A woman I assumed was his mother yelled, "What's the matter with him anyhow? McDonald's should refuse service to such a vulgar person."

Harley gave me a shamefaced look and groaned.

"Don't take it personal. You can see why they would be upset though. If everyone driving through yelled 'son of a bitch' into the speaker, parents would stop bringing their kids to McDonald's."

"I know. I know," he said, throwing me off-guard again by acting like a real human being.

Randall, on the other hand, seized the opportunity to bash the poor, old, dejected bastard by jumping on Harley's case really good. "That's right, man. You've got to be more considerate. Not only of kids and their mothers, but also hamburger managers and young ladies who just want to help you." Randall took a deep breath and stopped to collect his thoughts while he loaded up his scathing tongue. "The guy didn't mean anything by calling you 'Mister'. Sheesh! A lot of people call people 'Mister' all the time. Don't you know that, Harley? Hey man, I thought cussin' was out. People don't have to cuss to have a good time. Know what I mean, Harley?"

"Oh, man," I said to myself, figuring Randall's not knowing when to quit may cause him big trouble that would spill over to include me. I could just see Harley thinking about Randall as if he were a flea on a dog's back and, with a reflex action, sticking the revolver behind Randall's ear and blowing him away. Boom! There would be a loud noise. Bright red blood and splinters of white bone and chunks of meat would be splattered everywhere.

Much to my surprise, Harley looked at me with clenched teeth and made and seemed to be making an effort to smooth out the temper in his face. "All right, Son. Everything will be all right. Don't get so upset."

I looked at Randall and rolled my eyes, trying to convey my feelings about how I feared for his life if he continued to attack Harley.

Randall squinted his eyes and smirked at me as if he felt good about what he had done. "All right," I said to myself, as I stared at him and nodded my head, thinking how he had gotten by with the Harley-bashing for the time being. But he was sitting on the wrong end of the limb to keep cutting with the saw.

"May I help you, please?" the young lady called out over the loudspeaker again, sounding as sweet as honey and extra nice, considering.

"See, the McDonald's people like you, Harley," I said. "You were right about Kingman being a friendly town. Go ahead. Tell the lady what you want to eat."

Harley cocked his head to one side and studied the menu for so long I thought he might have gone to sleep. "Tell her what you want to eat, Harley," I said again, as I looked in the rearview mirror at the line of cars stacked up behind us.

Instead of placing an order, he leaned over close to my ear and whispered, "I don't know what to say."

"What's the matter?" I asked. Once again, it was obvious that either he could not read, was unable to see clearly, or had some kind of a short circuit in his brain which would periodically put his ability to think straight on hold.

At the same time that I started to ask Randall to order for all of us, Harley blurted out, "I want it all, nice lady. Give me everything you've got."

"I beg your pardon, sir?"

"All of it," Harley said. "I want everything."

"Do you mean you want to order one of each item on the entire menu?"

Harley jammed his cigarette out in the ashtray and leaned across Randall's chest. "Yes, lady. I want one of everything on the signboard." Looking over at me as he sat back in the chair, he wrinkled up his nose and smiled. "What's the matter with the nice young lady, Mark? Is she friggin' deaf?"

"Yes, ma'am," Randall said. "That's what he wants all right, one of everything on the menu. I'm sorry for the delay. We've had a rough morning." Randall ordered a couple of Cokes and two Big Macs with fries for him and me.

Honk! Honk! Someone, four or five cars back in the line, had finally lost his patience and was using his horn to hurry us along.

"That will be $62.78," the nice young lady said. "Please move forward to pick up the first part of your order."

"Does that include tax?" Harley asked.

Randall and I looked at one another sourly. Neither of us answered him.

He raised his eyebrows as he reached for his billfold after the speaker went dead. I knew it bothered him deeply to have to fork over money. He was one of the most miserable human beings to get stuck paying a third-party food bill who ever lived.

Randall pulled forward and handed the cashier his credit card. After signing the receipt, he grudgingly said, "Thank you, ma'am."

She handed back his card. "Please move to the parking area to wait for the rest of your order. Have a nice day, Mister." She closed the glass window and stepped away from the counter to get a better look at Harley.

"Who cares?" Harley said, stiffening up when he heard a loud thump at the back of the motor home. "What was that?" He raised the revolver up to his chest and looked back over his shoulder.

"Just some kid walked by and slapped the side of the big rig with his hand," I said, as I watched a couple of boys run across the parking lot, jump on their bicycles and pedal away.

"This place is too busy for me. I'll never come back to the 'arches' again as long as I live."

"You may change your mind after you sink your teeth into one of those burgers." My new goal in life was to keep Harley happy and as calm as possible.

"The cashier opened the window and handed Randall the first of six sacks of food and drinks, while a half dozen employees and a bunch of customers gawked at us.

"This should hold you for awhile, Harley."

"Everyone in the place is staring at us," Randall grumbled, as he pulled over and parked to wait for the rest of our food.

"I don't plan on eating it all right now," Harley said, defensively. "A man on the run needs to have some spare food around. Never know when we may have to hole up and fight off the law. Killing them could take days." Harley ripped open the first bag and grabbed a regular hamburger, cramming the entire thing into his mouth. He smiled at me with his eyes while he chewed. "You were right," he finally said. "That's pretty damned good meat."

A young man wearing a purple shirt with the golden arches embroidered above the left-hand pocket ran up to the window and handed Randall two more bags containing the remainder of our order. "Here's the rest of your order, sir. I put extra salt and pepper in the bag." He handed Randall a white sticker with a yellow smiley face on it and told him to have a really nice day.

I heard the kid laugh as he turned around and headed back toward the building. As he opened the door, I saw about twenty people inside that were laughing too. I thought Harley might get crazy with so many people making fun of him all at once. Later on I discovered on top of everything else, he had a problem with his hearing.

"Pull across the street to the gas station," Harley said, as he reached in the sack and grabbed a large bag of fries. "I need to get some smokes."

"When you go inside," Randall asked, "will you bring me back a pack of gum?"

"Yeah, right. I'm really stupid enough to go inside. Leave you two in the big rig alone. Pull up where the kid's standing. Tell him to get me a couple packs of Camels. No, make it five packs."

The full-service station was very busy and the kid in charge of pumping gas looked as if he were at his wit's end. When Randall pulled up beside him and said he wanted the cigarettes, I thought the kid was going to lose control.

"Can't you go in and get 'em yourself?" he snapped back at Randall. "I've got three cars waiting for gas."

When Harley leaned across Randall's chest, I figured the kid was in for the tongue-lashing of his life. I just hoped he didn't stick the revolver in the kid's face and get us caught up in the middle of a shootout. Instead of screaming and getting out of control, Harley calmly said, "It's worth ten dollars a pack to me, son. That's fifty dollars for a five-pack deal."

Without another word, the kid bolted for the front door of the station and was back with the cigarettes in about two minutes.

"That's nice of you to give him such a big tip," Randall said. "You must have a lot of money."

"I ain't got anything. You're the one payin' the nice young man. It's your punishment for thinking I was stupid enough to go inside."

"I'm about out of cash," Randall said, as he handed the kid the five tens in exchange for the cigarettes.

"Thanks a lot!" the kid said. "That's the biggest tip I've ever had. Come back every night if you want to."

"We'll sure stop in the next time we pass through," Harley said. "We'll for sure be back for the Route 66 Fun Run Weekend. One more thing, that little orange chain saw over by the curb, is it for sale?"

"Yeah, it is. Belongs to my dad. He wants $150 for it. He said I could keep twenty-five bucks if I sell it for him."

"Sold," Harley said. "Randall, give the nice young man your credit card."

"Now listen Harley, you can't just keep spending my money... Do you take MasterCard?" Randall asked quickly when Harley jammed the barrel of the revolver into his ribs.

The kid wrote up the transaction quickly. One of the cars that had been waiting for gas peeled out of the driveway, and another customer hung his head out the window and began to protest. Randall signed the charge ticket, Harley opened up the side door of the big rig, the kid handed him the chain saw and we were ready to go, armed with another potentially dangerous weapon.

At Harley's request, Randall pulled off to one side of the station's parking area and stopped. Harley wanted to finish eating his lunch before he started to drive. He crammed down a double bacon cheeseburger, a fish sandwich loaded with tarter sauce that squished out the corners of his mouth, a small order of fries and a hot fudge sundae. He washed it all down with a large Coke. Taking only five minutes to consume all of this food, Harley belched loudly and wiped his hairy face with the tail of his tattered red shirt. This left only a trace of mustard under the tip of his nose and a chunk of french fry about the size of a pencil eraser buried in the whiskers on his chin.

Having eaten enough food to feed a couple of starving dogs, Harley slapped Randall on the back and laughed "Well, my friend, get yourself up out of that seat. A truck-drivin' fool's about to hit the road."

"Are you sure you want to drive?" Randall asked Harley, making one last desperate attempt to try to save not only our lives, but also the lives of other innocent victims Harley might run over once he got behind the wheel. "There's no good reason for you to drive. I'm not tired or anything."

Randall groaned when Harley laid his hand on his shoulder and squeezed down hard. "I'm not only sure I want to drive, I'm driving. Now get the hell out of my seat." Harley crawled behind the wheel, laid the revolver in his lap, opened up the front of his shirt and looked down at the detonator taped over his belly button. "See this device, boys?" Harley put his finger right over the top of it as he looked at us and smiled. "I just want to remind you that it's still alive and well. Especially you Randall, you've been acting up and I'm not going to take it anymore. So say you're sorry."

"Say you're sorry!" I yelled when Randall just looked away.

"Sorry," Randall said, giving me a disgusted look.

"That's good," Harley said. "Sayin' you're sorry sometimes is good for the soul. Lord knows Randall's soul needs some patchin' up, don't you think, Mark?"

With that little bit of dues-collecting out of the way, Harley got down to serious business and scanned the instrument panel like a hawk.

He flipped down a lever mounted on the steering column and a blinking green arrow came on. He flipped the lever back up and switched off the left-hand turn signal. He pulled out a black knob and the flashers came on. He stared at the pulsing red light, made a fist and smashed it back in with his hand. "All right, Randall. You've had your fun. How do I get the damn thing to run?"

Randall reached over and turned the key, started the engine and pulled down the gearshift lever. "If you want to go forward, put the little red arrow on the letter D, which stands for drive. To go backwards, put the little red arrow on the letter R, which stands for reverse. Now step on the gas pedal and we'll be gone. Be careful and pay close attention to the traffic."

"We're on the road now!" Harley yelled, as the big rig rolled toward the entrance of the parking lot. "Glory-bound." He waved at a blond-haired little girl riding her bicycle down the sidewalk. She must have sensed danger because she hurried out of the way.

"You'll be okay, Harley," Randall said, "Just stay in your lane. Don't go over the yellow line in the center."

"How does it feel so far?" I asked. "Is everything under control?"

Bouncing over the edge of the curb, Harley steered the big rig out of the parking lot, made a wide sweep, which forced an oncoming car onto the left-hand shoulder, as he entered the frontage road and headed toward Interstate 40. "This is great, man. Really great."

Honk! Honk!

"Jack off!" Harley yelled, as a red Mustang zoomed past and the driver gave him the finger. "Why did he honk at me?" Harley sounded bewildered.

"Why?" Randall shouted. "You're riding the centerline. That's why. Now look at you. You're over the centerline completely. Look what's coming, Harley. My God, pull over! Pull over now!" Randall grabbed the wheel.

There was a loud blast from an air horn as a big gray monster swerved off the road, barely missing us as it zoomed past.

Harley knocked Randall's hand away. "Screw 'em! Bus drivers think they own the damn road."

The sound of gravel hitting the underside of the big rig was alarming as Harley ran off onto the right-hand shoulder, missing a speed limit sign by inches.

Randall grabbed the wheel again, saving us from running into the ditch. "Stop! Slam on the brakes!"

Harley looked bewildered. "What for? You just don't want me to drive."

"We've got to have a talk before we're all killed," Randall said, jerking the steering wheel to the right; Harley jerked it back to the left.

"Okay." Harley slammed down the brake pedal, throwing Randall and the yellow director's chair forward into the dashboard. The big rig slid to a stop in the middle of the road. "What is it, Randall? What is it you want to say?"

His voice quivering, Randall gasped, "We almost got hit by a Greyhound bus. You do know that, don't you? You do know we were almost killed?"

Harley looked at me and smiled. "I don't think we came that close. Did we, Mark?"

"I told you to stay in your own lane, didn't I?" Randall moaned. "If you can't do that, you can't drive."

"Give me a break. I just got started. I'll get the hang of it. Calm down before you have a heart attack."

"Did you say, give you a break?" Randall's hands were shaking. "What are you talking about? This is not a driver's training course."

Harley glared at Randall. His right eye twitched. He gritted his teeth. "You're as bad as my old man. You really are."

I could see big trouble looming on the horizon and decided to intervene before things got out of hand. "Everything will be fine if we all just calm down. What if we try this? Harley, you agree to pay more attention to the road and Randall, you agree not to get so upset. Okay, guys?"

The two of them staged a lengthy staring contest with Randall finally looking away.

"Thanks for your confidence in me, Mark," Harley said, giving me a smile. "Nice to know I've still got at least one person left that believes in me."

"Okay. Okay," Randall said. "Give it some gas. Let's get on down the road. We'll never get home at this rate. Just stay in your lane."

Hugging the steering wheel like a long lost friend, Harley pushed down on the gas pedal and the speedometer began to climb. Fifteen miles per hour. Twenty... Thirty... Thirty-five... At forty, Randall could not take it anymore. "Slow down! This thing's top-heavy. Don't go any faster. You'll never make the curve."

"Oh no," I said to myself when I saw Harley jerk the steering wheel to the right and heard the familiar sound of loose gravel hitting the underside of the big rig.

"Pull over, Harley," Randall said, sitting up on the edge of his seat. "Slow down, man. Slow the hell down."

"I think I've got it under control," Harley said, overcompensating when he jerked the steering wheel to the right. Dangerously close to the edge again, Randall grabbed the steering wheel for a third time, barely saving us from going down a steep embankment.

"Lordy, that was close," Harley said, as he and Randall steered the big rig down the entrance ramp onto Interstate 40, and we were on our merry way to Flagstaff, Arizona.

Chapter Five

Storm clouds rolled in from the South, blackening the midday sky. The corners of Harley's mouth tightened when a flash of lightning streaked down from the heavens and rain began to fall.

Randall pointed at the control mounted on the steering column and told Harley to turn the windshield wipers on. After a long pause with Harley acting spaced out, as if his mind had gone on a field trip, Randall leaned forward and twisted the knob on the end of the lever. The water cleared away just in time for Randall to see Harley was desperately close to the concrete railing of a bridge, and he jerked the steering wheel to the left. My head banged into the side window, and I felt a sharp pain just above my right ear. The discomfort was nothing compared to the pain in my back, but a nice-sized knot did appear.

I looked over at Harley and his face was sickly white. "What's the matter?" I asked, hoping he was having a stroke.

Gripping the steering wheel as if there was no tomorrow, he looked out the side window. "I'm afraid of lightning."

"Why, might I ask?" I figured I was about to hear an incredibly weird story might involve everything from the Devil to travelers from outer space.

His eyes darted back and forth as he looked out the side window again, anxiously watching the movement of the storm. "Mr. Lightning's got me under his spell." Harley's voice cracked, and he sounded like a scared little kid.

"You don't need to worry. As long as you stay in the big rig, you'll be safe. We're grounded because of the rubber tires." I pointed at the clear sky along the western edge of the storm. "Looks as if it will blow over soon. You'll be fine."

"I hope so," Harley said. "That's what ruined my life."

"What ruined your life?" Randall asked. "Lightning?"

Not wanting to let on I was really curious; I picked up a napkin and slowly rubbed some of the grease from the french fries off my fingers. "How did lightning ruin your life?" I asked, softly.

Instead of telling me the reason for his fears, what did Harley do? He began to sing an old Willie Nelson song, swaying back and forth, keeping time with the swishing windshield wipers.

"Mama, don't let your babies grow up to be cowboys. Let 'em be lawyers and doctors and such, but for God's sake, don't let 'em be scared of lightning like me."

"Stop it," Randall said. "You're all over the road again. I've had it with you, Harley. You can't drive."

My heart sank when I saw Harley reach down and open his shirt. One touch of the button and we were gone. I had always wondered if, when it came down to the end of my life, I would have enough time to cop a final plea. Only problem was, I couldn't think of anything to say that did not sound phony to me, as if it were something I had just made up.

"Can't drive, huh?" Harley grunted. "We'll see about that, Buddy Boy. We'll just damn well see."

"Look Harley," Randall said, his voice still sounding as if he were not afraid to enforce whatever had to be done, "you know you can't drive all over the road. You may not care if you live, but it's just not right to kill innocent people. Don't you agree?" Randall sounded a little less bold and not quite so confident now.

"Speaking of killing people," Harley said, "I found a little .22-caliber pistol hidden under a pillow in the bedroom. Had either of you thought about shooting me with the damn thing?"

"No," I said quickly. "I know I didn't."

"No matter, I threw it down the toilet before I came up front."

I looked in the rearview mirror and saw Randall flexing the muscles in his jaws. "I wish you hadn't thrown it away. It belonged to my grandfather."

Harley patted him on the leg. "Is your grandfather still alive?"

Randall bit his lower lip and looked up at the ceiling. "No. No, he's not. He passed away last year."

"Then he'll never know the difference, will he, Randy Boy?"

"It doesn't matter about the 22-caliber pistol," I said. "We don't have any shells."

"Yeah, that's right," Randall, said sharply. "So what's the big deal?"

Harley picked up the Colt 45 revolver from his lap and pulled back the hammer. "The big deal is Mark told the truth. You didn't, Randy Bud." He jammed the end of the barrel up under Randall's chin. "Lie to me again and you'll be missing the top of your head."

Peck, peck, peck. The old familiar sound of flying gravel was back tapping away inside my brain. I looked up just in time to see a big, green sign disappear under the front bumper. There was a loud thump, followed by a bang and the sound of metal scraping against metal. I looked in the rearview mirror and saw the crumpled up sign roll out from under the back of the big rig and come to rest on the side of the road.

"How far did that sign say it was to Flagstaff?" Harley asked, breaking into convulsive laughter. Randall and I looked at him with our mouths open.

"That's not funny." I saw Randall's hands and lips were trembling.

"Why not? It was just a sign. The highway people have gobs of stupid-assed signs."

"Did you say why not?" I said, raising my voice. "Something like that could come right up through the floorboard and kill you. That's why the hell not."

"Bull. A sign couldn't kill me."

"Fact is, I read a story in the newspaper last week about a guy who ran over a tire jack. It chewed its way right through the floorboard of his Jeep."

"What happened?" Harley asked, soberly.

"It killed him. It ripped his crotch out and he bled to death."

"So okay," Harley said, as he laughed and honked the horn, "I won't knock down any more signs. Better yet, I won't run over any car jacks."

"Here's one for you to think about, Harley," Randall said, barely able to speak. "If a highway patrol officer saw you run over a sign, he would come after you in a second. Is a shootout what you want?"

Harley paused for a few seconds and looked up at the ceiling as if he were giving the question some serious thought. "A shootout would be exciting," he laughed, causing Randall to moan loudly. "Come on, man. I already said I wouldn't do it anymore. Give me a break."

When Randall leaned forward, and I saw the empty look in his eyes, I knew he was about to suffer a meltdown. I saw a side of him I had never seen before, and it disturbed me to think about what might happen. If he were in his right mind, he never would have had such a dangerous attitude when dealing with a psychopathic killer. Randall seemed to be on the edge of being very dangerous. In the wink of an eye, he might do something that could include me as one of the victims.

Harley made a swishing sound as he sucked air in and out between the wide cracks in his ugly, yellow teeth. "Talk about a painful way to die. What could be worse than gettin' your dick gobbled off by a car jack? A person just never knows what's waiting up ahead to nail him to the wall."

I looked down at the revolver in his lap and wished he would hit a big bump that would cause it to discharge. Little chance of it happening, but with him continuously running off the road, who knows? The fun part would be driving around for six or eight hours playing like we were trying to rush him to a hospital before he bled to death. I continued with my pleasant daydream. God forbid we should try to dump him off at a hospital that only accepted patients covered by insurance. We would have to load him back up and haul him off to somewhere else. That would take more time.

"Yeah, it would be a poor way to go," I said, as I rolled down the window and stuck my head outside. The air was fresh with a sweet smell of ozone. I looked out across the rugged terrain. A red-tailed hawk was hovering overhead and a jackrabbit broke from a patch of scrub brush, narrowly able to escape by darting down into a ravine. "Man, this is great," I shouted into the wind. "I haven't seen rain since we left Kansas City." I wiped away the water droplets that had built up along the bottom edge of the mirror with the tip of my finger and smiled. The simple things in life really are the best, and for a brief moment, I was actually able to smile.

"I want some fresh air in my face too," Harley said, as he rolled down his window. "Lordy, lordy!" he yelled, licking his lips when a minivan passed us at a high rate of speed and covered his face with spray. I could tell by the way Randall grabbed the bottom of the director's chair and hung on for dear life that he wanted to jump on Harley for drifting over the centerline again. Having the revolver shoved in his face the last time he acted up, Randall had backed off considerably.

"If you think the rain feels good to you, Mark, think about this. I haven't felt water from the heavens in twenty years. This is a special day for me. It doesn't rain much in prison."

"I thought you were afraid of storms," Randall said, unable to resist trying to mess with Harley's mind again.

"What's the matter, man? Have you gone deaf? I'm afraid of lightning. Not storms. Isn't that what I said, Mark?"

"Yeah, that's what you said all right, Harley." I wondered what it would be like to finally feel rain again after a dry spell that had lasted twenty years.

Shaking his head like a wet dog fresh out of the water, Harley yelled, "Thank you so much, Lord. It feels so good to be free."

"Would it be all right if I lie down for awhile, Harley? My back is killing me. I haven't complained much because that's not my way. The pain has gotten terrible. If I keep sitting up, I'm afraid I may pass out."

Harley looked over his shoulder at the green couch behind the passenger seat. "Lay down right there."

"Why? The big bed in back is a lot more comfortable."

"I want to keep an eye on you, Mark. Even though I trust you a million times more than I do Randall, you still might get a wild hair to stab me with that knife lying by the toaster. Or who knows, you may even get desperate and fire up my chain saw. Wouldn't that be a bloody mess when I took it away from you and accidentally cut off Randall's head with the sharp, little, whirling metal teeth?"

"Funny," Randall said. "Really funny."

"I'm in too much pain to do any of that stuff. Do you think you'll give me a Percodan later?" I asked, sounding as if I were about to cry because I was.

Harley moaned a little while he considered my request. "We'll just have to see about that, Son. We'll just have to see."

"Can I at least take some Tylenol? There's a bottle in the glove compartment."

"Sure, go ahead. You best open the door slow and easy."

What a joke this is going to be compared to a Percodan. I dumped a half dozen capsules out of the bottle into the palm of my hand.

He must just be saving the Percs for himself. I washed the red and white Tylenol capsules down with what was left of my Coke from McDonald's. Walking over to the couch, I doubled up a pillow and slid it under my back as I lay down. It helped to ease the pain a little. Exhausted, within a few minutes I drifted off into a deep sleep. I dreamed I heard the sound of a siren and Randall was laughing hysterically in my face, telling me Harley had died of a heart attack.

When I awoke a couple of hours later, I still had a smile on my face. Some things had changed while I was asleep. Randall had become the driver once again and a young man, wearing a faded jean jacket with a red peace sign painted on the back, was now sitting in one of the director's chairs.

I raised myself up on one elbow for a better look and listened closely when I heard the visitor call himself Moon Love. Our big rig had become a magnet for attracting weirdo's.

"So, after your VW bus broke down, you talked to Mother Nature, and she stopped the rain until you could get a ride. Is that what you're telling us, Moon?" I heard Randall ask him, sounding very dubious.

"Well," Moon said in a high-pitched voice that sounded like a whining dog. He hunched up his shoulders and wiggled around in the chair as if he were eager to get someplace. "It was raining right before you guys saw me. Isn't that right?"

"Yes, that's right. It was raining, so what?" Randall said, as he waved at some kids in the back of a pickup who had held up a little black dog for him to see.

"Well, it wasn't raining when you picked me up, isn't that right?"

"No, I guess it wasn't raining. So what's your point?"

"Well, is it raining now?" Moon asked, and before Randall could say anything, he slapped Harley on the back. "That's right, it's not raining right now, so that proves I'm right."

"Yeah, you sure made your point," Harley said, his voice taking on a rough edge. "Now I'll make mine. Don't ever touch me again. I don't like to be touched—especially by strangers."

Jumping in the middle before Moon could say anything that might offend Harley even further, Randall asked, "Where did you ever get a handle like Moon Love?"

"Sounds like a name Frank Zappa might have given one of his kids, doesn't it? In this case, I gave it to myself. The Moon part has to do with a planetary phase of the heavens. The Love part stands for peace. I got into peace pretty heavy when I lived in Berkeley, California."

Randall looked at him and smiled. "It fits you well."

"So how long did you live in Berkeley?" Harley asked, scratching himself under the chin with the end of the revolver barrel.

"About a year. Actually, it was thirteen months, which is a year for me. I operate on my own lunar table."

"I can tell," Harley said. "I can just tell."

"By the way, Harley," Moon said, "what's the deal on that big revolver you keep waving around?"

"I use it to shoot rattlesnakes," Harley fired back an answer. "Somebody's got to. They scare away the tourists, you know."

"I don't like guns," Moon said, laying his hand on Harley's arm. "What do you say, since there aren't any snakes here—for now at least—that you put the revolver away?"

Harley sat there staring at Moon's hand until he removed it from his arm. I could not believe he didn't show Moon the TNT and threaten him with it the way he did with us. Maybe he is going to bypass that step and just go straight to the explosion.

"Where did you live after Berkeley?" Randall asked.

"Venice," Moon said, as he reached back and removed a rubber band from his ponytail. He shook loose his thick brown hair and let it fall down onto his shoulders. Leaning back in the director's chair, he pulled a thin little marijuana cigarette out of his shirt pocket and struck a match. "'Ere, man." He offered it to Randall after taking a long drag.

Randall looked at Moon and passed with a wave of his hand.

Harley grabbed the joint like a monkey snatching a banana, took a drag and held the smoke in his lungs until his ears turned red. Instead of passing it back to Moon, he took another drag and another. He was about to take another one when Moon grabbed the joint out of Harley's fingers. "Hey, Dude. Don't bogart that joint, okay? We've got other people around here wantin' to get high too." Moon got one hit out of what was left, snuffed the roach out on the bottom of his tennis shoe, stuck it in his mouth and swallowed the damn thing.

Harley tapped Moon on the shoulder with the barrel of the revolver and gave him a grim-faced grin. "Don't call me a dude, Buddy Boy. Keep messin' with me, I'll trim off your ears."

Moon must have thought Harley was only kidding. He just laughed as if it were all a big game.

"So why are you leaving California?" Randall asked, as he swerved to miss a big piece of rubber from a truck tire in the road. The big rig swayed from side to side, knocking me back down onto the couch.

Moon raised up out of his chair, looked at himself in the rearview mirror and rubbed his bloodshot eyes. "Too weird, man. California has just gotten too damned weird." A statement like that coming from a pony tailed, dope-smoking hippie with a name like Moon Love made me laugh, which caused a sharp pain to shoot up my spine. It felt as if someone had crunched down on one of my vertebrae with a nutcracker.

"You're awake," Randall said, as he leaned over so he could see around Moon. "Is your back feeling any better?"

"Not really," I groaned. "I'm just living with the pain. A Percodan would knock it out in about two seconds, if I had one."

"Where are you headed?" Harley asked Moon.

"Goin' to a little town south of Springfield, Missouri, to hook back up with my girlfriend and a buddy. They were followin' the Grateful Dead around until the Lord called

Jerome back home. Now there's no Dead to follow. The leader himself is dead."

"Jerome?" Randall said. "Who's Jerome?"

"If you don't know that much, I shouldn't even tell you," Moon said disgustedly. "Jerome is Jerry Garcia's first name. I thought everybody knew that much."

"I knew that," Randall said, trying to pass himself off as someone a lot more hip than he really was. "I just forgot. So that's why the sign was painted on the back of your bus."

"You mean the big peace sign?"

"No, I mean the message that read, Who are the Grateful Dead and why do they keep following me?" Moon groaned and shook his head. "How long have you been a Dead Head?" Randall asked.

"Started when I was seventeen. I'm twenty-four now. So that's seven years goin' on seventy. Feels that long anyway. It's been some kinda' livin', man. Some kinda' livin' indeed."

"Sounds like it," Randall said.

"Yeah. I've done my share of trippin' with the Dead. Went from California to Woodstock and back a couple of summers ago. Got busted twice along the way. Some cops just like to pick on Dead Heads. They're easy to push around, you know?"

"Yeah, no kiddin'," Harley said. "Lots of cops have a cruel mentality."

"Not all cops are that way," I said, feeling compelled to defend my departed uncle who had raised me as if I were his own son. "My Uncle Arthur was a cop, and he was really a good man."

Sounding as if he were about to cry, Moon looked up at the ceiling. "All I know is people who are into peace and love make an easy target."

"You're right there," Harley said. "Look what they did to poor Rodney King. Remember when he was shown on TV while LA was burning in the background? He said, 'Why can't we just all get along?'"

"You ever get into the Dead?" Moon asked Harley. "You look like some of the old-timers I met on the road—the kind of guy that might have dropped a few tabs of acid along the way."

Harley reached up and adjusted the big, wide mirror mounted above the sun visor in front of him so he could get a better look at me. He smiled really big and showed off his tobacco-stained teeth. "I think I was at Woodstock. I really do."

"You think you were at Woodstock? Do you remember who played?" Moon asked?

Harley squinted his eyes and rubbed his ear with the end of the revolver barrel, even stuck his tongue inside the muzzle at one point while he gave the question a great deal of thought. "What is Woodstock anyway? Something to do with a shotgun?" Moon laughed and Harley gave him a big, snaggle-toothed grin. "I believe Jimi Hendrix was there. I for sure remember Neil Young and Joe Walsh. Those were the only performers I knew personally."

"Oh yow," Moon said. "You're cool, man. You really were at Woodstock, weren't you, Harley?"

"Yeah, I was there all right." There was a little hesitation in his voice that sounded the way people do after they have convinced someone of something that was not really and in the process even convinced themselves. "I was considerably younger at the time, you know what I mean?"

The more Harley talked about his past, the more suspicious I became of what was real about him and what was not real. Too many things just did not add up. He had switched back and forth from being crazy as a loon to cagey as a fox and was almost normal somewhere in between.

"Stupid ass!" Randall yelled, honking the horn as he swerved to miss a coyote that ran across the road in front of us.

"That was close," Moon said. "I'm glad you missed him. He reminded me a lot of my buddy, Wolff."

"Who?" Randall asked.

"My buddy I told you about that lives south of Springfield. The one I'm going to visit. His real name is Wolffgang Pollen. We call him Wolff for short."

Randall looked back over his shoulder at Moon and laughed. "Why did the coyote remind you of him?"

"Well, Wolff has big hair and a fuzzy, coyote-colored beard. When he's not following the Dead around, he lives in a cave on the backside of his grandpa's farm. Don't both animals sound similar?"

"You've got some pretty strange friends," Randall said, sounding as if he wished he were one of them.

"Yeah, Wolff's really a cool dude. He grows his own smoke. Pretty much lives off the land. Only fitting, though, since he's half Native American."

"It would take a lot of balls to do something like that, wouldn't it, Harley?" Harley turned away and looked out the window without saying a word.

"What else could a person possibly ask for?" Randall sound weary and plumb worn out.

Sounding as pitiful as a kid in a candy store without any money, Harley raised his head and looked at me in the rearview mirror. He glanced over his shoulder at Moon, looked over at Randall and said, "A cave's about the only place I'd fit in anymore."

Instead of acknowledging Harley's downtrodden mood, Moon became ecstatic. "You really would fit in, Harley. I'm sure Wolff and his grandpa would be glad to have you."

"What's the name of the place where they live?" Harley asked.

"Deer Run, Missouri. That's the name of the closest town. Have you heard of it, Harley?" When Harley shook his head, Moon went on to describe the Ozark paradise with a great deal of enthusiasm. "It's just the neatest spot in the whole world. A spring-fed river runs right past the mouth of the cave where Wolff lives. A tall bluff shades a deep blue pool of water that's full of fish and a lot of bullfrogs live in a slough nearby. You like to eat bullfrogs, Harley? I love 'em. They're like brain food to me."

"Brain food?" Harley said. "Why are they like brain food?"

"I've been to Deer Run," Randall said, butting in on the conversation. "Beautiful place. My dad and I floated a river close to there once. I was about twelve. We must have caught a hundred smallmouth bass."

Moon broke in, "Mom sure did a nice piece of work there, didn't she, Randall?"

"Mom? What are you talking about?" Harley asked, sounding more than a little irritated that he had been kicked out of the conversation.

"Mom. Mother Nature. Who do you think?" Moon said sharply, adding insult to injury.

"Yeah. It's a nice spot all right," Randall said. "Treacherous as hell when the water runs high in the spring. We hit a boulder and ripped a big hole in the canoe. Lost most of our gear, too."

Harley reached over and pecked Randall on the arm with the barrel of the revolver, and with a voice that had grown cold, he said, "Moon didn't ask you if you'd heard of Deer Run, Randall. He asked me."

I hated to think about it, but I was afraid that Harley had worked himself up into a nasty funk again. Randall's taking him out of the conversation and talking about having a good time with his dad when he was young was not a good move. Harley didn't need much to push him over the edge, and Randall seemed bound and determined to give him a shove.

Moon held his arms up over his head and popped all ten fingers one at a time. Harley didn't say anything, but I could tell by the way he worked his jaw muscles that he was getting wound up.

"You seem awfully uptight about something, Harley," Moon said. "I hope it's not something I've caused."

"You asked me the question, not Randall. Isn't that right?" Harley whined.

"Yes, that's right, Harley, I did ask you the question. Have you heard of Deer Run or not?"

"No, I thought I had, but I haven't. It sounds like the place I need to be, though, if I make it out alive from my main mission."

"What main mission?" I asked.

Harley straightened up and looked back at me with his eye twitching again. "I can't talk about it right now, Mark," he said in a raspy voice, throwing his shoulders back.

"How did you guys get hooked up together?" Moon asked.

"My friend, Mark, back there and me, we're mechanical engineers," Randall said. "We've been on a goodwill tour, acting as ambassadors for the Environmental Protection Agency. We left Kansas City six weeks ago and worked our way out to the West Coast. Now we're headed back home."

Harley snickered. "Ambassadors. What's that mean? You guys are like royalty or something?"

Randall leaned forward so he could get a good look at me and smiled. "In a way we are royalty, aren't we, Mark?"

"I don't know. In a way we are, I guess," I said humbly, not wanting to get Harley thinking we thought we were better than he was again.

Randall was too full of himself to give a second thought to being humble and he was off and running. "Our senior year as engineering students at Kansas University, Mark and I applied for and received a federal grant. Working under the auspices of the Environmental Protection Agency, we designed and built the steam engine that's powering this motor home. Our primary responsibility for the past six weeks has been to demonstrate how steam power can be used as an alternative to the internal combustion engine." Randall had slipped back into the formal presentation mode we were accustomed to while on our tour, which had ended the day before at a big automotive show in the Las Vegas Convention Center.

"Holy smoke, Harley," Moon said, "these boys are not just another couple of blizzard brains like you and me.

Anyone that can do heavy-minded stuff like that has got some real smarts."

I had not given Randall enough credit for taking Harley's feelings into consideration. He followed up the glowing report of our importance by saying, "Harley here, he's our guest passenger, a unique and intelligent individual he is, too."

Harley looked at me in the rearview mirror again and smiled. "Well, since I'm your guest passenger, does that make me an ambassador too?"

"It sure does, Harley," I said loud and clear. "You're as much of an ambassador as we are any day."

Harley seemed content with just a reasonable amount of attention. A stroke or two here and there to build up his badly bruised ego would get us a long way down the road without big trouble. I knew it and Randall knew it. Moon, on the other hand, was a completely different story.

"Look at that big Sequoia cactus," Harley said, pointing out the right-hand side window. "One of those babies can hold six tons of water."

Instead of Moon acknowledging that Harley had given us some interesting information that probably none of us knew, he said, "Yeah, steam would be a nice way to go. Clean-burning and efficient. Your design seems to operate much quieter than other steam-powered engines I have known."

"My God," Harley said, "Moon knows everything about steam engines too. Hell, I'm totally surrounded by engineering geniuses."

"I'm not an engineer, sir," Moon said abruptly. "I am an environmentalist. My quest in life is a search for that which will provide the best conditions for our planet. I am a true student of MN."

"MN, what the hell's MN?" Harley said, sounding very defensive, making me think that the next time Moon opened his mouth he might find a fist stuck in it.

I saw Moon smirk at Harley as if he were nothing but a dimwit. I cleared my throat loudly and waved my arm, hoping he would look in the rearview mirror and see me trying to get his attention. Somehow I had to warn him to stop messing with Harley's mind. Every time he pissed him off he increased our chances of going up in smoke.

When I heard the sharp tone of Moon's voice, I knew it was too late. "MN stands for Mother Nature," Moon sniped at Harley. "I figured even you would know something as simple as that."

Harley squinted his eyes and gave Moon a look that would kill, but it did not slow down the love-and-peace man one bit.

"I hope you don't take this wrong, Harley," Moon said, as he wrinkled up his nose and sniffed the air. "On the road, when I was followin' the Dead, sometimes people didn't bathe for a couple of days, or maybe even a week. They'd stink a little, especially in the summer, but the whole damned group put together didn't smell half as rotten as you do. You might want to check your pulse, old man. You could be dead and not know it."

If Moon had even so much as cracked a smile, it would have helped. Instead he sat there like a know-it-all and it was just too much for old Harley to take.

Without hesitation, Harley got right into Moon's face and growled, "MN. MN. MN." He repeated the two letters over and over, as if they had caused a short circuit in his brain. "So you think it's all right to talk to people just using initials, do you? Even though only a dumb dick like you would know what the hell they mean. What's your game, Moon? To make other people feel stupid?"

"No. Not really. I didn't really think... " Moon stammered for words.

Before Moon had a chance to collect his thoughts, Harley reached over and grabbed the steering wheel as we approached Exit 121 leading to Seligman, Arizona, forcing Randall to steer the big rig off the interstate and down the ramp. All the while Harley was shouting, "MR. MR. MR. Long live MR."

Moon had finally pushed Harley one toke over the line and what was about to happen next was MS & T—Misery, Suffering and Trouble with a capital T.

Chapter Six

"Lordy," Randall said, as he stopped the big rig at the bottom of the exit ramp. His hands were shaking and his knuckles were white. "Just tell me the next time you want me to turn, Harley. You almost caused us to turn over."

"Okay," Harley said calmly, as he pointed up the frontage road that ran under the interstate toward the town of Seligman. "I'm telling you to turn here. That make you feel better?"

Randall covered his face with the palms of his hands and shook his head violently. "I'll never make it back home—not ever, never."

"What the hell's really goin' on here anyway?" Moon asked. When no one said anything, he mumbled, "Obviously a lot more than meets the eye."

"You want to know what's going on, do you?" Harley said, as he held the revolver up to his chest and stroked the barrel gently the way someone might comfort a pet. "MR, that's what's goin' on. I bet you don't even know what MR means, do you?"

When Moon didn't say anything, Harley cleared his throat and sat up straight in his seat, commanding a certain degree of attention. "You want to talk just using initials, do you, Moon Baby? Hell, I can talk initial talk with the best of 'em."

"All right, Harley," Moon said. "I got carried away. I'm sorry. What does MR stand for?"

"That's better. Much better. MR stands for Mother Road, Route 66. Don't forget it either." Harley gave Randall a scathing look and poked his arm with the barrel of the revolver. "I can't believe you didn't take MR out of

Kingman instead of the stupid interstate. I should make you turn around and go back."

Harley had become nervous and fidgety again. Waving the revolver around, he had worked himself up to a dangerous level of anxiety.

"Harley," I said cautiously, figuring it was only a matter of time before he shot the revolver, detonated the TNT or started up the chain saw and chopped off one of Moon's hands. "Can I reason with you for just a minute?"

"Sure you can, Mark. Nobody else can, though. Just don't try to pull something over on me. I'm not as stupid as Moon thinks I am."

"No one thinks you're stupid. If you think back to when we left Kingman, you didn't say you wanted to take Route 66. You said you wanted to go to the Grand Canyon, remember? Hell, we would have gladly taken Route 66, wouldn't we, Randall?"

Harley barked at me before Randall could say a word. "It's too damn late now. We'll just take 66 from Seligman to Ash Fork."

Still sitting at the stop sign with his mouth half open, looking as if he were in a daze, Randall made one final attempt to keep us headed straight for home. "Wouldn't it be better if we just went straight across this road? We could get right back up on the interstate."

"Better?" Harley blurted out, directing Randall toward Seligman with the wave of his hand. "Since when is an interstate better than something real? Route 66 is real, Pal. Get your kicks on Route 66. Haven't you ever heard that song in your whole life? Jesus, what do they teach college kids today?"

"Okay, we'll do what you say."

"Well do it then, man. You've been sitting here forever. Move this big beast. I bet you don't even know the year they opened the Mother Road."

"Was it 1945?" Randall said.

Harley smacked himself on the side of his head with the flat of his hand. "There you go again. Not knowin' anything about your own country's history. They opened Route 66 in 1926, ten years before I was born. My Uncle Shorty drove the entire route from Chicago to LA in 1939 in an American Bantam coupe: a midget auto with a curb weight of 1200 pounds, a 75-inch wheelbase, no trunk, no trip odometer, and no radio. It had a 22-horsepower engine that got 50 miles to the gallon and the car sold brand-spankin' new for 335 good old American dollars. What do you think of that, you bunch of know-it-alls?"

"I don't believe all of this is happening," I said when I saw the sign 'Seligman, Arizona. Population 900.' "The guy who will probably marry Ann if I die is from this one-horse town."

"Who?" Harley said.

"That stupid Ray Gilbert. He's from Seligman, can you believe it?"

"What are you talking about?" Moon asked. "What stupid guy? What do you mean 'if you die'? What are you doing to these guys, old man? What's going on?"

Harley held the revolver up over his head and pulled back the hammer. "Oh, no!" Randall yelled. I slapped my hands over my ears and cringed.

"Okay, Moon Dog," Harley said, "it's time for the old man to have show and tell."

Here goes, the long-awaited showing of the TNT—maybe the big blast. Just as I started to cop a last-minute plea, hoping for some spiritual consideration for all the things that I had done, stupid-assed Moon growled, "It's Moon Love, Harley. Not Moon Dog. What's the matter, are you deaf?"

"Lord," I said to myself, "I have tried to treat people nice. Remember when I mowed Mrs. Olsen's yard the whole summer for free? And remember when...."

"Oh yeah," Harley said, "sorry. I know how people hate to be called the wrong name."

He eased the hammer back down and laid the revolver in his lap, acting as if he had never been upset about anything.

"It's my own fault. I have a hard time remembering made-up names."

"It's okay," Moon said. "I understand."

As we rounded the corner and headed down Main Street, Harley slapped Moon on the leg and laughed. "You wanted to know what's going on, right, Moon? Well, we're in Seligman, Arizona—a town founded around 1887 by the Seligman brothers, who were a couple of bankers from New York that owned the Hash Knife Cattle Company." Harley pointed at a building on our left as we rolled down historic Route 66 past Lamport Street. "I gobbled down a couple of hamburgers there at the Snow Cap Drive-In when I was a visitor in 1959.

"See that barber shop? I got my haircut right there in that very shop. First crew cut I ever had in my life. Nicest guy in the world owned the shop. It only cost me $2."

"Why don't we stop in and see him?" Moon said, glancing over his shoulder at me and winking. I figured he thought we might be able to ditch Harley and be on our way. I winked back.

Harley took a good long look in the mirror. He wiped the mustard away from under his nose and flipped the chunk of french fry out of his beard. "I really should go see him. He's a good old boy. A really big supporter of the Mother Road, too."

Moon got up out of the director's chair and laid his hand on Harley's shoulder. "Stop the big rig, Randall. Let's all get out and go inside the barber shop."

Harley looked back at me and frowned. "I would," he said, as he pushed Moon's hand away, "except for the fact that I look too bad. I don't want him to see me lookin' this bad. When he saw me last, I was a much younger man." Pointing at a motel to our left, Harley took a deep breath and sighed. "I stayed right there in The Deluxe Court that same night. Nicest damned people in this town you'd ever want to meet."

"That's all well and good," Moon said, dismissing Harley's emotion-filled story. "All I want to know is why you've got the revolver. You seem like a person too high-strung to be trusted with a weapon."

I was amazed when Harley just laughed and rambled on. "Yeah, this town is the beginning of what's left of Old Route 66. It's 160 miles back west from here to Topock. How long would that take us if we turned around right now? Surely not more than four hours, am I right, Randy Boy?"

When Randall didn't say anything, Harley drank the last of a vanilla milkshake, wiped off his mouth and nonchalantly said, "Oh well, we can always go there another time."

That was a strange thing to hear from a man who had told us he only had a few months to live.

As we headed out of town past garages, motels and restaurants that lined the tourist-clogged streets, Harley was still rambling on about days gone by. His final observation was to point out what remained of the old A.T. & S.F. railroad stations and Harvey House structures, mumbling something about a redheaded waitress.

"Yow, Harley, you sure know a lot about this town." Moon sounded as if he was just humoring Harley.

Harley raised his eyebrows and smiled. "I'm a lot smarter than some people think. I've got brains held in reserve I've never even thought about using yet. You boys ever hear of such a thing?"

"No," Moon said, looking back at me over his shoulder as he laughed.

"How do you know so much about the history of the Mother Road?" I asked Harley.

"I'm a dues-paying member of the Historic Route 66 Association of Arizona," Harley said proudly. "Been affiliated with the organization since it was started in 1987."

"I'm very impressed," I said, wondering once again how he could have done so many things and still have spent twenty years in prison.

Harley looked at me in the mirror and yawned. "Yeah, well I know a lot about stuff I've never told you boys.

Probably never will either. I've only got so much time to live, you know."

"See," Moon said, "what's that all about? Are you dying, goin' on a trip or what?"

Harley just stared out the window and started to hum "Amazing Grace" again.

Just past an abandoned service station, as we headed out of town, we had the option to either go straight ahead onto I-40 or continue on Old Route 66 to Cookton Road exchange and on to Ash Fork, approximately 22 miles ahead.

"Last chance," Randall said. "We can still get back up on the interstate. Old 66 don't look to be in the best of shape."

I knew Harley was sick of Randall ragging him about getting back on the interstate.

"You might want to write this down, Randy Boy," he snarled.

"Unless you see a white rabbit jump out of my butt, we stay on the Mother Road, okay? If you want to wait here for it to happen, fine with me."

Randall threw his hands up in the air. "Route 66 it is, Harley. Just thought I'd ask."

"Look at that big baby," Harley said, pointing at a huge juniper tree on the left-hand side of the road.

"Yeah," Moon said, "it must be a couple hundred years old."

After we crossed the railroad overpass, Harley called our attention to the San Francisco Peaks, which at 12,670 feet were the highest mountains in Arizona. "There's no roadside services on this stretch, that's good," Harley said. "It'll be like the road was back in the old days."

Harley got a twinkle in his eye and started to tell us about a sexual encounter he once had back in the early sixties. It was with a hitchhiker girl he picked up outside of Oklahoma City on his way to California. He said the more he told her about it and the closer they got to the San Francisco majestic peaks, the friendlier she became. What consummated the deal for real was when she told Harley that it looked to her as if Mother Nature must have been thinking of a big erection the day the mountain got built? After that, there was no question about what they had to do, so they climbed to the top of the mountain. At that point in the story, something seemed to get cross-wired in Harley's brain, which caused him to stop talking about it altogether.

Even though we begged and pleaded with him to tell us the details, he flatly refused, his final comment being that he may tell us later—if we were good.

I looked down into one of the many McDonald's' food sacks that covered the floor and smiling back at me was Ronald, the happy-faced clown.

"Hey, Harley. Do you mind if I eat your Happy Meal?" I asked.

He reached around the seat and jabbed a finger at me, as if I were a piece of meat that he was about to fork. "I damn well certainly do mind. Don't you dare touch any of my food. In fact, all the rest of the McDonald's food is just for me. I told you before, I have to save it in case of an emergency."

"Well then, I need to stop somewhere," I said, pouting as I thought about how selfish Harley had been, not sharing my Percodan and hogging the big pile of food as if one little Happy Meal would make a difference.

"We can stop in Ash Fork," Randall said. "They'll probably have some good old home-cooked food."

"I can't believe it," I moaned. "You've got all this food. What would it hurt to share? Oh, my back!" I screamed when Randall hit a bump and it felt as if I had fallen from a rooftop onto the ground.

"Oh, go ahead," Harley said, "eat the damn thing. I don't even know what a Happy Meal is anyway."

"What's wrong with Mark's back? Something is really fishy around here," Moon said suspiciously when no one said anything. "I'm beginning to think I've hooked up with a bunch of nuts."

Randall pointed at a green metal box behind the driver's seat. "The handle was sticking up. He caught his foot and fell across that tool chest, twisting his back."

"Bummer," Moon said. "I bet that hurt like hell."

"Will someone roll down a window?" I said when I looked toward the back of the big rig and could barely see outside because of all the smoke.

"You want some fresh air, do you, Mark?" Harley said. "Tell you what, Son: I've got to stop and take a piss. So we'll all get out and stretch our legs a bit."

"Great idea," I said. "I was about to go in that cup like you did."

At Harley's suggestion, Randall pulled onto a narrow dirt road that ran alongside a dry gulch. He followed it until we had lost sight of the highway.

"Why did we go so far?" Moon asked, sounding more dubious of Harley than ever.

"'Cause I don't want strangers to see my tallywacker," Harley smarted off. "You boys can look all you want, though, since we know each other so well."

There was no doubt that Harley had recovered from what apparently was a sudden attack of shyness when we were trying to get him to tell about his sexual experience on top of the mountain.

"You're a sick old turd," Moon said. "You should be locked up."

"Language," Harley said, as he poked Moon in the ribs with his finger.

"Language?" Moon threw his hands in the air. "What the hell are you talking about?"

"Words just like that," Harley said, as he looked at me in the rearview mirror with a crooked little smile. "We don't tolerate no cussin' around here. Do we, Mark?"

"No, sir," I said. "No cussin' around here, that's exactly right. Those are Harley's rules."

"Okay, everybody out." Harley got up out of the passenger seat and on his way to the side door he kicked over a sack, scattering a large order of crispy brown French fries all over the floor. Harley yawned when he opened the side door and stepped onto the dry sandy ground. "That includes you too sleeping beauty."

"Why do all of us have to get out?" Moon said, not making any effort to move as Randall stumbled over him and hopped out the door.

"Because I want you to, that's why". Harley waved the revolver in the air like a wild cowboy.

I stepped outside into the quiet of the desert where the only sound I heard was... silence. I shaded my eyes with the flat of my hand against the glare of the sun. A small, gray lizard scurried across the sand in front of me and disappeared behind a rock, taking with it the only sign of life.

Harley looked shorter standing out in the wide-open space than he did in the confines of the big rig. He stood about five-nine and would push it to weigh in at a hundred and sixty pounds. What he lacked in stature however, he more than made up for with his rugged looks.

With everyone outside, Harley unzipped his pants and reeled out his sizable manly tool. For a good long time the perverted old bastard just stood there and gazed up at the sky, not dribbling a drop.

"Once, only once," Harley said, nodding his head up and down slowly, "maybe only once in a person's lifetime it ever happens. And that's if you're lucky, which most men are not."

"What are you talking about?" I asked, feeling like a voyeur standing there looking at him all exposed.

"What am I talking about, you ask?" Harley had lowered his voice and slowed down his presentation and he sounded like a preacher about to deliver a sermon on the seriousness of sin.

"She was seventeen. The love of my life, as it turned out. We had climbed to the pinnacle of the summit, the highest spot at the top of the San Francisco Peaks. Without speaking a word, we slithered out of our clothes, like a couple of snakes shedding their skin, and faced the setting sun. A soft summer breeze stroked her beautiful black hair. The sky was purple. Lazy white clouds drifted above us. The sounds of love were like a symphony."

Harley had gotten into the memory so strongly that he stopped telling the story to us and began to live it over again in his mind.

"What then?" Randall asked impatiently, getting Harley back on track.

Harley jerked his head back as if he had been awakened from a dream. "What then?" he repeated. "Oh, yeah, sure."

"Then what happened?" I asked, after Harley stopped talking and stared up at the sky again.

"It could have been just a figment in my mind, but at the peak of the sensual experience. When I looked out across the horizon, I thought I saw the face of Almighty God looking back at me."

"Oh my gosh!" Moon gasped. Reliving the old memories has caused Harley to get aroused. Moon was laughing so hard he was barely able to stand up. Randall, on the other hand, seemed to be enjoying the show. "She must have been a real pretty girl, right Harley?" Randall said sheepishly.

Harley's response brought back memories from the first time I discovered The Song of Solomon at church one Sunday when I was a kid.

"Behold, she was beautiful," Harley said. "Breasts like two fawns, twins of a gazelle. Eyes like doves, lips like a scarlet thread. Lordy, what a nice long, smooth neck she had." Harley took a long deep breath and sighed. "The sweet smell of her garments was like the scent of Lebanon. She had round thighs shaped by a master hand. Her belly was like a heap of wheat. Navel like...."

"Come on, Harley," I said, "we get the picture. Let's get back on the road."

It took a few seconds for Harley to come back to the real world. When he did, all of the beauty and pleasant memories he had bestowed upon us quickly turned to sour grapes.

After a brief adjustment, Harley directed the yellow flow to splatter on the flat, green petal of a cactus plant a few feet away from where we stood. Being the crudely inventive creature he was, Harley decided to write the girl's initials in the sand with his stream. He managed to finish the M and was rounding the curve on the bottom of the S when a gust of wind blew some of the spray back onto Moon's pant leg.

"Hey watch it, Mister!" Moon yelled. "You're pissin' on the wrong dude."

Harley's eyes narrowed. His face turned red. He flipped his driver back into his pants and screamed, "I'm sick of your trivial crap, Moon. The world can do without a crumb brain like you."

Just that quickly, Harley leveled the revolver and fired a round over Moon's head. The sound of the blast split the still desert air like a sonic boom. A second shot, aimed at the ground, hit a couple of inches in front of Moon's tennis shoe, kicking dirt up on the pant leg of his jeans.

"Oh my God!" Randall yelled, as if it were him who Harley had almost shot. Moon, however, just stood there gazing up at the sky as if nothing out of the ordinary had happened, like he had nerves of steel.

"This is the final straw. I was going to part company with you boys in Kansas City. Now I've decided to take you with me to Chicago."

"Chicago! I thought you were headed for Deer Run," Moon said. "What happened to the idea of you living in a cave?"

"I might after I finish my Chicago mission. That's the first thing on my list. After the way Moon has treated me, I just don't think I can trust him anymore."

"He can trust you, can't he, Moon?" Randall said, his voice dripping with the sound of desperation. Moon stared at Harley, but he didn't say a word.

"Yeah, it's a shame," Harley said. "I thought I only had one more killin' to do. Looks like I was wrong."

I started to plead with Moon to tell Harley he was sorry. All he had to do was be a little more civilized and the old man would be all right. Before I could say anything, Harley started to talk mean and ugly again.

"You want to know why I'm going to Chicago, Moon?" Moon just looked down and kicked at the sand, so Harley answered his own question. "I'm goin' to kill my brother. That's why. So what do you think of that, Moon Pie?"

Chapter Seven

Things took a sudden turn for the worst when Harley heard a rattling sound behind him. He whirled around, pulled the hammer back on the revolver and with one well-placed shot to the head, blew away a coiled-up rattler.

While Harley looked down at the dying snake as it twisted and turned in the sand, Moon ran around the front of the big rig, jumped behind the wheel and tried to start the engine.

"Get out of there, you little hippie prick!" Harley yelled, as he hurried around to the driver's side with the revolver pointed at Moon's head.

The threat did not bother Moon one bit; he just switched to suicide mode, gave Harley the finger and calmly said, "You may be able to kill me, old man, but I'm way too tough for you to eat."

Harley walked up to the window and stuck the end of the revolver barrel between Moon's eyes. "Get your skinny tail out of there right now." Harley's voice was so filled with anger that he sounded like he was going to boil over.

"Please don't shoot him, Harley," I begged. "He doesn't mean any harm. He's just a free spirit like you are."

Moon was so cool. He just sat there, stone-faced, and looked at Harley as if he couldn't care less about what was going on.

"Well, Moon Beam," Harley finally said. "Are you going to get out of there or what?"

What did Moon do? He just smiled and honked the horn repeatedly. Beep, Beep, Beep, three shorts. Beeeep, Beeeep, Beeeep, three longs. Beep, Beep, Beep, three short beeps again. He taunted Harley by sending an SOS signal using Morse Code.

"Get out right now or I'll pull the trigger," Harley's voice quivered. His hand shook so badly he could barely hold the revolver steady.

Moon slowly opened the door. The second his feet hit the ground; he lowered his head and lunged forward into Harley's chest, knocking him down. Running like a jackrabbit, Moon headed toward a ravine, yelling, "Free at last! I'm free at last!"

"Son of a bitch!" Harley growled, as he scrambled to his feet. Boom! There was a deafening roar when he fired the revolver and sand flew up to the left of his zigzagging prey. Boom! A second shot kicked up sand on the right. Boom! A third shot found its mark, and Moon went down like a heart-shot deer.

"Harley, you rotten bastard!" Randall yelled. "You've shot Moon."

Harley turned the revolver on Randall. With a cold, hard voice he screamed, "That's right, Buddy Boy. Here's one for you too!"

Before Randall could say anything, Harley pulled the trigger. Boom! The bullet hit the right-hand corner of the windshield and Randall dropped to the ground.

"Holy smoke!" I shouted. "You've shot Randall too."

"Stay here!" Harley shrieked at me, as he hurried toward Moon, who lay flat on his back holding his foot and moaning.

I looked down at Randall, who I thought had been critically injured. He was propped up on one elbow, staring back at me. "Moon's still alive," I said. "He's cussin' at Harley like a wild man."

"Good. That's good." I was amazed Randall had remained so calm, considering the circumstances.

"Are you okay?" I asked, as I reached down, grabbed him by the arm and helped him to his feet.

"I'm okay. A little shook up, but glad to be alive."

"You turned your head just in time." I reached over and pulled a thin sliver of glass from the top of his ear. "Your face could have been cut up really bad. As it is, you've only got a few scratches."

"You could have killed me, you crazy old fart!" Moon yelled, as Harley ran up beside him.

"Looks as if Moon lucked out too," I said. "We've got to stop Harley before he kills all of us."

"You're right. I'm surprised he hasn't accidentally detonated the dynamite. That stupid button is sticking out like a big wart. Got any ideas on how we are going to stop him?"

"One of us has to go inside the big rig and get the butcher knife. Stab him when he walks through the door." I thought Randall might get a sudden burst of courage and go for it, considering Harley had almost blown his head off. When he didn't make a move, I laid it out for him again. "You need to plunge the knife into his heart. Kill him instantly before he can set off the dynamite."

I looked at Randall with great anticipation, hoping against hope that he would take advantage of the situation. When he gave me the wide-eyed look of a man who had just been asked to sign his own death warrant, I knew my plan to celebrate a nice heartfelt, legal murder in self-defense had failed.

"Are you okay?" I asked, as Moon limped back toward us with Harley close behind.

"He's lucky to be alive," Harley said. "Stay here, all of you. I'll be right back."

Harley went inside the big rig and reappeared a couple of minutes later holding a lit stick of dynamite. Harley wrinkle up his nose and squinted his eyes as red sparks flew from the burning fuse and the air began to fill with smoke.

"Oh no!" Randall said, as he turned around to run and knocked me down. As I scooted backward in the sand, frantically trying to escape, Moon grabbed my arm and helped me to my feet.

"What in the hell are you doing?" I yelled.

"Only what you boys have forced me to do." Harley held the dark brown, wax-coated stick of dynamite out in front of him and smiled.

"Please, Harley," Randall begged. "We'll do anything, if you won't blow us up."

"I thought I was your friend," I said, pleadingly. "Why would you want to kill me?"

Even though Moon was not badly injured, he did look a little pale around the gills.

Harley was having the time of his life, flicking his tongue in and out like a snake, as the glowing red fuse burned down closer to the dynamite. Holding the stick above his head, he stood there looking as proud as the Statue of Liberty. At the last possible moment, he threw the stick into the ravine.

Boom! A deafening blast shook the ground as a mixture of sand and smoke boiled up into the air.

Waving his arms madly above his head, Harley danced around in a circle, laughing and snorting like a pig.

I had not cried from fear since I was a kid, but a grisly feeling of panic deep down in my gut caused my eyes to fill with tears.

Once again, I wished more than anything that I could get even with Harley for what he did. I had changed my mind about wanting him to suffer a slow painful death. At that stage of the game, any form of death would do.

I just wanted it to be over quickly so a healing process could begin. I thought about Ann and what a comfort it would be to lay my head in her lap. All I had to do was stay alive long enough to catch Harley off-guard.

"What the hell's the matter with you, Mark? Were you crying?"

"Nothing's the matter, Harley," I said, as I looked away.

"All I did was put on a little dynamite display. I just wanted to show you boys how powerful TNT can be."

"We know now, that's for sure," Randall said, trying to sound brave, even though I knew he had probably dribbled in his pants.

"It would behoove all of you to remember this one thing: Even if you shoot me, stab me, choke me, or try to kill me in any other way, in my final seconds on this earth I'll detonate the blasting cap and take the whole bunch of you with me. You know what I mean?"

"We hear you all right, don't we, boys?" Randall said, and I forced a smile.

Moon, on the other hand, seemed obsessed with irritating Harley, no matter the cost. "Yeah, good old Alfred would sure be proud of you. Alfred Nobel," Moon said when Harley looked at him and shook his head. "I can't believe an explosives expert like you doesn't even know who invented dynamite."

"I know who he is. You just caught me off-guard. People accused him of doing the Devil's work because so many people got killed with nitroglycerin. That was the forerunner to TNT. They called it blasting oil, and it was highly unstable. Dynamite is a Greek word that means power. Did you know that, Moon, you little piece of crap? I also know somebody who won the Nobel Peace Prize, too."

"I take it back. You know a lot more about it than I thought," Moon said, sounding more humble.

After a long silence, Harley looked at Randall and said, "Now that we're all one big happy family again, Randall my boy, you go sit yourself down behind the wheel."

Randall hurried around the front of the big rig and climbed into the driver's seat. Moon and me climbed in the side door and sat down on the couch while we waited for Harley.

"What are you doing out there?" I was worried he might be thinking of lighting another stick, only this time tossing it inside the big rig.

"Yeah, what's going on?" Randall asked nervously.

Harley climbed back inside with a big smile on his face. "Waiting on me, are ya? I had to reload. All the shooting burned up my last bullet. All right boys, we're back to business as usual. Mark, I want you to tie Moon up and lock him in the crapper." Harley slammed the door and walked over to the counter by the sink. Ripping open a McDonald's bag, he picked up a Big Mac and began to scarf it down like a hungry dog. Between bites he said, "I always get hungry when I set off a charge. How about you boys? You want something to eat?"

"Tie him up with what?" I asked.

"Use a shoestring." Harley pointed at one of my hiking boots lying on the floor. "Strip it out and get started. You better do a good job, too, or I'll tie you both to the bumper and see how fast you can run."

I glared at Harley as I pulled the string from the boot and wrapped it around Moon's wrist. I wished that hate could kill, Harley would explode.

"Is that too tight?" I asked Moon when I tied the second knot.

"I'll be the judge of what's too tight," Harley said, as he crammed down the rest of the hamburger and checked out the knot. "Hell no, it's not too tight," he mumbled, as he walked toward the front of the big rig. "Nothing's too tight for that little freak."

Not seeing any blood, I asked Moon where he had been hit.

He gave me a loony-faced grin. "I got hit in the heel. The bullet knocked my foot out from under me."

"You lucked out, man. You really did."

"What did you say about me, Moon?" Harley asked suspiciously, as he looked back at us over his shoulder.

"Moon's foot hurts where you shot him, and my back is killing me. So can we have a couple of Percodans now?" I asked boldly, figuring that I had nothing to lose.

"Show me where you're shot," Harley demanded, as he walked up beside Moon and hunkered down. "Where's the hole? Where's the blood? I want to see the wound right now."

Moon slowly raised his leg and I pointed at his tennis shoe, which looked as if someone had taken a knife and cut a chunk of rubber out of the heel about the size of a quarter.

Harley snorted like a bull. "You big faker. You only got hit in the shoe. There'll be no Perc for you, Moon. I'll tell you another thing too...."

Arf! Arf! Harley stopped in mid-sentence when he heard a dog bark.

"Well, Howdy Doody. Would you look at what we've got out here, boys?" Harley said with a big grin, as he opened the door.

Moon and I looked out the side window and standing there, wagging a broken tail, was the most god-awful, ugly-looking dog I had ever seen—worse even than anything I saw when I worked at the city dog pound one summer.

"Come here, boy," Harley said. "Come here, Long Dog."

"You're not going to bring that dog in here, are you?" I said.

Harley actually snarled at me and showed his teeth. "Damn right I am. I've already named him. Long Dog's mine now. You best treat him with human respect too."

Randall tried to talk him out of the dog. "Just look at him, Harley. He's got some kind of terrible disease. If you want to shoot something, put that mutt out of his misery."

Harley grabbed Randall's arm. "Tell you what, Buddy Boy. I want Long Dog in here a whole lot more than I do the three of you. Just keep that in mind, if push comes to shove."

What an incredible transformation had just occurred. A bitter man, on the verge of killing all of us one moment, had become a compassionate fanatic the next—all because of a nasty little dog that looked like an overgrown Polish sausage with patches of hair.

Harley patted his leg again and begged Long Dog to jump through the door. The poor thing made a heartfelt leap, came up short by a couple of inches, smashed his head into the edge of the step and fell back onto the ground with a yelp.

"He's either too weak to go the distance, or too blind to see the doorway," I said, figuring it could be a little of both.

"Poor boy," Harley said, as he jumped outside and cradled Long Dog in his arms.

Considering how consumed with affection Harley had become, I decided to play on his emotions. "I'm going to let Moon lie down on the big bed in back," I said, as he climbed into the motor home. "No good reason to lock him up in the bathroom, okay, Harley?"

"Go ahead, Mark. Do whatever you want. Just don't bother me for awhile, okay?" When we walked to the back of the big rig, Harley sat down on the edge of the couch and rocked Long Dog back and forth as if he were a little baby.

"You're happy now, aren't you, Harley?" I said, expecting him to give me a glowing smile.

Instead, he stopped the cradling and looked at me with tears in his eyes. "I had a beagle when I was a kid that somebody killed just for meanness. I think it was my brother. I never knew for sure." Harley put Long Dog's runny nose against his cheek and hugged him so tightly that the poor thing moaned and tried to wiggle free.

"I'm sorry about your dog," I said. "I know how it feels. I've lost a couple I really liked myself."

"Bastards never let me have another one either," he sobbed and looked away.

"You've sure got yourself some specimen there, Harley," I said, when I realized what looked like a collar was actually a strip of raw skin, apparently a condition caused by a bad case of the mange. "Long Dog has the mange, you know," I grumbled, as I watched a patch of hair on the dog's hip move like a wave on the water and wondered how long it would be until we humans would be attacked by fleas.

Harley nodded his head without even looking at us when I told him that Moon and I were going to the back of the big rig. I loosened the knot on the shoestring that bound Moon's wrists when we sat down on the big bed.

"Thanks, man," he whispered. "You're a real pal."

"Let's go," Harley said to Randall, slurring his speech as Long Dog flicked his quick little tongue in and out of Harley's mouth like an anteater.

"I thought you got hit bad the way you went down on that last shot," I said.

"Me too," Moon said. "I think I tripped over a rock at the same time the bullet hit my shoe."

"Why don't you put that dog outside, Harley," Randall said, as he started the engine. "We might get a disease."
You would have thought Randall had been talking about Harley's mother.

"What the hell! Are you crazy? Long Dog's my only real friend. At least I can trust him. That's more than I can say for you jack-offs. Now hit the road before I slap you upside the head."

"What about me, Harley?" I said. "You know you can trust me, don't you?"

"A lot more than I can Moon and Randall, that's for sure."

"I'm glad you feel that way. Since my back's hurting something awful, can I please have a Percodan, old friend?"

Harley laughed quietly to himself. "You can have one, Mark. But Moon Love can't. He is being punished for being a bad boy."

I tapped Moon on the shoulder when I saw Long Dog lick Harley on the lips. "That a sick sight, or what?" I said when I saw Harley lick him back.

"I hope the old bastard gets the mange from that broke-dick little dog," Moon said with an empty look of disgust.

"What did you say?" Harley grumbled, pulling a hamburger from one of the sacks. He bounced it off the wall beside Moon's head, leaving a glob of ketchup about the size of a ping-pong ball. "I know you was talkin' bad about my sweet little dog."

"He didn't say anything about your dog, Harley." I picked up the burger meat and put it back on the bun. Moon opened his mouth and I gave him a bite. "Let's let him calm down," I whispered to Moon. "It won't do any good to get him upset."

"Rotten piece of crap," Moon said in-between bites of the hamburger.

Broke-Dick Dog is a perfect name for such a strange looking creature, I thought, as I patted Moon on the shoulder. I hoped he would hold his tongue and not cause Harley to have any more flare-ups, but I had my doubts.

With Long Dog cradled in his arms, Harley jumped to his feet as if he had been goosed by the Devil. "Where the hell are those scissors?"

"What scissors?" I blurted out, backing up against the headboard of the big bed as Harley rushed toward us. Getting tangled up in his own feet, he fell down on the floor. The revolver Harley had shoved down in the waistband of his pants slipped out and slid across the floor at the same time Long Dog flew through the air like a shot out of a cannon. Lighting on Moon's chest, the weird-looking dog began to frantically lick hamburger juice off Moon's face with his quick little pink tongue.

"Where are they, Mark?" Harley shouted, as he picked up the revolver and scrambled to his feet. He rushed to the cabinet mounted on the wall beside the big bed. When he jerked open the door, a roll of tape fell from the top shelf and bounced onto the floor. "Oh, I see they're right here."

"Are they there?" I asked, as if I had not heard what he said.

Harley turned around with the sharp-pointed barber's scissors in his hand, walked over beside the big bed, snipped them a couple of times in front of Moon's nose and laughed nervously.

"I can't believe you got in such a panic," I said, taking advantage of having the upper hand. "No way in hell would I try something as stupid as stabbing you with a pair of scissors. How did you know they were in the cabinet anyhow?"

"I found them when I was sitting back here awhile back. I should have thrown them in the toilet like I did the .22-

caliber pistol." I smiled to myself when he laid the scissors back on the shelf and closed the door.

Harley snatched Long Dog off Moon's chest and headed toward the front of the big rig. "I can hardly wait until we roll into Flagstaff," he said, looking back over his shoulder at us with a grin. "Have I got a big treat in store for you boys."

"Why are you so anxious to get to Flagstaff?" Randall asked, as he turned the big rig around and headed toward the highway.

Harley looked back at me and smiled. "You can untie Moon now, Mark. I want both of you to come up front with me. I may have overreacted, shooting at Moon and setting off the dynamite. There's no reason why we can't all just get along."

"Oh, that's okay," I said, as I slapped my hand over Moon's mouth to keep him from stirring up trouble again. "Everybody makes a mistake now and then."

"That's one of the things I like about you, Mark," Harley said smugly. "You follow the golden rule. To err is human. To forgive is divine."

Moon looked at me and moaned. I raised my eyebrows and shook my head back and forth.

"Okay boys, let's go. Mark, I want you in the passenger seat," Harley said. "Moon, you'll occupy the yellow director's chair."

"Why me in the director's chair?"

"You remind me of a director, that's why. You're always ordering people around. So why not?"

Moon glared at Harley, his nose twitching like a rabbit about ready to jump from cover. "Whatever you say, man. It's your party."

"That's more like it," Harley said pompously, raising his chin. "A little bit of kindness goes a long way in this world, Moon Beam. Let that be a lesson you don't forget."

"No one would know better than you," Moon said coldly.

"Well thank you, Moon. I'll just sit here on the couch with my sweet little dog. We'll play like we're all one big happy family."

"Thanks for being so nice, Harley," I said, as I untied Moon's wrists, and we walked up to the front. After we sat down in our assigned seats, Randall drove us back to the main road and we headed toward Ash Fork.

Harley was in such a good mood that he handed me a couple of Percodans, gave one to Moon, took one himself, and told us to let him know when we needed more.

For the next twenty minutes, Randall motored us down the final leg of old Route 66 toward the Crookton Road overpass. There we would join up with Interstate 40 again. Nothing meaningful was said except for Moon telling us that Jerry Garcia was buried in a sweat suit.

After hearing that bit of interesting information, Harley raised a clenched fist and solemnly proclaimed, "The king of the Dead Heads has moved on to higher ground," after which Moon gave Harley the peace sign. "Long live the Dead!"

"How's the back?" Randall asked, as he headed east past a sign that read "Ash Fork 5 miles, JCT 89 6 miles, Flagstaff 55 miles."

I glanced in the rearview mirror at Harley, who was sitting on the edge of the couch with Long Dog on his lap. "I never thought I would feel this good again," I said with a big grin, and Harley smiled back. "Thanks for the magic pill."

As we passed the "Welcome to Ash Fork, Flagstone Capital of the U.S.A." sign, Harley began another Route 66 commentary.

"This town was settled around 1880 as a stage depot under a group of ash trees at the fork of Ash Creek. See that gas station over there?" Harley pointed at the roadside attraction. "It's been around since the beginning of Route 66. There's a really neat old settler's cemetery here, too. First man buried there was Tom Kane. He got shot by mistake. Wouldn't that be a bitch of a way to die? What would the killer say? 'Oh, hey man, I'm sorry?'"

"No good way, I guess," Randall said, as we pulled out of town, got back on Interstate 40 and headed for Williams, then on to Flagstaff.

Harley just kept on doing it. How could anyone who seemingly should know so little, know so damn much?

"If we're still alive after we stop in Flagstaff, I want to drive through the Petrified Forest. It's just on the other side of Holbrook. One of my buddies in the slammer told me that petrified wood could bring a person good luck if they lick it. I don't see any problem with that, do you, Randall?" Harley asked.

"Licking it or driving through?" Moon asked with a snicker.

"No, I don't see any problem with that," Randall agreed, and I moaned.

"How much time will that take?" I asked, thinking only about how much longer it would add to the trip before I saw Ann.

"I've done it a couple of times with my dad," Randall said. "It doesn't take that long to drive through. Thirty minutes at the most, if we don't stop and mess around."

"The wood in the Petrified Forest is protected by law," Moon said. "You're not even supposed to pick it up, let alone take any with you. That's a bunch of bull about licking it bringing good luck."

"I'll tell you what then, Moon," Harley said, with a touch of sarcasm in his voice. "When you see me pick up a piece, you can do a citizen's arrest. Meanwhile, me and my dog are going to just lay back and get better acquainted."

"Let me ask you something, Harley. What did you mean when you said 'if we're still alive after Flagstaff?' Is there maybe some trouble up ahead that we should know about?"

Harley threw his head back and looked at me in the mirror with cold dark eyes. Finally, letting a hint of a smile creep through his stone-faced exterior, he said, "Nothing that a revolver, a few sticks of dynamite and a chain saw won't be able to control."

Chapter Eight

For the first time since Harley became our unwelcome guest, the atmosphere in the big rig had become almost normal. He seemed perfectly content to just lie on the couch and pamper Long Dog.

Moon clicked on the radio and tuned in to a rock station, even turned the volume up some when the DJ played "Sugar Magnolia" by the Grateful Dead. Harley smiled and commented on how good it felt to be back feeling right about things again. He even hummed along with the tune as he stroked his new dog and swayed back and forth.

Moon had rebounded from the shock of his near-death experience and he was feeling so good that when the song was over and after he had informed us that Robert Hunter was the lyricist, he decided to tell a joke. He asked if any of us had heard the one about the three-legged pig.

"Can't say as I have. But I sure would like to," Harley said, claiming that most of the really good jokes were made up in prison. He claimed that it was because inmates had so much free time.

"That's what I've heard," Moon said. "I really doubt it though."

"Why's that?" Harley asked him, defensively.

"Because most guys in prison are barely smart enough to tie their own shoelaces, let alone be creative enough to make up a good joke. I would be more inclined to think a lot more are made up by lawyers and college professors."

Harley did not say anything, but there was no doubt Moon had driven one more nail into his coffin.

Moon went on to tell his joke about a guy who walked into a bar with a three-legged pig. When the bartender asked why the pig only had three legs, the guy told him how the pig had saved his life. Once the pig had dragged him from a burning building; another time the pig had shoved him from the path of a speeding car. When it came time for the punch line, Harley sat up on the edge of the couch. "Did the guy say, I bet if you had a pig like that, you wouldn't eat him all at once either? I told you most jokes were made up in prison. The guy in the cell across from me was the joke author of that one."

"Oh brother," Moon mumbled. "I don't even know why I waste time talking to you."

Harley was feeling so good that when I asked him if I could have another Percodan, he handed me the whole bottle. Everyone settled in as we rolled on down the interstate, past Williams, Arizona. Harley pointed out that this was the last Route 66 town to be bypassed by Interstate 40. We passed Highway 64, a main road that led to the north rim of the Grand Canyon and on toward Flagstaff. Harley said Flagstaff got its name from a tall pine tree that was used as a trail marker for California-bound wagon trains. That trail eventually became U.S. Route 66.

Harley sprang to his feet as we entered the city limits of Flagstaff. "There's a bar down the road a couple of miles called the Silver Saddle," Harley said to Randall. "When you see it, pull into the parking lot and stop." Harley was so excited that he actually giggled and gave Long Dog a big kiss on the mouth.

"Why are we stopping at the Silver Saddle?" Randall asked.

"Why, you say? I've got my reasons, which is reason enough." Harley sounded so smug I wanted to slap him silly.

"Since I'm driving, it seems like I should get to know something about what's going on."

Before Harley could say anything, a police car zoomed out of a side street in front of us and gave chase to a speeding red Mustang. I expected Harley to get really upset and start cursing and yelling about how much he hated the cops. Instead, he was perfectly calm. "I'm stopping at the

Silver Saddle to drink me a beer. That and the fact I've got a prearranged meeting with a woman lined up—a red-headed Mama who knows how to swing."

Harley waited for a reaction with a big smile on his face, and we gave him exactly what he wanted. Randall spoke up first. "Are you serious? How do you know about this place?" Pushing Harley a little further, he said, "What is it, a strip joint? A dance hall for drunks and druggies?"

"So tell us all about this redhead. She's a real beauty, is that right, Harley?"

Moon chimed in, sounding very dubious, "How do you know some woman in Flagstaff? Did she correspond with you in the joint? Is she a whore or what?"

Harley reached up and flipped Moon on the ear. "Like I started to say before you so rudely interrupted me, my cellmate was a full-blooded Native American Indian named Night Hawk. He was born and raised in Flagstaff. His sister works at the Silver Saddle. As if it's any of your business, Moon Shine."

"A red-headed Indian," Moon said. "I can hardly wait to witness such a sight."

It was obvious that Harley was really nervous and becoming annoyed with us for asking so many personal questions. I figured the thought of meeting up with a woman after all these years had him a bit on edge.

"How will I recognize the place?" Randall asked.

"You can't miss it. There's a big silver saddle about the size of a car on top of the building. This is not some loser's den. It's a classy joint."

"What about us?" I asked. "What are we going to do while you're in the Silver Saddle drinking and messing around with your girlfriend?"

"Yeah," Moon said, "do we get to go inside with you?"

"I'll tell you when we get there," Harley said, raising his voice. "Just shut up for a minute. I'm tired of being pushed to have an answer for everything."

Harley reached over my shoulder and jerked the bottle of Percodan out of my hand. "You can't be trusted with any more drugs."

I glared at him in the rearview mirror, but I was too chicken to say anything.

"What's the woman's name?" Randall asked.

"I think Hawk said her name is Julie, either that or Judy. I can't remember for sure." Harley smacked himself upside the head with the flat of his hand.

"I can't remember diddly anymore. I should have written it down."

"There it is, Harley," Randall said, pointing at a silver neon sign in the shape of a saddle on top of a brightly lit, dark green building surrounded by a huge parking lot about the size of a football field.

A half dozen guys wearing cowboy hats stood off to the right side of the front door, laughing hysterically as if someone had told a funny joke. I wondered if they knew that most of the jokes were made up in prison. How impressed they would be if they knew we had one of the authors in our big rig.

Moon leaned forward and looked up at the big neon sign on top of the roof. "Harley was right. The silver saddle really is as big as a car."

"I told you it was. You boys better start believing me from now on."

"Man, this is redneck city," Moon said, as Randall pulled to within fifty feet of the front entrance to the big hall and stopped.

"Pull the beast in and park it right there," Harley said, pointing at the front door.

"We can't park a big rig right in front of the entrance," Randall said. He pointed at a large, red sign with hand-painted white letters mounted on a tall metal pole that read, DON'T EVEN THINK ABOUT PARKING HERE!

"Hey, Randall. Read my lips." When Randall turned his head, Harley shouted, "Park the Mother right now!"

Without further delay, Randall pulled up to within a few feet of the front door and turned off the ignition.

We sat for some time, nobody saying a word, and watched the action as a stream of pickup trucks, most sporting a gun rack displaying the driver's weapons of choice in the back window, began to fill the parking lot.

Harley must have had some really strange thoughts meandering through the dark corners of his mind because when he broke the silence, he was all pissed off at Randall over something they had never even discussed before.

"I don't care what else we do tomorrow, Randall. We're going to get me a CB radio. I'm tired of only talking to you three know-it-alls."

"I didn't know you wanted a CB," Randall said, sounding bewildered by Harley's surprise attack.

"I want to be able to talk to some of those people." Harley pointed at a couple of the good old boys in the crowd. "Cowboys and over-the-road truckers."

"Why don't you just crawl into one of their pickup trucks?" Moon said sarcastically, as he looked back over his shoulder. "Every one of these guys has already got a CB."

"I would miss you too much, Mooney."

"Who's going to pay for a CB radio?" Randall asked.

"You are, Randall. Who the hell do you think would pay for the damned thing?"

Harley pointed at a ten-foot whip antenna on the back bumper of a shiny red pickup truck that had pulled in on our right. "I want two big, long antennas just like that, one mounted on each side of our front bumper."

Guys and gals dressed in tight-fitting jeans and fancy western-style shirts had to turn sideways before they could squeeze past the big rig and get in the front door. "Assholes. Pricks. Jack offs." There were plenty of curse words and nasty looks being directed at us because we were parked in the sacred spot.

Harley loved the ringside seat. He stared down at the women like a scientist looking at a new discovery through a microscope. He even pressed his nose against the windshield to watch one particularly well-endowed young lady twist and turn to avoid rubbing up against the front of the bug-splattered big rig as she worked her way toward the front door. "Look at that candy-apple ass," he sang out sweetly as she disappeared inside.

"Is that the way you used to talk about some of the guys in prison?" Moon asked, and we all laughed, which was a mistake.

"All right, head for the back, all of you!" Harley screamed.

"What's the matter?" I asked as I struggled to my feet.

"What's the matter? I'll tell you what's the matter. I'm the one who's going into the bar and you're not. So what do you think of that, Mr. Moon Hog?" Harley laughed loudly. "Nobody makes fun of me and gets by with it."

"Why are we going to the back?" Randall asked. "What are you going to do with us?"

Harley grabbed Randall by the shoulder and turned him around so that they were face-to-face. "Lock you in the bathroom. What do you think?"

I panicked at the thought of being locked in that little bathroom with two other people for hours. "Please don't lock me up, Harley, I'm claustrophobic. It will be horrible."

"Just take us with you," Randall pleaded.

"Are you crazy? You'd cause me big trouble."

"No way," Moon said, "you've taught us a lesson once and for all. It's not any fun to be shot at or blown up. We'll be straight."

"Don't bother me right now," Harley said, as he rocked back and forth while he studied a dark-haired beauty wearing black leather pants and a silky white blouse leaning against the front fender of a pickup truck parked next to us. She nervously puffed on a cigarette and watched a couple of guys standing back in the shadows by the corner of the building.

"I wonder why she seems so nervous," Randall asked, as she turned her head from side to side. Standing up on her tiptoes, she looked over the bed of the truck at a couple of people as they walked toward her.

"Look at that, man," Harley said, pointing to the corner of the building. "There's a drug deal going down."

The cowboy wearing a black hat handed some money over to a skinny man with a joint dangling from his lips. He slipped a brown paper bag into the pocket of his jean jacket, walked to the front of the truck, put his arm around the girl's waist and they walked through the door into the Silver Saddle.

"That guy sure looked familiar," Harley said when the cowboy that took the money disappeared around the corner of the building. "Any of you guys recognize him?"

When we did not say anything, Harley changed the subject. "Maybe I should take you boys inside with me. Be handy to have you around if a fight breaks out."

Randall and I looked at one another and frowned. I had not given any thought to getting caught up in a fight, which was shortsighted on my part. For someone who looked as scruffy as Harley did, smelled like a goat and would probably become a drunken, loud-mouthed, obnoxious fool, the odds of not getting into a fight were probably about five hundred to one.

"Maybe I would rather be locked in the bathroom," I said, after thinking about how bad going into the dance hall with Harley could be.

"What's the matter? Afraid of a little trouble?"

"No, I just figure my chances of staying alive will be better if I stay here—unless someone decides to set the big rig on fire because we're blocking the entrance to the hall."

"Oh, I doubt that will happen."

"Stranger things have happened," I said, figuring it probably would not come about until late in the evening after some drunk had stumbled out the door and gotten pissed off because he banged into the bumper and knocked himself down. He would go to his truck; get a can of gas and the big rig would be history.

Harley tried to persuade us. "Look at it this way. Even though some people in the bar will probably have guns or knives, and some may have even killed someone, there's no reason to be afraid."

"Why?" Randall asked with a troubled expression. "Why should we not be afraid?"

"Use your head, Son. We'll be the only people in the whole place with dynamite." Harley laughed as he stood up and unbuttoned his shirt so we could look at the TNT detonator button. "Makes you feel a lot safer, doesn't it, Moon?"

Moon did not say a word.

I thought to myself, Harley is so romantic. He's going inside to try and score the sister of his friend from prison and all he can think of is possibly blowing the place up.

Harley walked over to the side door and stood there scratching his head. "All right, here's the plan: Long Dog stays in the big rig. I'd take him with us, but I don't want him shot or cut up if there's flying glass. Moon, since I trust you less than anybody, you'll be out in front of me at all times. Randall, you'll be on my left. Mark, you'll be on my right. That's the formation. Don't forget it and don't be anywhere else for any reason. If one of us has to piss, we all go piss. Hear what I'm sayin'?"

"Yeah," Moon said. "I hear what you're saying. I'm out in front, so I get hit first."

"Let's hope so," Harley said with a smile. He reached over and pinched Moon on the cheek.

Moon was getting impatient with Harley. "What if I have to do number two while I'm inside the Silver Saddle? Will all four of us get inside the stall?"

Harley never responded and I moved on to a more pleasant subject. "Would it be okay if I call home when we get inside? I'm sure Randall would like to make a call too. Would that be all right?"

"What for, Mark?" Harley asked suspiciously.

"Because Saturday's my mother's birthday. She thought we would be home by tomorrow night. I'd like to call my fiancée, Ann, too."

"Sure you can, if I can talk too." After a long pause, Harley said, "I barely remember my mom. I bet you boys have moms that treated you like little golden gods. Just let me know when you're ready to make the call."

"On second thought, I would rather make the call later," I said when Harley opened the door and we stepped out into the parking lot.

"Howdy folks," Harley said, as he grabbed his crotch and jiggled his acorns up and down a couple of times so they would hang just right. His jiggling had dislodged a big, white patch of dog hair from the front of his shirt, and it drifted away on a summer breeze, up toward the floodlights above the front door. The grim-faced crowd looked at us as if we were a bunch of lepers and began to back away.

Harley shoved Moon toward the front door of the Silver Saddle and told him to get up front where he belonged. Moon opened the heavy, black door cautiously and stepped inside a huge, open building where cedar shavings covered a wooden floor. The pounding beat of a rockabilly band was so intense it echoed in my head. I could feel the throb of the music through the soles of my shoes. The sweet pungent odor of marijuana and the stale smell of beer permeated the air.

I looked across the dimly lit room through a cloud of smoke that looked like a war zone and saw a man who looked like Duke, the cowboy from the restaurant parking lot, leaning back against the wall talking to the good-looking girl in the black leather pants.

Harley grabbed me by the arm when he spotted him and put his mouth up next to my ear. "We've got big trouble already. Make sure that cowboy doesn't get behind our back. He's Duke from The Best Food Anywhere Restaurant. That's a very dangerous man."

Chapter Nine

The cowboy tipped his hat when he spotted Harley, as if nothing out of the ordinary had gone wrong.

Harley kept a close eye on him as we tried to maintain our formation and shuffle through the crowd. We tried to keep a low profile, but it did not work very well.

Faces soured and people backed away after a tall, lanky guy with thick black sideburns and a big brown Stetson hat pointed a finger at us and yelled, "Them are the fools with the motor home blockin' the front door."

By the time we reached the bar, the camaraderie of the wild and rowdy crowd had Harley hyped up pretty good. It could not get any better for him than standing at the bar smoking cigarettes, drinking beer, talking loud and having a chance to score with a woman. Duke, and danger in general, be damned. Harley was psyched up and he was ready to rock on.

"Does a Ms. Judy or a Ms. Julie work here?" Harley shouted at the bartender so he could be heard over the brain-numbing sound of the band. He said it at exactly the same moment the band stopped playing, so Harley's booming voice carried loudly throughout the hall.

The laughter fell silent when Harley whirled around and the crowd got a full view of the real star of the show. What they saw was a highly unstable, animal-like, disheveled-looking creature, and knew immediately he would not be a fun fella' to reckon with.

Sensing a change in the mood, Harley slipped a hand under the front of his denim jacket and wrapped his fingers around the handle of the revolver.

I imagined if he actually pulled the trigger, the first shot would rip through someone in the packed crowd, killing at least one person. The deafening boom of the second and third shots would barely be heard over the screams and shouts of hundreds of people as they trampled each other trying to escape the dance hall.

As if an earthquake had struck, a rumbling sound from out in the parking lot caused heads to turn away from Harley, and everyone stared at the front door.

"What in the world is that?" Randall said, as he craned his neck to get a better view.

"It might be the end of the world," Moon said calmly. "The Everlasting Church of L.A. said it would be all over before the end of the month."

Raising his hand above his head when the rumbling stopped and a hush fell over the crowd, Harley smiled as if he had become the proud parent of an original idea. "I know exactly what it is. It's a big bunch of Hell's Angels."

The front door banged open and one by one, at least fifty leather-clad bikers and their old ladies marched inside the building. They staked out the south end of the hall and lined up at the bar. They looked mean and surly and ready for a fight.

"Oh no," I said when I saw one of the bikers turn sideways and squeeze through the door. It was none other than the big, the bad and the ugly shotgun-tottin' monster man who had chased cowboy Duke from the parking lot at the Best Food Anywhere Restaurant earlier that morning.

When the steroid king spotted Duke, he smiled and tipped his hat. This exchange was followed by a buzzard-meat glare between the two of them.

The crowd of cowboys and their girls moved to the north end of the dance hall, leaving a wide-open space for a rumble between the two groups. I figured the fight would begin with the big fella' dragging Duke to the center of room where he would rip off his straggly-haired head.

The bikers hunched their shoulders and smirked a lot. The cowboys puffed out their chests and shuffled their feet.

"I'm cooked no matter who wins," Moon said, sounding a bit more concerned than usual. "I'm the only flower child in the whole damned place."

Before I could suggest to Moon that he might want to use the power of the peace sign to try to stop the ruckus, Harley tossed his arms in the air and yelled, "Tomorrow's Mother's Day! The drinks are on me." Jumping up in the air, he did a little jig and sang, "The rooster's in the henhouse peckin' at the hens. Mr. Brown's goin' to town to pick up his girlfriend again."

People stared at him momentarily as if he were some kind of a madman. One of the cowboys finally gave out a loud 'Yee Hah!' and broke the silence. A biker followed him with a louder rebel yell. The fiddle player ripped the bow across the strings and lit into a version of "Old Joe Clark" that started hundreds of happy feet a-dancin'.

A cowboy grabbed his honey and swung her around while a biker shuffled his old lady across the floor. The crowd lined up five deep at the bar for the free beer Harley had ordered.

Emotions were running high between the bikers and the cowboys. I even saw the big guy lumber across the floor and give Cowboy Duke a friendly slap on his back.

A dark, rather heavy-set woman with a large wart on the side of her nose gave Harley a sloppy, wet kiss on the lips and waddled away into the crowd.

Harley got all excited and pushed Moon along quickly in front of him as he tried to catch up with the woman that he thought could be either Julie or Judy, but she was nowhere to be found.

Moon looked back over his shoulder and yelled in my ear. "These crazy bastards were ready to kill each other. Look at them now. Harley has become the doctor of peace."

I smiled and nodded my head at him as I shouted back, "I doubt he'll be the peace doctor for long."

After about fifteen minutes of being out of control, dancing and yelling like a wild man, Harley was soaked with sweat, his lips were gray and he was puffing like a locomotive.

I thought about grabbing for his revolver when I saw the handle sticking out from under his coat, but I chickened out. Even in his weakened condition, I figured he could still activate the dynamite.

I leaned close to Randall's ear. "God forbid, Harley looks as if he might have a heart attack. If he goes down, let's run like hell for the front door."

"How are you going to pay for all the beer?" Randall asked Harley with a big smile. "You probably owe at least three hundred dollars."

"You can put it on your credit card."

"When we charged the chain saw, it maxed out my card," Randall said. "You're on your own, Harley."

Harley's mouth dropped open when I said, "The bill will soon be five hundred dollars if they keep drinking."

Harley jerked the three of us into a huddle and muttered, "Let's get out of here, right now." He shoved Moon in the direction of the front door, and we worked our way though the gyrating mass of people and out into the parking lot.

"Mark's right, you probably owe at least five hundred dollars, maybe more. It's a mistake to buy the house beers when there's more than hundred beer drinkers," Moon said, "unless you've got a lot of money."

Harley hung onto the open door while he caught his breath and pushed Moon into the big rig. "Get in there right now, you little prick."

"I can't believe you're shoving me around," Moon shouted back over his shoulder. "I just saved you from having to pay a big bar bill."

"Get this thing started. Let's get the hell out of here!" Harley yelled, as he stepped inside and plopped down on the couch.

Randall climbed into the driver's seat, started the engine and turned on the headlights. "This thing doesn't take off very fast, remember? So don't expect a quick getaway," Randall snapped back at Harley.

"Good boy. Good boy," Harley said, as he reached down and picked up Long Dog, who had been frantically scratching on his pant leg. Harley gave the dog a quick little kiss on the lips as he stroked his back. Fleas jumped up in the air like popcorn in a hot, greased pan.

I looked out the window at the lineup of big, black steeds waiting for their leather-clad masters to stumble out the door, mount up and rumble off into the cold, dark night.

I wondered how all those drunken crazies could keep from running into each other even before they got out of the parking lot.

"Stop, you son of a bitch!" I heard someone shout outside my window. It was one of the burly bouncers who had been guarding the front door.

"Get goin'!" I yelled at Randall. "We've got to hurry."

Randall stomped down on the gas pedal and hovered over the steering wheel as if that would help the big rig move faster. "I'm going as fast as I can!" he yelled, as the big rig slowly began to pick up speed. When we reached the far edge of the parking lot, near the frontage road, he was still not going fast enough to outrun the bouncer, who was banging on the passenger door with the butt end of a cut-off pool cue.

Harley did not waste any time springing into action. He tossed Long Dog onto the couch and pulled his beat-up, green canvas duffel bag out from under the passenger seat. Grabbing a stick of dynamite, he struck a match and lit the fuse. He stood behind my seat and laughed like a madman as a shower of sparks and a strong odor that smelled like burning hair filled the air.

"Holy smoke!" I yelled, leaning forward to get away from the sparks as I rolled down the window, hoping he would have the good sense to toss the TNT out the window before it was too late.

"Watch this," Harley hissed, as he stretched across my lap and tossed the dynamite outside. "There you go you big idiot!" he yelled, as the big guy made a running dive for the ditch.

We were so close when the dynamite exploded that the concussion from the TNT caused the cabinet doors above the sink to fly open and half dozen plates fell out, smashing on the floor.

I watched closely in the rearview mirror until Randall pulled out onto the main road, but I never saw the bouncer reappear. "I think you may have hurt him really bad," I said to Harley. "I never saw him get up after he dove into the ditch."

Harley gave me a weary little smile, as if it were all just a game to him. "I scared the hell out of him. That's all I did. So don't make me out to be a bad guy. Tough, if he can't take a joke."

"You can't throw dynamite at people for the hell of it," Moon said. "They'll come after us now, big time."

Harley grabbed Moon by the earlobe and pulled his head backwards. "Shut your hippie mouth, or I'll shut it for you. You think you know everything. You don't know crap."

Randall's voice quivered. "What do we do now, Harley? You know they'll come after us. We won't be hard to find. Where do we go?"

Harley tossed Long Dog onto the couch and hunkered down beside Moon so he could get a better look out through the windshield. Pointing at a big, blue sign with white letters, he directed Randall to turn right at the intersection and drive toward the University of Arizona Medical Center.

"Why are we going to the Medical Center?" Moon asked. "Have you decided to commit yourself to the Psycho Unit?"

Harley laughed loudly and slapped his leg. "That's funny. We'll hide in the parking lot. Those Silver Saddle jerk offs will never think to look for us at a hospital."

"That's one hell of a good idea, Harley," I said. "We just might get out of town alive."

"This place is huge," Randall said, as he drove into the parking lot entrance and headed toward the far side of the parking lot. We pulled in close to a blue and red bus that belonged to the medical center so we would be hidden from view. Randall shut off the engine.

Maintaining his carefree mood, no matter what insanity was going on around him, Moon slapped his chest with the flat of his hand and acclaimed loudly, "The big bird has landed. The good Lord has delivered us from death and destruction once again."

"This is our home for the night, boys," Harley said happily. "What a peaceful place it seems to be, I'm sure you will agree."

"What time is it?" Moon asked, as he grabbed Randall's wrist and checked his watch. "It's 9:30 p.m. I'm hungry as hell. Let's walk across the parking lot and eat at the hospital, okay?"

Harley looked puzzled. "Eat at the hospital? What would they have for us to eat?"

I encouraged the food idea. We hadn't had a good meal since morning. "A medical center this big would have lots of places to eat: a coffee shop and a cafeteria. They will have a morgue, plus a pharmacy where I can get my Percodan prescription refilled."

"A morgue?" Harley said, sounding too serious for comfort. "I've always wanted to go to a morgue. It would be kind of exciting, don't you think?"

"Are you crazy or what?" Moon said. "I'm not going into any damned morgue."

Harley laid his hand on Moon's shoulder, cocked the revolver and stuck it in Moon's ear. "You'll go one way or the other."

I could not believe I had been so stupid as to mention the morgue. What was I thinking about? I knew better than to say anything like that around Harley, even in fun.

"I'm not hungry," I said. "In fact, I'm sick." I lowered my head and faked a gag.

"What made you sick?" Randall asked.

"I don't know. I'll stay here and rest my back."

When I raised my head and looked over my shoulder, Harley was staring at me like a father about to scold his son.

"You know something, Mark? I could care less about what happens to these other two guys. You're different. I think of you as the son I never had. How do you feel about that, my boy?"

I gave him a halfhearted smile. "Oh, really? That's an interesting thought. No one has ever said anything like that to me before."

"Yes, Son. It is an interesting thought." Harley gave Long Dog a couple of quick strokes and another patch of hair flew off his back onto the floor. "So you see Mark, I would be really lonesome if you stayed in the big rig. Plus, there would be a hole in our formation."

"Our formation?" I was still preoccupied with thoughts of Harley making us go to a morgue.

Harley grinned at me and winked. "Hell, Son, without you, there'd be nobody to guard our right flank. We'd have a lopsided formation. Lord knows what we might run into."

"Okay. I'm ready when you are, Harley," I said, realizing there was no way out of my going on the trip.

Harley patted me on the shoulder tenderly. "You stick with me and you'll learn about the call of the wild. I'll teach you how to talk to animals."

When Moon grunted, I looked at Randall and he rolled his eyes. "That would be something all right, Harley. I've always wanted to be able to talk to a squirrel."

"That's easy. It's not that much different than talking to a rat."

Maybe someone will recognize how dangerous Harley is once we are in the medical center and throw a net over him or at least call the police.

"Okay, then. Everything's settled, let's roll." Harley motioned for us to get out of our seats and head out the door. "I've never been in a really big hospital before," Harley said, as he patted his pants pocket. "Just wanted to make sure I still had my sharp knife. They may want me to do some surgery."

Chapter Ten

"Now don't forget the travel rules," Harley said, as he talked about the importance of maintaining a close formation, once again reminding me to stay on the right since I was his right-hand man.

It was about four hundred yards from the back of the parking lot to the emergency room door, the closest entrance into the reddish-colored brick building that covered an entire block.

Directly in front of us was a hedgerow about three feet tall and a couple hundred feet long.

"Would it be okay if I jumped that hedge?" Moon asked. "I need some exercise. I'll wait for you on the other side. Promise."

"No. Absolutely not," Harley scolded, giving Moon a shove forward.

Moon flared up at Harley for trying to boss him around. "Why not? What can it hurt?"

Harley raised his voice. "I don't trust you for one thing. Plus it would break up the formation. We've got to stay together as a group. Go on along before you really piss me off."

I decided to make a bold move and test my favorite-son status. "What would it hurt, Harley? You'll only be a few feet away. If Moon takes off across the open parking lot, you can shoot him."

"All right, Mark," Harley said, calming down some. "I'll do it because you want me to. So it will be your fault if anything happens." Harley slapped Moon on the back and gave him a push. "Go ahead, Moon Man. Show us how high you can jump."

Moon jogged around Harley a couple of times in a tight little circle, playing like he was warming up before the big bolt. "You'll be proud of me, old man. I was a high-hurdles track star in high school."

"Stop dead still once you're on the other side," Harley spluttered out at Moon. "I'll stop you cold if you don't."

"I hear you, Mr. Harley, sir." Moon jumped up in the air and lit out for the hedge.

"Come on, let's get closer. I don't want the little bastard trying to run away. The revolver will attract too much attention when I shoot him." Harley grabbed Randall and me by the arm and we hurried toward the hedge as Moon gracefully leaped up in the air and cleared the top of the hedge by a couple of feet. Only thing was he did not bounce back up once he was on the other side.

"Moon," Harley called out his name, but there was silence. "Where the hell are you, Moon?" Harley called again, only louder.

We rushed up to the hedgerow and discovered that there was a woven wire fence just on the other side. It had apparently been placed there to keep people from accidentally falling into a concrete drainage ditch. Moon not only cleared the shrubbery, but also cleared the fence and fell into a hole about six feet deep.

"Are you okay?" I said when I heard him moan. He did not answer. "I'm coming down, hang on." I had spotted some steps off to my right under an overhanging streetlight.

"Be careful," Randall said, as I climbed the fence and started down into a dark hole that was filled with dancing shadows.

"Damn it!" I yelled when I missed the last step and fell to my knees.

"Are you okay, Mark?" Randall called, as he leaned over the top of the hedge.

"I'm okay." I stood up and felt my way along the damp concrete wall until I reached the spot where Moon had jumped over the hedge.

"Did you find him?" Randall asked. "Do you want me to come help?"

"I found him," I said when I kicked something soft and saw the outline of a body stretched out in front of me. "Sorry, Moon. I didn't mean to kick you. Are you okay?" He did not answer. I reached down and put my hand where I thought his face would be, only to discover that a lot of it was missing.

Where a nose should have been, there was just a flat, squishy spot that felt like tenderized steak.

"Hey, I'm over here!" I heard Moon's voice several feet away. I jumped backwards and got tangled up in my own feet, falling face down on top of a cold, dead stranger.

"What's the matter?" Harley yelled when he heard me scream. I scrambled over to Moon on all fours and cowered beside him. My teeth were clenched shut. My heart was pounding like a drum. I grabbed Moon by the arm and squeezed it tight when I heard the wail of a siren.

Moon patted my hand, trying to reassure me. "That's an ambulance, not the police. Everything will be all right. Take some deep breaths and you'll feel better."

I leaned back and looked up at the stars as I sucked in a deep breath of air. I exhaled slowly and did it again. That calmed me down enough so I could talk. "What about the guy I fell on?"

"I don't know. I jumped right on top of the poor bastard myself. Lucky for me he was there to break my fall. I might have been hurt a lot more than just being dazed for a couple of minutes."

"He's got no face. He must be dead."

"Yeah, I know. He seemed pretty lifeless to me."

"Are you guys okay?" Randall yelled down at us. When we didn't answer, he started for the steps. "I'm coming down to help."

"No, don't. We're coming up right now." Moon and I helped each other up and stumbled toward the steps.

"Stop a second," Moon said, as we started to walk past the corpse. He reached in his pocket and pulled out a lighter, leaned down close to the man's head and flicked the wheel.

"Oh my God," he moaned and turned his head away. "It looks like he took a shotgun blast at close range."

Standing up, Moon looked at me in the shadow of the flickering light, and I said, "Do you think we'll get out of this mess alive?"

Moon squinted his eyes and whispered, "I think we've got a better chance than Harley does. I've got a plan that will make him wish he was never born."

I didn't even ask him what it was, since he had told me before about having a plan and I had yet to see any action. When we reached the top step, Harley grabbed Moon by the arm and pulled him out into the parking lot.

"Plotting against me again were you, Moon Puppy? I heard you say my name."

Moon screamed and jerked away. "Come on, Harley," I said. "Take it easy, okay? He might have been killed if he hadn't landed on a dead man."

Harley squinted his eyes, looked at Moon, looked at me and cleared his throat. "A dead man? What are you talking about, Son?"

I took a couple of steps into the light and pointed at the drainage ditch. "There's one right down there, Harley. He's not just dead, he's mangled meat."

"Bull hockey," Harley said, as he picked up a wad of newspaper lying by the hedgerow and set it on fire. Tossing the flaming mass over the wire fence, it fell within a few inches of the dead man's head.

"My God, Harley," Randall said, "is there no end to this insanity? Look what you've done! You've caught the poor guy's hair on fire."

"Nice touch, Harley," Moon said. "What a great end to a perfect day."

"The day's not over yet," Harley growled. "I may set the hair on your ass afire before I'm through. We'll see how you like that, Moon Ass."

"You're a sick man, Harley," Moon said, "a danger to yourself and everyone around you. How about we talk to someone in the hospital about getting you some help?"

"Come on, you guys," I pleaded. "It's stupid to hang around a murder scene. Let's get the hell out of here."

Without another word, Moon, Randall, and I started for the big rig, but Harley stopped us in our tracks. "Hold up, all of you. Nobody else will be jumping the hedge between now and daylight. So nobody will discover the body. This is the safest place we could be."

"Maybe," I said, thinking he was probably right.

"Maybe, my ass! How doubly stupid would it be to go out driving around? Every cop in the Flagstaff area and even worse, those crazy bastards from the Silver Saddle will be out trying to hunt us down."

After thinking it over for a couple of seconds, I had to agree. "Good thinking. No one is going to find the corpse before morning."

"I wonder what happened to the guy?" Randall asked.

"He sure as hell didn't die from jumping over the hedge. Isn't that right, Moon?" I said. "A ten-foot fall doesn't rip a man's face away."

"It looks like someone blasted him in the head. Probably used a shotgun at close range," Moon said. "One of the biggest mysteries to the police may be trying to figure out why his hair was set on fire. That will be how he's remembered—hairless—sad as it is."

"Things are pretty bad when you're not even safe in a hospital parking lot," Randall said. "What the hell's the world coming to anyhow?"

Moon put his hands on top of his head and moaned. "I've got a splitting headache. I think I better get it checked out."

When Harley didn't say anything, Randall grabbed Moon by the arm and started toward the hospital. "You need to go to the emergency room, right now. You may have a serious injury."

Harley ran up to Randall and grabbed his arm, jerking him backwards. "This is just one more example of the way you guys overreact to everything—going off half-cocked without being in proper formation."

As we approached the emergency room entrance, an ambulance with red lights flashing sped into the driveway. The EMT slammed on the brakes and jumped out of the cab. Running around to the back, he threw open the doors and shouted at Moon, who was only a few feet away, "My partner's been shot! I need some help." When he pulled a stretcher out onto the driveway, Moon grabbed the front end, and with us close behind, they hurried toward the big, wide-sliding glass doors.

"I'm an EMT too. Let me know if I can help," Randall offered, as the big glass doors opened with a swishing sound.

Getting a whiff of the antiseptic smell, my mind flashed back to the painful way my day had begun with me being the one stretched out on a hospital table in Las Vegas—my back hurting so badly I could hardly stand the pain.

An orderly grabbed the stretcher away from Moon and pulled it into an unoccupied room directly across from the nurses' station.

"What happened, Virgil?" Nurse Janet asked the EMT, as she wrapped a blood pressure cuff around the injured patient's arm and we moved closer to get in on the details.

"Some crazy bastard shot Billy. He pulled up beside us at the 10th Street stoplight, pointed a shotgun out the window and blasted him in the chest. He must have been high on PCP or something."

"How do you know?" Nurse Janet asked, as she dialed the phone and told the operator to page a Code Blue.

"After he shot Billy, he just sat there giggling. Once I got over the initial shock, I pulled out my own shotgun from under the seat and blasted him in the head."

"I didn't know you guys were armed," Nurse Janet said, opening the door to a cabinet mounted on the wall and removing some medication.

"I got permission to carry a gun. We've been robbed twice in the last six months by hopheads looking for drugs."

"Did you wound the guy badly?"

"It looked like I blew half his face away. I don't know how he managed to drive off. I figured he'd show up here since he turned onto Elm Street headed this way."

"No, Billy is the first gunshot wound we've had tonight," Nurse Janet said, as she began to cut away the blood-soaked shirt. She looked over at Nurse Julie and frowned. "Someone needs to call his wife."

"I had hoped the most critical case we'd treat tonight would be that weird little guy from LA with the obstruction," Nurse Julie said as she picked up the phone, asking the operator to page Father Lewis.

When I heard her call for the priest, I knew Billy was past the Code Blue stage.

The doors swished open and two policemen rushed into the emergency room hallway. The tall one walked up to Virgil and began to question him about the shooting while his partner wrote down the information on a pad.

Harley gave me a wide-eyed look and turned away from the patrolman as Virgil described the shooter to be a cowboy-type wearing a black, wide-brimmed hat and driving a red Chevy pickup truck.

"Let's get on along," Harley whispered out of the side of his mouth. "Do it right now."

"Father Lewis, report to the emergency room," the hospital operator called from a paging speaker above my head. We slipped out of the ER and turned a corner into the main corridor where we stopped to figure out what to do next.

Moon couldn't resist pushing Harley. "Bet it made you nervous being so close to the cops, didn't it?"

I jumped in before Harley could answer Moon. "What do you want to do next?" I hoped to distract him from doing anything that would attract more attention. I could just see him involved in a hallway shootout and me getting hit by a stray bullet.

Harley glared at Moon and shoved him out in front of us. "What I want to do next is eat."

I stuck my head around the corner and looked back down the hallway to make sure the police had not followed us. "What about your injury, Moon? Should we get someone to examine your head?"

"It feels okay now. I think I'm going to be all right."

"Pretty quick recovery," Harley smarted off. He gave Moon a little shove to speed up the pace.

When we came to the second corridor, Moon pointed at a blue sign with white letters on the wall that read Pharmacy. "Do you want to get the Percodan prescription filled before we eat?"

"Would that be okay, Harley?" I asked. He gave me a nod and we walked through the pharmacy's double glass doors.

"Mr. Andrew's prescription for Seconal is ready," the pharmacist said to someone on the phone. "You will? Okay, I'll tell him. I'm going to the ER, Tim," he spoke to someone in the back. "Someone from 2-West will pick up a prescription in a few minutes. I'll leave it by the cash register."

"Okay, Sam, I'll mind the store," a coworker called out from the back room.

"Tim will be with you in a minute," Sam said, as he unlocked the gate beside the counter and walked past us, headed for the ER.

I grinned when I saw the bottle of Seconal; I knew how to kill Harley! All I had to do was divert the pharmacist's attention while I took a few sleeping pills out of the bottle. At the opportune moment, I would slip them into Harley's drink. Once he was asleep, I could do all of the horrible stuff I had thought about doing to him.

After what he had done to us, I figured nothing short of cutting off his head would be too severe.

"I'll be with you in a minute," Tim called from the back room.

"That's okay. We're in no hurry," I said, as I stepped to one side and saw the pharmacist still at work pouring pills from a tray into a brown bottle. I turned around to make sure no one had walked into the room and I diverted Harley's attention by pointing at the door. "I just saw the most beautiful woman in the world walk by. She's wearing one of those open back hospital gowns."

When Harley started toward the door, I grabbed the pill bottle and unscrewed the cap. I dumped four capsules into the palm of my hand. I screwed the cap back on and put the bottle down by the cash register just in time. A nurse had walked through the door and was standing behind me.

"Thank you, Tim," she yelled toward the back of the room as picked up the bottle of Seconal and left the room.

"What can I do for you, gentlemen?" The pharmacist asked with a smile when he came up to the counter.

I smiled back at him. "I need to get my prescription for Percodan filled."

"May I see some identification, please?" he said, after taking a look at Harley.

I showed him my driver's license, but that wasn't good enough. I pulled out the ID card issued to me by the Environmental Protection Agency. "Call the 800 number if you need further verification. I'm an employee of the federal government." He filled the prescription, rang up a charge of $27.50, and we were out the door.

"I wonder how Billy's doing," Randall said as we walked down the hallway.

"Not very well, I would imagine," Moon said. "It's gettin' hard to leave your house without running into crazy people. You know what I mean?"

I stopped a guy in a white lab coat carrying a tray filled with glass tubes containing blood samples. "Can you tell us how to find the cafeteria?"

He gave us long, careful directions to the extent I wished we had never stopped him in the first place. He ended by saying he thought the cafeteria was closed.

"We'll check it out for ourselves," Harley said abruptly. "Probably doesn't know what he's talking about anyway."

"We want something to eat," Harley demanded in a gruff voice, as we walked into a huge, deserted cafeteria that would easily seat 400 people.

A wiry little guy wearing a baggy green scrub suit was mopping the floor. He gave us a startled look when he saw Harley. "Cafeteria's closed, Mister."

I looked at Moon and Randall and we frowned at one another, knowing what was probably going to happen because the janitor had called Harley 'Mister'. To us it was just another case of Harley having a severe mood swing. To the poor little guy who had turned his back and continued to mop the floor, it was going to be one of his worst nightmares.

Harley got the guy's undivided attention when he screamed, "Closed! What do you mean closed?"

The janitor hunched over and looked as if he had shriveled up inside. He realized he had gotten himself crossways with a genuine, certified crazy person who could be dangerous.

"You've got bread!" Harley shouted. "I can see it, and what's that, good old Mister Ham?" Harley pointed at a half dozen loaves of bread on a shelf and a pile of ham on a big white plate.

When the guy started to back away, Harley ran over to the counter, stuffed a fistful of meat in his mouth and began to chew vigorously. Little pink pieces of ham rolled out of his half-open mouth, some sticking in his beard and the rest falling onto the nice clean floor.

With a quiver in his voice, the janitor said, "The cashier's gone, sir. There's no way to ring up a sale."

Harley threw his hands up in the air. "Screw the cashier! Randall, give this kind man twenty dollars. Hell, we're not beggars. We've got money, and we pay our own way."

After Randall whipped out his billfold and handed over the money, Harley jerked the revolver out of his pants and stuck the end of the barrel under the trembling janitor's nose. "If you tell anyone about what happened, you'll never mop another floor."

The guy's face was chalk-white. His hands were shaking so badly that he dropped the mop handle. "I won't... I won't tell a soul. Take anything you want, Mister."

"Come on, Harley," I said. "Let's take the food and go. Someone might walk in and call the cops." I looked at the janitor solemnly and forced a smile as I patted him on the back. "Believe me when I tell you that you're very lucky."

"Why is that, sir?"

"Because you don't have to go with us, that's why."

"I'm starved," Randall said. "Let's go back to the big rig and eat."

We headed out of the cafeteria with a loaf of bread, a pound of cheese, a jar of mustard, the big stack of ham, a gallon of milk and four glasses.

As we started to walk through the door, Harley stopped and turned around quickly, looking at the janitor as if he were about to give him another round of grief. In a soft voice, he asked him how we could find the morgue.

The guy gave us directions and we headed down the hallway on what had a good chance of being the most disgusting and potentially disease-ridden experience of my life.

"What are you thinking about?" Randall asked, as if Harley had to have a reason for what he did.

"You're crazy," Moon said. "I'm not eating in some damned morgue."

Without another word, Harley stuck his finger in Moon's back, shoved him forward and we were off to the morgue for a late-night dinner.

When we reached the end of the hallway, Harley stopped and turned around to make sure we were not being followed. "This is where we catch the elevator to the basement. Don't try anything stupid like pushing the emergency button."

"Why are you doing this to us, Harley?" I asked. "As a big favor to me, would you please let us go to the big rig and eat? Please?"

"Now Mark, I'd do almost anything for you, if it were reasonable. You not wanting to eat in the morgue is where I draw the line." Harley smiled and gave me a friendly nudge in the side with his elbow. "Hell, Son, you brought it up in the first place, remember?"

Crazy bastard. I rubbed the tips of my fingers over the outline of the Seconal pills in my pants pocket. "I guess you're right." I smiled at the thought of being free from Harley forever.

Harley laid his hand on my shoulder and grinned. "That's more like it, Mark. It doesn't hurt to humor an old man."

The elevator opened and we stepped out into a deserted, dimly lit hallway. A white sign with blood-red letters on a door directly across from us read MORGUE—AUTHORIZED PERSONNEL ONLY!

"I bet the door's locked," Randall said. "What will we do if it is?"

"What will we do?" Harley said mockingly, as he pulled Randall over to the left to maintain the integrity of our formation. "Maybe we'll break it down with your head."

I looked at Randall when Harley snickered, and the muscles in his jaw were working overtime. I rolled my eyes and nodded my head at him slowly, trying to signal him to cool it just a little bit longer. As with most of our attempts to relay visual signals, he just humped up his shoulders and gave me a confused look.

Moon walked up to the door cautiously and reached for the knob! Bang! The door flew open with a jolt that knocked Moon backwards. His head made a loud thump when it smashed into the red brick wall.

"Oh my God!" he yelled, as he stumbled forward, pushing Randall into Harley, who grabbed me by the arm to keep from falling down.

A tall, thin man with dark, shoulder-length hair darted through the doorway and ran down the hallway. His arms were flailing the air as if the spirits of the departed residents were chasing him.

"What was that all about?" I gasped when I was able to catch my breath.

"I don't know. I don't care," Harley said. "Just get inside. I'm ready to eat."

When Harley slammed the door, I heard a loud click as he turned the dead bolt knob. I had a terrible feeling that none of us would ever leave the morgue alive. My nose wiggled when I caught a whiff of formaldehyde.

Every light in the place was turned on, including the high-intensity surgical lamps hanging over each of the three autopsy tables. Light was bouncing off the shiny white tile that covered the walls, ceiling and floor. The blinding clarity made our skin look pale as a ghost.

I half expected to see body parts strewn all around the room, but there was not a trace of blood, tissue, or even a hair to be seen anywhere.

We put the food down on one end of an autopsy table. Harley walked to a far corner of the room and stopped in front of a big, double-door refrigerator. A cabinet filled with surgical scrub clothes and a red laundry hamper stamped MORGUE were on the left-hand side. A stainless steel table with a dozen plastic specimen jars stacked up along the back edge was on the right.

I closed my eyes when Harley grabbed the door handles. "Wonder what we'll find in here?" He opened the doors slowly. Much to everyone's surprise, with the exception of a brown paper bag, the refrigerator was empty.

"Open it up, Harley. I know you're dying to see what's in it," Moon said, as he walked closer.

Harley grabbed the bag and ripped it open like a bear after honey. A half-eaten hotdog plopped out onto the floor.

Moon laughed. "I bet you're really disappointed, aren't you, Harley? I know you had your heart set on eating a nice juicy piece of liver."

Moon's cute little game ended abruptly when Harley slapped him on the head with the flat of his hand. "I've still got your liver to eat anytime I want, Moon Furry Pie."

Harley slammed the doors shut and walked over to a row of vaults lining the wall behind the autopsy tables.

"I don't want to look at any corpse," I said. "I'll fix the drinks and get the sandwiches ready for dinner, okay, Harley?"

"I don't want to look at any either," Randall said. Harley grabbed him by the arm and jerked him back when he started to walk away.

"Mark's excused since he's fixin' the food. You and Moon Pie are stayin' with me," Harley growled, as he pulled out one of the vaults, picked up the toe tag, and asked Randall to read the guy's name.

Randall looked at the tag and gagged as if he were going to throw up. "John Doe. It says right here this dead man is named John Doe."

"John Doe. Hell, I knew a guy in prison named John Roe. I wonder if they could have been related?" Harley slapped his leg and laughed with such force that spittle flew out of his mouth. A couple of drops beaded up on Randall's forehead.

"Standing in a morgue reading toe tags, waiting to eat dinner while a killer makes jokes and spits in my face? Tell me, Lord," Randall said wearily, as he looked up at the ceiling, "is it going to get any worse?"

"Oh, it can get a lot worse, Mr. Randall Smart-ass," Harley snapped back at him. "You've only seen one toe tag. Hell there could be twenty."

I could tell by the way Randall's eyes narrowed that his hatred for Harley was about to make him explode. I just hoped that he didn't do anything stupid before I had the chance to concoct my witch's brew.

I prepared four ham and cheese sandwiches and laid them down on paper napkins that I had spread out on one of the autopsy tables. I poured four glasses of milk. Turning my back to Harley, I emptied the Seconal powder from the capsules into the last glass and stirred it up with my finger. Smiling as I turned around, I offered Harley my special mixture. "Here's a nice glass of milk for you," I said. "Come on everybody, let's drink up and eat."

Chapter Eleven

My nerves did a tap dance when Harley looked at me suspiciously and hesitated to take the glass. I stared at the granules of Seconal that had collected along the rim, hoping he did not sense something was wrong and make me drink it.

"What's the matter, Mark?" Moon asked. "You look as pale as that milk."

The glass clanked loudly when I sat it down on the table, and I forced a grin. "What's the matter?" I repeated quickly, as I tried to think of an answer. "What do you mean?"

"You look really strange," Randall said. "Are you sick?"

Sick! Why would I be sick? Why would eating dinner on an autopsy table in the morgue with a killer that I was about to put to sleep make me sick?

I took a deep breath and cleared my throat, stalling for time while I tried to think of something convincing to say. "I want to propose a special toast to you, Harley." I handed him the glass again and picked mine up when he grabbed his from my hand.

"What's the toast about, Mark?" Randall asked, causing my mind to go blank.

"It's just a special toast," I said, giving him an evil eye. "Come on everybody, raise your glass." At that point, I still had no idea what I was going to say. All I knew was it had to be something wondrous enough so Harley would drink the milk right down.

"Yeah," Harley said, as he raised his glass and clanked it into mine. "I deserve a special toast more than anyone I know."

Still uncertain about what to say, I raised my glass even higher and Harley followed suit. After a pause that lasted so long my lips stuck to my teeth, I looked deep into Harley's eyes and went in for the kill. "In spite of our differences, for the most part Harley, you're really a pretty good old guy."

When Harley patted me on the shoulder and grinned, I knew I had him hooked. "All right everybody," I said joyfully, "let's all drink our toast."

Harley drank all of his milk in three big gulps and banged the glass down on the table. "That's the only toast anyone ever made to me," he said solemnly and let out a loud burp. "Fact is, though, I don't remember milk tasting like that at all. But I don't drink much milk."

"I'm glad you were pleased, Harley." My voice quivered with excitement. "Now let's eat our sandwiches."

Harley picked up his sandwich and took big bites as he walked slowly around the room. He opened every drawer and checked out every little bitty thing he could find. He fixed another sandwich and continued to look around, after gobbling down the last bite, he came back to the table. He yawned and blinked his eyes. "Maybe we should go back to the big rig," he said. "I've gotten sleepy all of a sudden. I don't know if I can... If I can...."

Harley slumped over and rested his body on the edge of the table for a few seconds, then he slid down onto the floor. Randall and Moon looked at me wide-eyed when I said, "Guess what, boys, I've drugged Harley. We're free to head out the door." I was so relieved; it was all I could do to keep from crying.

"Are you sure he's knocked out?" When I nodded my head, Moon ran around the table and gave Harley a swift kick in the side. "You crazy old bastard," he yelled. When Harley didn't move, Moon kicked him again. "After all he's done to us, we should do something awful to him. Just leaving him here asleep is not nearly punishment enough."

"What about you Randall?" I asked. "What do you think we should do?"

My friend Randall, who had always been a levelheaded guy, someone who would not hurt a fly, turned on me like an animal protecting its young.

His eyes filled with rage. The right one began to twitch and his voice tightened. "Harley did the unspeakable to me." He started to say something else, but he was so upset he just looked away.

"What was it that has affected you the most?" I asked, thinking about some of the terrible things that probably flashed through Randall's mind. Harley had shot at him, spit on him, cursed him, yelled in his face and nearly caused him to have a heart attack discharging the revolver and setting off dynamite. He scared him half to death driving the big rig recklessly, and now a band of Hell's Angels, a horde of cowboys and a bunch of pissed-off bartenders were stalking us. Not only that, since we were about to set the old man up to be killed, Randall was morally obligated to take care of Harley's disease-ridden, flea-infested dog.

"Harley blew smoke in my face. That's what he did," Randall said. "I hate that worse than anything."

"How strange." I was so disgusted with him I wanted to smack him. "Okay then, let's just get out of here. We'll head for Kansas City and not look back."

"I agree with Moon," Randall yelled at me, as if I had done something wrong. "Harley deserves anything he gets for all he's done to us."

"Yeah," Moon said, "he really does."

"What slow and painful death did you have in mind, Moon, my friend?" Randall smiled.

"Come on, you guys. You sound like Jeckyl and Hyde. We're not criminals. Let's just go."

Randall smacked the table with the flat of his hand. "No, sir!" he shouted at me. "I'll handle this myself. If anything goes wrong, you can claim to be an innocent victim."

"I know you, Randall," I said. "You're not a murderer. This will haunt you the rest of your life."

"What medication did you use?" Randall asked.

"Seconal. I dumped the powder from four capsules into his glass of milk."

"Where did you get it?" Moon asked.

"I took it from the bottle sitting by the cash register in the pharmacy. Snatched it before the nurse picked up the prescription."

"How long will he be knocked out?" Randall asked.

I shrugged my shoulders. "I don't know. At least six or eight hours, I guess."

"It's ten o'clock now," Randall mumbled to himself, as he walked over to a wall-mounted phone and ask the operator to dial the pharmacy. "My name is Jim Martin. I'm a student at the university doing a term paper. I need some information about the long-term effects of a drug. How long will a 160-pound man stay asleep if he has been given four Seconal tablets?" After a long pause, he thanked the pharmacist and hung up the phone.

"What did he say?" Moon asked.

Randall gave him a wicked-looking smile and rubbed his hands together. "We have plenty of time gentleman. Help me get Harley up on the table. Mark, you grab his feet. Moon, get your hands under his back and lift him up. Stay clear of his belly button. We don't want to detonate the TNT."

"Wait a minute," I protested, "what are you going to do?"

"Just get him up on the table," Randall said. Without any further questions, we carefully lifted Harley's limp body up off the floor. "All right, let's get his clothes off."

"What the hell for?" Moon asked. "I'm not doing anything else until I know what you've got planned."

Ring! Ring! I jumped backward, almost falling down when the telephone rang. "Who would call here this time of the night? Come on, let's get out of here right now."

"Who cares who called?" Randall said, grinding his teeth, tightening the muscles in his jaw.

"What's gotten into you?" I tried to sound calm, even though my stomach was a big knot. "This is stupid, undressing Harley. What if we were to set off the dynamite?"

Once again, Randall acted as if he had not heard me. He began to unbutton Harley's shirt.

"Look at that," Moon said, and we all stared at a small, tastefully done, yellow butterfly in the center of Harley's chest.

"This job would be a lot easier if you two would help," Randall snarled.

Moon threw his hands in the air. "All right, let's help him so we can get out of this creepy place."

"What do you want us to do next?" I asked.

"I only need help with a couple of simple things," Randall said, as he turned around and opened a drawer behind him. Pulling out a pair of bandage scissors, he slid them down the table toward me. "Cut the tape holding the dynamite around Harley's leg." When I hesitated, he raised his voice. "Cut it off right now!"

"What am I supposed to do with the dynamite?" I hoped he could not come up with a good plan and would abandon the insane project.

"Put it in the refrigerator. Be careful not to blow us up."

I slammed the scissors down on the table and the sharp crack of metal smashing against metal echoed through the room. "First you tell us what you're about to do."

"No, I won't tell you," Randall said, calmly. "I'll show you instead." Opening a half dozen drawers, he finally found what he was searching for. He plugged the electrical cord attached to the device into an outlet. He squeezed the trigger and watched the circular blade whirl around at a high rate of speed. Satisfied it would do the job, he pulled the plug from the outlet and laid the bone saw down on the counter. He picked up a pen and wrote furiously for a couple of minutes. When he turned around, he was holding a toe tag in one hand and an official-looking form he had filled out in the other.

"Why haven't you got that TNT off his leg yet?" Randall asked, as he walked toward me.

"What about the wire running to the blasting cap?"

"Go ahead and cut it." He sounded like he knew what he was doing.

"Are you sure? How do you know that's okay?"

"I saw a bomb squad cop do it one night when I was on an ambulance run. I'm still here, right?"

I took a deep breath and snipped the wire with the bandage scissors. With the detonator disengaged, I cut the tape and removed the dynamite. I stashed it in the refrigerator with the half-eaten hotdog. When I walked back to the table, I picked up the tag that Randall had tied around Harley's big, yellow-encrusted toe and saw he renamed him John Doe.

"I realize you've been under a lot of strain," I said. "I know that you want to get even with Harley. But don't you think your going too far?"

Randall smiled as he walked over to the telephone and dialed the operator. "This is Mr. Bianchi with the FBI. I would like the name of the county coroner. Dr. Mannee, is that what you said. Okay. I also need to talk with a pathologist. You say Dr. Baron is the resident on call. Can you connect me with him? Yes, I can wait."

Randall stared at the floor and bounced the toe of his tennis shoe off the wall while he waited for the operator to make the connection.

"Dr. Baron, this is Dr. Mannee with the county coroner's office. I have a John Doe in the morgue we need clinical results from by morning, if possible. We're dealing with a hush, hush federal investigation. All of the big boys are involved, FBI, Drug Enforcement, CIA and the Federal Witness Protection Program. The John Doe's body is stripped and on the table, ready for you to begin. A signed copy of the autopsy authorization form is laying on the counter beside the bone saw."

After more probing questions from Dr. Baron, Randall, alias Dr. Mannee, went into greater detail, which made his story even more convincing, by telling Dr. Baron the evidence they were looking for pointed to death from a cocaine overdose. Randall, alias Dr. Mannee ended the conversation by getting a general agreement from Dr. Baron that the logical thing to do would be to open the cranium first.

My heart sank when I fully realized that Randall had actually laid out a plot to murder Harley in cold blood, a plan that might very well work. Faced with the stark reality of being part of a conspiracy to kill another human being, I weakened at the knees.

"Randall," I said, "I know Harley has been a bad man, but setting him up to be killed this way... You might think about the consequences of what you're about to do."

"Yeah," Moon said, "like having to sleep with the lights on for the next five years because you're afraid of Harley's ghost."

Randall gave me a blank look. His eyes rolled back in his head and he sank to the floor. When I grabbed his arm, he was shaking so badly I thought he might be having a seizure.

"Deep breaths, Randall," Moon said, as he grabbed the other arm. "Take some deep breaths."

"Let's lay him down," I said.

"What? Are you crazy? Dr. Baron will be here any minute." When I didn't say anything, Moon raved at me some more. "Here we are with dynamite, a revolver and a live body set up for an autopsy. This is serious, man, really serious." Moon got right up in Randall's face. "Can you walk, or do we need to carry you?"

"We can't drag a big lug like him through the hospital," I said, as I hurried over to the sink. "People will get suspicious. Hang on to him. Maybe this glass of water will help."

After a couple drinks of water and some deep breaths, Randall came around enough so that with our assistance, the three of us shuffled our way out through the door of the morgue. We caught the elevator to the first floor, leaving Harley drugged on the autopsy table, waiting for the whirling blade of the bone saw.

Chapter Twelve

When we reached the emergency room there was an attendant wheeling a stretcher out into the hallway, which he parked, beside the wall. As we walked past and saw a body covered up with a white sheet we hurried on out through the sliding glass doors.

The lump that had been stuck in my throat the whole time we were in the morgue disappeared when we started across the parking lot. I wanted to scream, jump up and down and cry all at once. It felt so good to be free.

Moon patted Randall and me on the back and smiled. "You guys did it. You set us free from Harley forever. Bless you. Bless you."

"Do you think we should call the cops once we get down the road? Tell them about the dead guy in the drainage ditch and the TNT in the refrigerator?"

"We really should tell them about the dynamite," Randall said, as he looked back over his shoulder at the hospital. "It would be a bitch if the place blew up."

"It's okay, Randall," I said softly, figuring he was teetering on the edge. "We all hated Harley and wished he were dead. I killed him at least a hundred times in my mind. Moon and I just didn't have the guts to do what you did."

"Something just snapped down there in the morgue," Randall said. "It was as if one of Harley's evil personalities took over my soul. A part of me, who hated him so much, wanted him dead. Luckily my good sense kicked in just in time to stop me from using the bone saw myself."

Long Dog barked and jumped out into the parking lot when I opened the side door.

"I forgot about that damn dog," Randall said. The sorry-looking creature sniffed around his feet and raised his leg as if he were going to wet down Randall's shoe.

"You can tell that dog's been Harley-trained," I said, and we all laughed.

"What are we going to do with him?" Randall asked.

"Someone will have him picked up and killed if we leave him here," Moon said.

"What are you saying?" Randall asked, his voice raising. "You don't think we're taking him with us, do you?"

"I'll get some mange medicine tomorrow. Treat him until he's cleared up. I'll take him with me when I leave you guys."

Before Randall could say anything, Moon picked up the dog and climbed into the motor home.

"It's a strange world," I said, as I slid into the passenger seat and Moon sat down in the director's chair.

"It doesn't get much stranger than what we've been through," Moon said, and we all laughed again. "I wish you guys would seriously consider spending a couple of days with me at the farm."

"Maybe another time. Mark has to get married next Saturday, you know," Randall said, as he fired up the engine. We drove across the parking lot, out through the gate onto Elm Street, and back onto Interstate 40 headed toward home-sweet-home.

I looked out the window and remembered that there was a full moon the night Ann and I had our first date. I wished I could snap my fingers and be sitting in her living room. Surely nothing else bad will happen to us. I leaned back in the seat and closed my eyes.

"How far are you going to drive before we stop for the night?" Moon asked.

"How about I go to the outskirts of Flagstaff, pull into a parking lot somewhere and shut it down? To tell you the truth, I'm exhausted."

"It would be good to get off the Interstate," I said. "We can call our folks, and I can check in with Ann, let her know I'll be home in time for the wedding. We'll get some food, get a few hours sleep and take off early in the morning."

"We've got ourselves a plan," Randall said. He pulled into the left lane and passed an eighteen-wheeler hauling a load of cowhides that were stacked up to the top of an open-bed trailer. Even though the smell was so terrible that it took my breath away, I didn't care. I was so happy to be shed of Harley and still be alive that I would have gladly ridden on top of the stinking pile the rest of the way to Kansas City and not complained.

"I don't mean to judge you, Randall," I said, as I pinched off my nose with my fingers to stop the smell when we passed the truck, "but I really thought you had lost your mind back in the morgue. I've never seen you get upset about anything—let alone be mad enough to kill someone."

"A person can only put up with so much abuse. Harley finally shoved me over the edge."

"I guess you're right." I truly realized, for the first time, that given the right circumstances, anyone could be pushed into committing murder.

"Oh my God!" Randall yelled and slapped his chest when a couple of bikers roared up beside us. "I thought the one on the right was Harley. Just look at him."

Moon scooted his chair forward and I leaned across Randall for a better view out the window. The guy looked about as much like Harley as Pee Wee Herman did. Not wanting to upset Randall any more than he already was, I humored him. "He resembles him a little, I suppose."

"Yeah, I guess he does," Moon said, as he looked at me and grinned.

The so-called Harley look-alike and his buddy cruised along beside us for a quarter-mile or so before throttling their hogs and rumbling into the night.

"We need to get off the interstate," I said nervously. I pointed at a church up ahead with a brightly lit neon cross hanging above the entrance to a large parking lot. "Let's pull in there. A church lot should be as safe a place as any."

"This is great," Moon said when we pulled into the lot and he pointed at a restaurant a couple hundred yards up ahead. "We can eat at Denny's."

"I'll probably order a cup of coffee, a glass of milk, a Coke, a milk shake, a hamburger, a steak and a ten-egg omelet. Do I sound like Harley or not?" Randall said, and we all laughed.

When Randall stopped the big rig at the backside of the church parking lot, a set of headlights flashed on and a beat-up old pickup sped out of a graveyard onto a frontage road and disappeared over the hill.

"I hope this isn't a hangout for a bunch of drunken, loud-mouthed kids," Randall grumbled, as he stopped close to a big pine tree and shut off the engine. "I need a few hours of uninterrupted sleep."

"It was probably just a couple of kids playing kissy-face," Moon said. "They won't be back."

"Let's go get some food," I said. I opened the door and slid out of the seat onto the asphalt parking lot. "I'll call the police and let them know about the dynamite in the fridge and tell them about the dead man in the ditch. We'll call home so people won't worry, and we'll be in bed, asleep, by midnight. I bet you're really disappointed there's no hedge to jump over, aren't you, Moon?" We squeezed out a couple more laughs of relief before we reached the door of the crowded restaurant.

The waitress seated us at the only table that was open in the very back of the room by a window. I already had my mind made up about what I wanted to eat without even looking at the menu. I ordered the pancake, sausage, bacon and eggs special.

As I looked out the window, I caught a glimpse of something that looked frighteningly familiar. I jerked my head around quickly.

"What's the matter?" Randall asked when he saw my mouth fall open as I looked away.

"It was nothing. It will take me a while to get over being so jumpy."

A tall, pretty waitress with long, red hair and a cross-tattooed on her right forearm took our orders. Without even asking, she poured coffee all around. The cup froze in front of Moon's face when he started to take a drink and he stared at the front door.

"What is it?" Randall asked. "What's wrong?"

"I can tell you without even taking a look," I said, feeling sick to my stomach again. "I thought I was seeing things when he drove past the window. It was the cowboy parked in the graveyard, wasn't it, Moon?"

"What are you talking about?" Randall asked.

"Don't turn around," Moon said, as he scooted his chair to the right to avoid being seen from the front door. "It looks like the two guys with the cowboy both have shotguns."

I scooted my chair to the left so I would be hidden from view and looked back over my shoulder. "That's scary, but it's a lot harder to escape a scatter gun blast than it is to dodge a single bullet."

With a cigarette dangling from the corner of his mouth, the cowboy played cock-the-hammer on a lever-action 30-30 rifle while he watched the girl behind the register put money in a brown paper bag. He pulled the hammer back and let it back down a half dozen times while she worked feverishly to empty the cash drawer.

He grabbed a candy bar off the shelf, bit off a big chunk and chewed it up, wrapper and all. Pulling a half-pint bottle of whiskey from the pocket of his faded jean jacket, he took a long swig. His face puckered up and he yelled, "That Wild Turkey's a powerful bitch!"

"That's all the money there is, Mister," the cashier said, her voice quivering as she dropped the last greenback into the bag.

"I'll take that timepiece too, honey." He held out his hand.

Tears ran down her cheeks as she hurriedly stripped the watch from her wrist and dropped it in the moneybag.

"Please don't hurt me," she begged. "I did what you said."

The cowboy's running mates looked like a couple of inbred losers. Both of them together did not look like they would make a pair.

The short, heavyset one was wearing bib overalls that stretched at the seams across his big belly. His responsibility was to guard the front door. Taking his job seriously, he paced back and forth, darting his head from side to side like a nervous chicken. He was definitely wound up too tight to be trusted with a loaded shotgun. Bang! Crash! Bang! Whirling around quickly, as if he thought someone was about to sneak up on him, the pear-shaped creature knocked over a wooden chair, then dropped it twice while hurriedly trying to set it back up before anyone noticed.

The cowboy unleashed a bitter tongue-lashing, calling him, among other things, a complete idiot and a joke among criminals. I thought he was going to cry when the cowboy threatened to take his shotgun away.

The second marauder was a tall, dark fella' with curly, black dreadlocks that made him look as if he were wearing a Bob Marley wig. He stood close to the cowboy's backside with his head hung low, like a dog that had been made to heel. There was no doubt that he was also an accident waiting to happen.

The clerk screamed and stumbled forward when the cowboy jabbed her in the back with the end of the rifle barrel and yelled, Bang!

"Please don't kill me," she begged with tears running down her cheeks.

Wanting to get in on the act, the hangdog-looking guy stepped up behind the girl and snorted like a bull. When she shrieked, he got so tickled that he shook all over, accidentally squeezing the trigger and discharging the 12-gauge shotgun.

Blood-curdling screams filled the room as shredded bits of white tile, which looked like snowflakes, floated down from the ceiling.

"It'll be your face next time," the embarrassed shooter shouted at no one in particular, as he tried to compensate for the stupid accident.

To make the threat even more dramatic, he pumped out an empty green hull that bounced across a tabletop and fell into the lap of a pretty young girl wearing a red and white cheerleader's sweater. She screamed and pushed her chair backwards, knocking over the Please Wait To Be Seated sign behind her. The shooter smiled as he pumped another live shell into the chamber.

"We'd better do something before the cowboy spots us," I said quietly, as I watched him play cock-the-hammer again with a teenage boy. "He'll recognize us for sure. He thinks we're Harley's friends. You know how he hates Harley."

"Did you say do something?" Moon asked, giving me a desperate look. "Like what are we going to do?"

"The restroom doors right behind you. Let's sneak in there and hide." When Moon didn't answer, I reached across the table and squeezed his hand. "Come on, damn it. Let's go."

"Okay," Moon said, as the cowboy started toward the back of the room.

Not wasting any more time, I slid forward out of my chair and under the table. Crawling on my hands and knees, I scrambled across the hallway and through the restroom door with Randall and Moon close behind.

We had temporarily escaped being gunned down, but our safe haven had a serious defect. There was only one stall and no place else to hide.

"We have to do it," I said, trying to imagine how three grown men would be able to huddle together on a wobbly stool lid without falling off. "If the cowboy looks underneath the stall and sees a bunch of feet, he'll shoot right through the door and kill us all."

I climbed up first and situated myself on the back part of the stool lid, facing front. Moon grabbed my right arm and I helped him up onto the side. We pulled Randall up on my left and there we stood like three stooges. As if enough hadn't already happened to mess with my mind, on the back of the stall door someone had written, For A Good Time in KC Call Ann. It was just one more thing to kick me in the ass.

Boom! Another shot rang out. People screamed and the cowboy yelled, "Just shut the hell up." Seconds later the door to the restroom banged open and someone stepped into the room. He levered an empty 30-30 cartridge from the chamber of his rifle. The metal casing clattered its way across the white tile floor, bounced off the wall and came to rest in our stall.

"Anybody in here?" he yelled, as he levered in a live cartridge and waited for a response.

I looked at the ceiling and took a deep breath of air when I felt faint. My heart was beating so hard I could feel it pounding in my throat. Moon and Randall looked at me wide-eyed, their faces frozen with fear.

The footsteps started toward our stall, stopping when the restroom door banged open again and one of the cowboy's running mates said, "Bubba Boy wants you out front."

"Well, all right, I'm comin'." A couple of seconds after the door to the restroom had slammed shut, shots rang out and there were screams of mass hysteria. At the same time, the lights went out and it was pitch black.

"They're killing everybody in the place," Randall said. "We're the same as dead."

"They can't have killed everybody," Moon said. "There were only two shots fired."

"They're probably stabbing and clubbing the others. They'll come in here next."

"Be quiet," Moon whispered. "I think I heard something."

The restroom door creaked open again and a stream of light streaked across the ceiling. I slapped my hand over my mouth and swallowed deeply, hoping I could stop myself from throwing up.

I could just see our picture on the front page of the Flagstaff newspaper. What a nice remembrance for our families, the three of us heaped up in a pile around a white porcelain stool in a pool of blood. I took some more deep breaths, but I didn't get much relief.

"Anybody in here?" someone with a deep voice asked, as a beam of light streaked across the ceiling, came down the wall behind us and stopped under the door to our stall. "I know someone is in there," the mystery man said after a long pause. "Come out with your hands up right now."

A pain so severe I wanted to scream tensed up my calf muscle and I stood up on the ball of my foot, hoping to get some relief. When I reached down to rub my leg, I got off-balance and my foot splashed into the water bowl. I threw my arms in the air, knocking Randall and Moon off the stool lid onto the floor.

The next thing I knew someone was shining a powerful flashlight in my eyes and a revolver barrel was pointed at my nose.

A police officer gave us a disgusted look and motioned for us to come out of the stall. "What were you three doing in there?" he asked suspiciously, as he lined us up along the wall.

"We were just waiting to eat," I said. "Some guys came in to rob the place. So we sneaked in here and hid."

"Are they still out there?" Randall asked.

"Two of them are dead," the tall man in blue said, as he holstered the revolver. We followed him through the door into the restaurant. Cowboy Duke and one of his friends were lying on the floor covered with matching red and white-checkered tablecloths.

"What happened?" Randall asked.

"My partner and I stop here a couple times a day for coffee. The place gets robbed a lot so we always come in the back door. We saw what was going on before they saw us. We nailed these two," the policeman said, looking down at the bodies.

"We're sure glad you did," I said, as I wiped the sweat from my forehead. "They would have got us good."

"How come they didn't find you in the restroom?" the patrolman asked.

"We were standing up on the stool lid," Randall said. "The cowboy never opened the door."

The policeman chuckled. "All three of you on one stool lid. That must have been some sight."

"What happened to the other guy?" I asked. "The one wearing overalls by the front door?"

The policeman looked at me and frowned. "Unfortunately, he got away. We'll catch up with him though. We know who he is and he's dumber than a box of rocks. Most of these robber guys are pretty stupid. That's why so many of them get caught."

I looked at Randall. "With our luck, he'll probably be waiting for us when we get back to Kansas City."

We hung around about ten minutes while the policeman collected the information he needed for his records. He let us go on the promise that we would not leave Flagstaff until we checked in with headquarters on Saturday morning.

I felt like a cat with nine lives when we walked out of the restaurant into the cool night air. "Saved by the bell again. This is like something out of movie." I looked up at the stars and sighed as we headed across the parking lot.

"I hope they don't run a check on me," Moon said. "It will be curtains for me, if they do."

I started to ask him what he had to hide, and then decided that I didn't really want to know. "Bubba could be watching us right now," I said, then started out in a dead run for the motor home.

Once we were safely locked inside, prepared for bed, it dawned on me that with all the excitement, we had forgotten to call home and I was afraid to go back outside. Poor Ann, I've got to call her first thing in the morning.

"We didn't get any food," Randall said, sounding as if he were about to cry.

"We didn't call home either," I said. "I'd go do it now, but it's too late. We'll do it first thing in the morning."

"You know something else?" Moon said. "We didn't call the police about the dynamite or the dead man in the ditch."

I looked over my shoulder at Moon lying on the couch and hunched up my shoulders. "It's too late to help the man in the ditch. Whoever finds the dynamite will be sharp enough to leave it alone. Health care professionals are pretty smart people."

"Yeah, you're right," Moon said, raising his head up off the pillow and waving at me as I headed for the back bedroom, stepping over Randall who was curled up in a sleeping bag on the floor.

In a few minutes I drifted off to sleep thinking about Ann and how it would be our last night away from each other for a long, long time.

Chapter Thirteen

A sparkle of sunlight shone through the back window as I woke up.

I sat up in bed and yelled, "What's that smell?" There was a stench so foul it made the odor from the truck hauling cowhides seem like a flower garden by comparison.

"Something's rotted," Randall shouted, as he crawled out of the sleeping bag and jumped up from the floor. By the time we reached the door, everyone, including Long Dog, was heaving and wheezing as if they had taken a whiff of ammonia.

The fact that Randall and I were wearing nothing except our jockey shorts was bad enough. Moon leaped out onto the pavement with nothing on at all but a pair of socks and began to heave up his guts. A busload of senior citizens, which had arrived for the church service, witnessed our morning sickness.

"What's all the ruckus about?" one of the elderly gentleman asked, as he made the mistake of opening the door and stepping outside. Long Dog headed toward the poor guy, dragging his crippled hind leg and growling as if he were going to eat him alive.

"Get back here!" Randall yelled at the same time that Long Dog bit the old gentleman on the foot, tearing off his loafer as he tried to escape back inside the church bus.

"That's going to be big trouble," I said when I saw one lady snap our picture and another one dial her cellular phone. The driver started up the bus and moved closer to the church.

"They probably figure Long Dog has rabies," Moon said. He reached down and picked up a discarded Dunkin'

Donuts box and held it in front of his private parts. "You know they called the police."

"Hell, he damn-well could have rabies," Randall said. He kicked at Long Dog and yelled at him to get back inside the motor home, which prompted the mutt to run around in a circle barking.

"We'd better get inside and put on some clothes," I said. "Moon's probably right about them calling the police."

"I can't go back in there," Moon said. "I'll throw up again if I do. Run in real quick and get my pants for me, will you, Mark? You've got a lot stronger stomach than I do."

"We've become the center of attention," I said, as I pointed at a crowd of about forty people that stood outside the church. One of them was watching us through binoculars.

"Let's at least get out of sight," Randall said. I started to walk around in front of the motor home, but it was too late. A police car, with red lights flashing, had turned into the parking lot and was headed toward us.

I never imagined the police being so upset that they would jump out of their patrol car with revolvers drawn and threaten to shoot us if we didn't put our hands above our heads. They acted as if we were common criminals.

"We have a good reason for looking like this," Randall said.

"Put 'em up right now," a big officer said, as he glared at Randall. His name badge read Singleton.

As if Long Dog were protecting us from the big bad cops, he ran out from under the motor home, assumed attack position and growled. Officer Singleton pointed his revolver at Long Dog and pulled back the hammer. "If your little dog attacks me, he'll be dead."

"He won't hurt you," Moon said. "He's just scared because he's blind. That's all it is, sir."

The short, heavyset officer with a long, crooked nose that Officer Singleton had referred to as Officer Andrews, squinted his eyes and snarled, "Is that the dog that bit the elderly gentleman?"

"It's the dog all right," Moon said. "But he only bit him on the shoe."

"Maybe I should rephrase the question," Officer Andrews said. "Is that creature actually a dog?" He looked at his partner and they laughed.

Officer Singleton made Moon turn around in a circle while he gave him the once-over. "Why are you standing out here without any clothes on? Did the people on the church bus see you naked like this?"

"No sir," I answered for Moon quickly, figuring there would be no telling what he would say. "He covered himself with a donut box."

"Like I told you earlier," Randall said, "there's a good reason why we're standing out here in the cold."

"It better be real good," Officer Andrews said.

"When we woke up this morning, something in the motor home smelled so bad it made us sick. He even threw up," Randall said, pointing at Long Dog. "Look at the proof over there."

"That's a good one," Officer Singleton said, laughing as he looked at his buddy.

"If you don't believe me, just go inside," Randall said, taking a couple of steps towards the motor home to open the door.

Having pretty much determined that we were just a bunch of idiots and not criminals, Officer Singleton holstered his revolver. "The odor must be awfully powerful. I better check it out for myself."

We smiled at one another as he opened the side door of the motor home and stepped inside.

"My God!" he yelled, as he ran outside gagging. "He's not kidding, Paul," he said to his buddy. "Something is rotten to the core. How long has it been since you emptied your holding tank?"

I looked at Randall, he looked at me and we both looked down at the pavement, away from the officers' piercing eyes.

"Do you think that's what it is?" I asked.

"That's exactly what I think it is. Why are you boys parked here anyway? This is private property," he said, getting huffy with us again.

No doubt about it, unless we came up with a really convincing story, the three of us were goners.

"It was because of our mothers," Randall blurted out.

The officers smiled at one another, and Officer Singleton said, "Oh really? I can hardly wait to hear this story."

"I pulled into the parking lot last night because I knew today was a special day," Randall said. "Do you know why?" he asked, sounding a little too cocky.

"It's Mother's Day," Officer Andrews said. "So what about it?"

"That's correct. Because of that, we wanted to drive straight through to Kansas City and be home by tomorrow. But we couldn't, because something critical came up, so we pulled in here knowing that our moms would want us to go to church on Mother's Day and we would be close to the building, just in case we overslept."

The two officers rolled their eyes at one another, and Officer Andrews said, "Sounds like a wild story to me, but a good one. What's the rest of your tale?"

Randall smiled and rambled on. "After we parked the motor home last night, we walked over to Denny's for a bite to eat. We wanted to call home and tell our moms that we wouldn't make it home for Mother's Day, but that we were spending the night parked in a church lot so we would make it to Sunday morning services. We didn't get to call because we got involved in a robbery and a shootout where two men were killed."

"Hold it right there, motormouth," Officer Singleton said. "I've heard enough about your moms. You guys were at Denny's when the two robbers were shot?"

"That's right. We hid in the restroom until the shooting was over. A patrolman came in and found us. We thought we were going to die."

"Okay, that's enough," Officer Singleton said.

"Can I get my clothes on, please?" Moon begged, his teeth chattering.

Moon pinched off his nose and ran inside the motor home when the patrolman gave him a nod. He reappeared quickly with a pair of Levis and a black sweatshirt thrown over his shoulder. He put on his clothes, sat down on the retractable step and slipped on his tennis shoes.

"We're supposed to check in with police headquarters before leaving town," Randall said. "Could you please give them a call and ask if it's okay for us to go?"

"Sure," Officer Singleton said, as he walked around the back of the big rig and wrote down our license number before walking over to the police car to radio headquarters.

"What's the story with you boys?" Officer Andrews asked, sounding as if he still doubted our credibility.

"What do you mean?" I asked, wondering why he had not mentioned anything about the big ruckus at the Silver Saddle.

"You said you're going to Kansas City. Where have you been? If you have a criminal record, you may as well tell me right now. It will pop up when Officer Singleton talks to HQ."

I started to show him my ID card from the Environmental Protection Agency but then decided to see if we would get a fair shake without having to pull any strings. "Nothing will show up," I said, hoping that anything in Moon's past did not cause him serious trouble.

"That's good," Officer Andrews said solemnly. "There was a man found dead in the parking lot at the medical center this morning. The ER doc told us he saw a big RV like this one parked in the general area last night. Were you boys around the hospital anytime during the evening?"

We shook our heads, and Randall said, "Like I told you, we are just passing through."

"We're going to let you go now," Officer Singleton said, as he walked around in front of the police car. "Your license number is entered into the computer. Any more trouble involving an RV and we'll track you down."

"There won't be any trouble," I said. "Thank you for letting us go."

"Where do you plan to empty the holding tank?" Officer Andrews wanted to know.

"At an RV park, I guess," I said. "Is there one close by?"

Patrolman Andrews looked at his partner. "There's one on the other side of town. It's close to the Silver Saddle nightclub. You probably noticed the place when you drove through town."

"I didn't notice it," Randall said, as he looked at me and raised his eyebrows.

"No, I didn't either," I said. "But we can find it, I'm sure."

"Look at those assholes," Moon said, as the policemen pulled away laughing. "They thought we were a bunch of freaks."

We climbed back inside the big rig holding our noses while we opened all the side windows, cranked open the two roof vents and turned on the exhaust fan. The cross-ventilation gave us enough relief that we were able to slip into our jeans and sweatshirts and breathe at the same time without getting sick again.

I waved at the half-dozen parishioners standing outside the church as we drove past. All of them looked away except the guy that Long Dog had bitten. He shook his cane at us until we were out of sight.

Randall stopped at the frontage road and sat there looking around; as if he were trying to figure out what he should do next.

"I'm not going back across town to the Silver Saddle," he said. We decided to just dump the holding tank into the ditch under the bridge, get back on Interstate 40 and be on our way.

Once we were rolling down the highway again, I looked out the window and thought about all that had happened to us since we left Las Vegas. The thing that would be hardest to forget was what we did to Harley in the morgue. Even though he may have deserved to die, we still had committed a murder.

"Look at that," I said when I noticed the dark clouds rolling in from the east. "It looks like we may run into another rainstorm."

"Did you see that flash of lightning?" Randall said. "Harley would freak out."

I looked at him and shook my head without saying a word. I started to remind him of the old saying that time heals everything. In the case of Harley, I didn't know if it would really be true.

Except for some eighteen-wheelers, the occasional cowboy in a pickup and a few families headed for church in their Sunday best, the traffic was light on the interstate compared to what it had been the night before.

"Winslow is only an hour away," I said, as I pointed at a billboard advertising a restaurant called the Home Of The Big Short Stack. "What about that place for breakfast?" I said to Randall. "It's all-you-can-eat. You should like that. We can call home from there and be on our way."

"Great idea," Moon said when Randall didn't answer. "Let's stop for sure. I'm really hungry."

"Is there anything you want to talk about?" I asked Randall after about ten minutes of silence, during which he just gritted his teeth and stared down the road.

"It's too late now," he snapped at me. "Who cares anyway?"

"What are you talking about?"

"Harley. I hate it because I didn't make the call."

"I was afraid this would happen. I thought we agreed he deserved what he got. He almost killed us about ten times."

"I know he did. But he had some good qualities too."

Moon looked at me and frowned. "Like what?"

"Like saving that poor dog," Randall said, looking over his shoulder at Long Dog.

"Yeah, I guess," I said, thinking about Harley's rough life and how terrible it would be to have your own brother send you to prison.

"I dreamed about him last night," Randall said. "Just like you guys told me I would."

I reached over and patted him on the arm. "It'll be okay. It's not as if the world will miss him much."

The wind picked up, and swirling, dark clouds blackened the sky. Heavy rain pelted the windshield, and it became difficult to see the road. I jumped away from the door when a black plastic garbage bag flew out of the ditch and smashed into my side window.

I turned on the radio and pushed the search button, hoping to find a weather report. It stopped on a country station playing a Johnny Cash song and I turned the power switch off. "I guess we don't need to hear about Folsom Prison right now," I said.

"I can hardly keep this thing on the road," Randall said, fighting the wheel as he scooted up toward the edge of the seat. "It's not worth it. I'm going to stop." He pulled onto the shoulder and we sat there for thirty minutes, rocking back and forth as the storm bashed us with its fury.

We reached the city limits of Winslow, Arizona around 1:00 p.m., hungry as a pack of dogs. There was a sign on the front door of the restaurant informing the general public that the Health Department had closed the Home of the Big Short Stack. We drove a couple more blocks and pulled in at a place called The Red Rooster, which was a run-down-looking eating establishment that reminded me a lot of The Best Food Anywhere Restaurant. The Red Rooster had been freshly painted by what may have been the sloppiest painter in the world. The green foliage and shrubs that grew along the edge of the building were splattered with red paint, and the sidewalk looked as if someone had been stabbed to death on it. We sat in the parking lot for a few minutes and debated if it would be a mistake to go inside.

Our mind was made up for us when a couple of truckers, who looked well-fed, walked out the front door chewing on toothpicks and laughing.

When Randall and I called our moms to wish them a happy Mother's Day; we told them we had run into some trouble with the steam engine in the motor home, but that we were safe and would be home in plenty of time for the wedding. As most mothers would be, they were glad to hear from us; they said for us to be careful and they gave us their love.

Ann, on the other hand, did not take the report of our delay nearly so well, and I couldn't blame her. The prospect of having a church full of people at a wedding without a groom would be about as bad as it gets. To calm her down when she started to cry, I told her that the motor home had broken down in a remote section of the desert. I said we were lucky to be alive. I begged her to stop crying and promised that everything would be okay.

When she didn't ask if I was hurt or how I was getting along, I figured her attitude had been strongly influenced by her mother.

I took back any bad things I might have thought about The Red Rooster because the food was delicious. As we left, we asked about the paint job. It turned out that the owner had hired some guy to give the place a fresh coat of red paint while he closed down for a week's vacation. He said the problem seemed to be that the painter drank about a gallon of whiskey for every gallon of paint he used.

I stood out in the parking lot beside the motor home and looked up at the sky as a light rain fell on my face. I remembered how as a kid growing up on the farm I used to stand out in the warm summer rain and lick the raindrops from my lips. Everything smelled so fresh and sweet. There would usually be a rainbow, and I would daydream about someday finding a pot of gold. I thought about how nice it would be if Ann and I were to raise our kids on a farm, a place where they could be outdoors a lot, go fishing in a pond and have a dog—maybe even some more animals like chickens, a horse and a cow. It would be somewhere far enough away from Ann's mother so that she would only visit us a couple of times each year.

Traffic had begun to pick up. I watched the cars and some bikers go by.

"I'd better run back inside real quick and use the restroom," Moon said.

"Why don't you use the one in the motor home?" I asked suspiciously.

"The smell is still pretty bad. I would hate to lose my breakfast."

"All right. Hurry up though. I'm on a life-or-death schedule." Randall and I got into the big rig.

Moon came back looking relieved and content.

Randall pulled out of the parking lot and back onto the highway. He was very quiet.

He turned away from me and stared out the window. "I can't live with what I've done. When we get back to Kansas City, I'm turning myself in to the police. In my dreams, I was standing by the table last night when the pathologist started up the bone saw. Blood flew everywhere, even in my eyes."

I patted him on the shoulder. "Even if you did, no jury in the world would convict you—not after what Harley did."

Before Randall could say anything else, a car pulled up beside us and the driver honked a horn that played a bugle call like they play before the start of a horse race.

I leaned across Randall's lap for a closer look and saw a large, black woman wearing a white muumuu-style dress about the size of a pup tent. She smiled at me, stuck her hand out through the sunroof of an old Lincoln and waved. I pulled back and buried myself in the seat, barely able to maintain my composure.

Randall ducked his head and looked up at me through bushy brown eyebrows. "That's the biggest woman I've ever seen. I'm serious, man. She must weigh at least four hundred pounds—maybe more."

"She's not really that big, is she?" I asked.

"Her head's as big as the steering wheel," Randall said, as he sneaked another quick look and reconfirmed his findings with a nod.

I eased up to the window again for another look and waving at me from the backseat of the big Lincoln was a white woman wearing the same muumuu-style dress as her running mate, only it was black, and she was at least fifty pounds heavier. She caught me off-guard. Like an idiot, I waved back. I looked at myself in the rearview mirror and my face was beet-red.

"I bet they're road whores," Randall said.

"They can't be. Who in their right mind would chase after those two?"

"Truckers. They get really bored just driving up and down the road."

He could be right. I remembered listening to a report on Public Radio about truckers in India or someplace that picked up at least one loose woman every day. They said the heat from the truck engine kept their sexual desire stirred up and they were always primed and ready.

The question was answered for us when the white gal in the backseat yelled, "Come on out, pretty young boys. Mama's got some sugar for your love spoon."

"What's goin' on, Dude?" Moon asked, as he leaned forward to look out Randall's window.

"There's a couple of cheerleaders over there that want to talk to you," I said, proud of myself for keeping a straight face.

"Yeah, right."

"Go see for yourself. I think you'll really like 'em."

Randall pulled over and the girls pulled up in front of us.

"Okay, I will," Moon said with a sheepish grin. He walked around in front of the motor home and cautiously approached the car.

I figured he would take one look at the big mamas and we would get on down the road. Instead, he looked over the top of the car at Randall and me. He actually seemed to have a sparkle in his eye.

I opened my door and stepped out onto the parking lot so I could sneak around the back of the Lincoln for a closer look.

The trunk was smashed in where the car had been rear-ended. A greasy, white rag was stuffed in the gas line and rust had eaten away the rocker panels under the doors. To finish off the native beauty of the beast, a dirty white bumper sticker with faded green letters read, Save Water Bathe With A Friend.

While Moon was talking to the girls on the driver's side, I sneaked up by the rear door on the right and looked inside the open window. The floor was covered with fast food containers. Candy bar wrappers and milk shake cups were everywhere.

"Come on, let's go," Randall said, as he started the engine and tooted the horn.

"Okay, girls," I heard Moon say, as he looked over the top of the car at Randall and smiled. "You guys go on," he said with a chuckle. "Me and the girls will be close behind."

"You can't be serious, Moon." Randall sounded as if he had just had the shock of his life.

"Yeah man, I am. Me, Maybeleen and Gertie, we'll follow you boys to the Petrified Forest. Stop when you get to the entrance and I'll get back inside."

"Okay," Randall said. "That's about thirty miles on the other side of Holbrook, Arizona, in case you and your friends get lost."

Moon smiled as he opened the big, heavy door and slid in behind a steering wheel with a sheepskin cover. His new girlfriend scooted over by the window and Moon fired up the engine.

I climbed back into the big rig at the same time Randall made one last plea. "For all you know, Moon, those girls could be criminals."

Moon raised up out of the seat and grinned as he stuck his head up through the sunroof. "A Lincoln with suicide doors can't be all bad. I always wanted to drive one."

"You're crazy," Randall said. "That's all I've got to say."

Moon pointed his finger down the road and like a commander directing a charge he shouted, "You lead, Randall, my boy. Me and my people will follow."

"Why don't you come with us, Mark?" Moon yelled at me. "You'd have a good time."

"Yeah, come on, Marky honey," Gertie said. "It's been ages since I've had a tender young prize like you."

"No thanks," I said, feeling my face start to flush again, and it was at that moment I realized what it took to qualify as a free spirit. Moon had it; Randall and I definitely did not.

Randall shook his head and started down Interstate 40 again with the big Lincoln close behind.

"I can't believe Moon's in that car," Randall said. "What is he thinking about?"

"I can believe Moon might do just about anything. He's truly a free spirit, not like anyone I've ever known."

"A lot of it must have come from him following the Dead."

Long Dog began to whine and scratch at something under the seat. "Look what I've got," I said, as I pulled out a green canvas duffel bag and looked inside.

"What's the matter, Mark?" Randall asked, as I scooted it back under the seat. "Isn't that Harley's old bag? What's in it?"

"Two sticks of dynamite, a half dozen shells for his revolver and a hairbrush. Kind of a weird combination."

Randall looked panicked. "Throw the damn thing out the window."

"No way. What if a kid found it? What if someone ran over the damn stuff and it exploded?"

"Then what do you suggest?" Randall hissed at me as if I had done something wrong. When I didn't answer him, he calmly said, "We could blow up some rocks or something. You Know Who would be really proud of us if we did."

"Let's just not do anything. I'll stash it in the back the next time we stop. It won't bother us, if we don't bother it."

"Not until we're rear-ended and the big rig catches on fire. With our luck, that could happen easily."

"Maybe we're finished with our run of bad luck. It could be someone else's turn."

Honk! Honk! The sunshine girls laughed and waved at us when Moon pulled up beside the motor home. They went into a convulsive fit of laughter when we waved back.

Gertie poked her head out through the hole in the roof and started to say something. Her flowing black muumuu got sucked up by the wind and flew up all around her, flapping in the wind. Vehicles honked and waved at the unusual sight as Moon drove along beside us.

"Can you imagine Moon's view?" I said to Randall, as Gertie plopped back down into the seat. Moon dropped back into the right-hand lane behind us, and we didn't see the Lincoln again until we reached our destination.

Randall pulled over and parked at the entrance to the Petrified Forest. He shut off the engine while we waited for Moon and the girls.

I glanced in the rearview mirror and saw a string of fifty or sixty motorcycles roaring down the interstate toward us. "Look behind us."

"Oh my God! Is it that bunch of crazies from the Silver Saddle?"

"I hope not, but I bet it is though."

"If they start trouble, we'll give them a surprise," Randall said, as he looked over at me and smiled.

"Oh sure, like what?"

"We'll use Harley's TNT. Get it out of the green bag. We need to be ready."

I lucked out when I reached down for the bag. I got hold of my good sense first and put an end to the insanity. "No!" I pushed the bag away. "We're not going to make things any worse."

"How could they be worse? It doesn't get any worse than us being dead."

"My God, Randall! What have we become? We're thinking about blowing people up. This is crazy."

"It was just a thought," he said with a frown. "We couldn't blow them all up anyway. We've only got two sticks of TNT."

"Look at that," I said, as I pointed at a highway patrolman running at a high rate of speed in the westbound lane with his red lights flashing. I had hoped that he may be after the bikers, but instead of cutting across the median and pulling in behind them, he disappeared over the hill.

Within seconds after the last biker had stopped at the intersection, Moon pulled the big red Lincoln in and stopped right outside my window. His eyes were wide and filled with panic. A dark cloud of smoke bellowed out through the grill and flames shot up from under both sides of the hood.

Moon jumped out and threw his hands in the air. "The engine's blown," he screamed, as he hurried away from the accident waiting to happen. "I told you we should have stopped, Maybeleen."

"Remember what I told you about the dynamite and a fire?" Randall asked, as he started the engine and pulled away to a safe distance with the bikers following our move.

As I jumped outside to witness the action, Maybeleen and Gertie were rolling out through the big suicide doors, looking like a couple of buffalo about ready to stampede.

Seconds later, an explosion shook the ground and a strong, acrid-metallic smell of burning paint filled the air.

"Far freakin' out!" Moon yelled. "I've never seen a real live car fire before."

A biker smiled at Moon and clapped his hands. "Far freakin' out is right, man. This calls for a get-down party."

When someone in the back of the crowd laughed and whistled, everyone else joined in, yelling and clapping and stomping the ground as we watched the big Lincoln become engulfed in a cloud of black smoke and dancing yellow flames.

Maybeleen was a pretty cool old gal. She raised her arms toward the heavens and with the thick, slow, reverent drawl of a Southern Baptist minister's daughter, she said,

"God bless my high-spirited children. Because of folks like you, real people can remain free."

That earthy philosophical message caught the attention of a biker with a long gray ponytail and "Black Is Beautiful" tattooed on the shoulder of his left arm. Sounding like a product of the Deep South himself, the wiry little dude said, "Don't worry your pretty head about the burned up car. Just climb on this here Harley hog. You an' me, we'll crisscross America together."

When he blew Maybeleen a kiss and took a slow graceful bow, one of his road mates shouted, "Go for it, Molten! You've got yourself a real woman now."

"Yeah, Molty," another rider yelled, "she's a living treasure!"

"Molten?" Randall said, as he looked over at me. "Whoever heard of such a name?"

Maybeleen walked over to her newfound soul mate and wrapped her big brown hands around his tight little ass. She embraced him with so much gusto that Molten's feet came right up off the ground. He broke away and backed up with a wild look in his eyes as if something were wrong.

"Only one thing concerns me about the ride," Molten said solemnly, as if once he had gotten a good look at Maybeleen up close, he had changed his mind.

"What's that, my little lamb?" she said with words that sounded as sweet as honey.

"It's my tires. I'm afraid they might blow."

Maybeleen held out her hands and licked her lips. "No problem there, Sugar Pie. With what I've got planned for you, I'll lose a bunch of weight really fast."

When the two lovers laughed and hugged each other again, one of the bikers yelled, "You got yourself a good one, Molty, my man!"

Moon batted his eyes at me and grinned. "Have we just been witness to a biker marriage?"

"Believe so. Seems like there's even a musky smell of love in the air."

A smile as wide as a river spread across Gertie's face when another one of the older bikers, outfitted in black leather from head to toe, said, "If you'll be my old lady, I'll be your biker man."

I was amazed at how courteous the hard-core-looking crowd was. They just up and moved away so the two newfound soul mates could have a private talk. It wasn't long before the conversation turned into a hug and a kiss. Gertie climbed on her biker man Slim's Harley hog and they headed off down Interstate 40.

"Yeah, let's get the hell out of here before the cops come. They'll blame us for settin' the damn car on fire." That command came from the really big guy who had shot at the now-dead Duke in the parking lot of The Best Food Anywhere Restaurant. The same guy from the Silver Saddle had migrated to the entrance of the Petrified Forest. It was as if this crazy band of restless renegades were following us. The bikers roared away down Interstate 40 toward Gallup, New Mexico. I thought about how much simpler it would have been if Ann and I had chosen a less complicated wedding ceremony like the bikers'. We could have cut her mother out altogether.

"Do you guys still want to drive through the Petrified Forest?" Randall asked, as he started the engine.

"No," I said, "keep on going down the road."

"Come on, let's do it, man," Moon said. "What's thirty minutes? Hell, we may never come this way again."

"Moon's right," Randall agreed. "Thirty minutes isn't going to hurt us none."

When I didn't say anything, Randall pulled across the road in search of petrified logs.

"Well Moon, other than smoking a little dope and acting silly, what else happened during your ride with the girls?" I asked. Moon opened his mouth as if he were going to say something, and then changed his mind. He just winked at me and smiled.

"What's the matter, boy?" Moon said when Long Dog ran to the back of the motor home and scratched on the restroom door.

"Too much excitement, I guess." I looked over my shoulder and watched him lay down on the floor.

"Look, there's a petrified log!" Moon shouted, pointing at a dark gray tree trunk that looked as if the wood had turned to concrete.

"Harley would have liked this part of the trip," Randall said. "Remember how he talked about taking some wood?"

After a couple more sightings, I convinced Randall we'd had enough of the Petrified Forest. He turned around so we could head back down Interstate 40 toward home.

Long Dog scratched at the bathroom door again. I got out of my seat and walked to the back so I could take a leak and see what was going on. I tried to scoot him out of the way with my foot so I could open the door, and he bit my foot. A reflex action caused me to kick him in the side hard enough that he yelped and ran under the couch.

I heard a click on the other side of the door and I froze. I looked down and saw the handle turn slowly.

"What's going on?" Moon yelled, as I grabbed the handle and jerked open the door.

"Oh my God!" I screamed and slapped my chest when I saw a revolver pointed at my head.

Boom! There was a blast so loud that I thought the dynamite had exploded. At the same time, Moon had run up beside me and I grabbed him by the arm. In an instant, we both fell to the floor.

Chapter Fourteen

We looked up. There stood Harley in the doorway of the restroom with a cigarette dangling from the corner of his mouth. A smoking revolver was pointed at Moon's head. If a cold, hard stare could kill, Moon would have been dead.

"Please don't, Harley," I begged, as Long Dog ran over and began to lick blood off the floor. The blood was dripping from Moon's injured hand.

Randall pulled off to the side of the road so fast that it felt as if the motor home might turn over. Like an idiot, he looked back at Harley and yelled, "You mess with my friend, I'll kick your ass." With that bit of foolish, suicidal posturing, Harley turned the revolver on Randall and pulled the trigger. Randall dropped to the floor.

"You're a bunch of rotten bastards," Harley yelled, as he flipped the cigarette and it bounced off Moon's forehead. I screamed when sparks flew in my eyes. The fear of dying, which had kept my stomach tied in a knot when Harley was with us the first time, had come back—only this time it was even stronger than before. He was doubly pissed off about our leaving him.

"Moon needs to get his hand stitched up, Harley," I said, as I finished wrapping a blood-soaked gauze pad with tape. I squinted my eyes and stared at the red streak across Harley's forehead.

"I'll tell you what Moon needs more than anything," Harley said with a big grin.

Before Harley could say anything else, Moon pointed at him with his hurt hand. "I'll be okay, Harley. I never used the little finger on my right hand much anyway. I'm left-handed, you know what I mean?"

"How about you, Randall?" I asked when I saw him sit up in the aisle and put his hand up to the side of his head. "Are you okay?"

"Yeah, I think I am." He stood up and looked in the rearview mirror. "If I hadn't turned my head the instant before he shot, I'd probably be dead."

"We'll probably all be needing some of those pain pills now," Moon said, and it dawned on me that I had forgotten about my hurt back. There wasn't any pain, not even a slight tingle. As though a miracle had blessed me, I was back to normal again, so to speak. I had always heard that was what happened in many cases with severe back pain. One day you're crippled up and in pain, the next you feel like jumping fences.

"All right," Harley said, "let's get up front while I decide what to do with you band of traitors."

We sat down in our respective places, Randall driving, me in the passenger seat, Moon in the yellow director's chair and Harley on the edge of the couch, holding Long Dog. In a mean tone of voice Harley said, "Killing you pricks quickly would be too easy. You deserve a slow death."

"How in the world did you find us?" I asked Harley.

"Some bikers were hanging around the hospital checking on a buddy and they offered to help me catch up with you guys. They found the big rig without any trouble. Why did you leave me in the morgue on the table?"

"Moon thought he heard somebody in one of the vaults moan, so did Mark and so did I," Randall said. "After that we ran out of the morgue because we were afraid."

"So you ran away and left me on the table?" Harley said suspiciously. "Why didn't you take me along?"

"You passed out and we couldn't get you to come back around," I said.

"I almost got cut up in that place where you pricks left me. I almost died."

"So what happened to make you think you almost died?" Randall asked.

"It was like a dream, except I knew it was real. It was like I had been drugged or something. I tried to sit up, but I couldn't. Whir. Whir. Whir. That's the sound I woke up to when I was on the table in the morgue. The place where you pricks left me for the night. Guess what happened though, man? Like something only the Lord could do, I got saved."

"This sounds like it's right down my alley," Moon said. "Go on with the story."

"So anyway, the next thing I hear when I start to come around are a couple of guys standing at the foot of my table talking about somebody named Dr. Baron."

"What did they say about Dr. Baron?" Randall asked.

"He had a heart attack and died. So nobody showed up during the night to do an autopsy on guess who. Me, that's who. That was until this morning when the backup pathology team showed up to carry out the orders of cutting me up."

"Are you kiddin' me?" Randall said.

"That would be scary," I said.

"A weaker man would not be here," Moon said, as he looked up toward the sky.

After a moment of silence, Harley continued with the story. "I thought I was having a dream. I heard people talking and then their voices would fade away."

"I thought you heard the Whir, Whir, Whir sound of a saw," I said.

"I did. One of them fired the thing up and ran it for a few seconds then shut it off. It was lucky for me that one of them walked down by my feet. The Lord caused my toe to twitch and it moved the tag. I came around and sat up so fast that I bumped my head on the blade of the saw. The docs helped me sit up and treated the cut on my forehead. They were pretty shook up that I was alive and they were about to saw me up."

"Lucky you," Randall said, as he leaned over and looked in the rearview mirror at the place where the bullet had scraped the side of his head, leaving a permanent part.

"You almost got even with Randall big time. You could have killed him, you know," I said, hoping to stop Harley from feeling so sorry for himself that he would turn on us again.

"Bull. Lucky for him I'm a good shot. I could have plugged him right in the face. Come on, let's get on the road."

"So the toe tag actually saved your life," Randall said. "How very weird."

"Yeah, that's right. I woke up just in time to keep the guy from cutting my skull open with a bone saw. I'll hear that Whir, Whir, Whir sound until the day I die." He reached forward, grabbed Randall by the arm and yelled as he pointed to his forehead. "That cut right there is how close I came to losing the top of my head! I'll get even with all of you for what you did. I just haven't decided yet what awful thing I'm going to do." Harley touched the ugly red cut above his eyebrows tenderly and whimpered like a pup.

"What the hell are you so concerned about, Harley?" Randall said, trying to reassure him. "You're making a big deal out of nothing. That wound will heal up in no time." Randall rolled down the window and yelled, "Get over, you complete idiot!"

The guy driving alongside the big rig gave Randall the finger and sped away.

"Randall knows what he's talking about, Harley. He used to drive an ambulance. He saw plenty of cuts worse than yours, isn't that right, Randall?" I looked over at Randall and he forced a grin.

With fire in his eyes, Harley jumped up and grabbed hold of Randall. "Just shut the hell up! You pricks tried to kill me. Now you're makin' it into a joke. For two cents I'd blast all of you plumb to hell. That would teach you a damned good lesson none of you'd ever forget." Harley's hand was shaking when he cocked back the hammer.

Once again, good old Randall took care of the problem. "Now Harley, I know you're upset. I know what I'm about to tell you may be hard to believe, but its every bit the truth. Just hear me out, okay?"

Randall blinked when a trail of smoke from Harley's cigarette floated into his right eye.

Harley sat back down on the couch. "You better hope I believe you and Mr. Smart Mouth, or you're.... " Harley was so upset he could not finish the sentence. After a long mental lapse, he moved the cigarette close to the side of Randall's cheek. "Because if I don't believe you, I'm going to stick this cigarette in your eye and grind it out. You know something, Son? After what you boys did to me, the screams won't bother me one pissy-assed bit."

Randall swallowed and cleared his throat. He looked up through his eyebrows as if he were hoping for divine guidance then glanced over at me for any help I might be able to offer. I just frowned, and he started his story. "Harley, do you remember what happened after we drank the milk?"

"Hell yes! I remember I passed out. I also remember the three of you were still standing beside the table lookin' pretty damned healthy."

"Not for long, Harley. We didn't stand there for very long, I can assure you. You've got to believe me when I tell you we didn't stand there for long." Randall was repeating himself, stalling for time while he tried to come up with more parts to his unbelievable save-your-own-ass, do-it-or-die story.

"Randall's telling the truth, Harley," I said. "He really is telling you the honest-to-goodness truth."

"How do I know it's true?"

"I'm about to tell you. Just have a little patience," Randall said. "I'm sure you remember the janitor in the cafeteria, the one you scared half to death?" Randall was really cool. He had put Harley on the defensive.

"What do you mean, the one I scared half to death? I never did no such thing."

"Come on, Harley. You scared the guy so badly he pissed his pants. I saw the wet spot. You made the poor guy feel like dirt. How would you like it if someone humiliated you the way you did him?"

Randall rolled down the window again and swerved the big rig toward a black Cadillac, running the car off onto the shoulder of the road. "What are you trying to do, you lame-brained prick?" Randall yelled out the window. "That stupid turd should have his driver's license taken away."

It finally dawned on me that Randall was trying to attract attention, hoping that someone would call the highway patrol.

"Maybe I scared the guy a little, so what? A lot of people scare a lot of people every day. There's no crime in scaring people. You know what the hell I mean, Randall?"

"Well guess what, Harley. That little guy had a lot more courage than we figured. Not only did he give us milk laced with sleeping pills, he...."

"Wait just a damned minute," Harley said, cutting Randall off. "Just hold it right there. Why would he have a gallon of milk around laced with sleeping pills? How stupid do you think I am?"

Moon jumped into the conversation. "You really don't get it do you, Harley? You really don't get it at all."

"Get what? What the hell are you three trying to pull?" Harley poked Moon in the back with the nose of the revolver.

"Guys like that janitor get tired of loudmouths like you being mean to them. They've got special ways of getting even," Moon said.

"Yeah, like how do they get even? Hit people with their broom?" Harley laughed loudly and poked Moon again with the cold steel.

"Think of this for a minute," Moon said. "I know a guy that waits on tables in a classy restaurant. He gets even with people like you who treat the little people like crap. You know how? He puts disease-ridden stuff in their food."

"Like what?"

"His favorite is the lowly cockroach. He zaps them in the microwave until they're crispy. He grinds them up into a powder that looks like pepper. When people are mean and nasty, he puts cockroach pepper on their food." Moon looked at Harley and smiled. "It's a big mistake not to treat guys like the janitor with proper respect—a big mistake indeed."

"You're an ass, Moon Rat. You just want to...."

"Moon's right, Harley," I interrupted him. "I knew a guy who worked in a drive-in restaurant during high school that got even with people who hassled him by pissing on their pickles. If they were really bad, he would tell them a red star came up on their cash register receipt and they had won a free hamburger. It's hard to taste piss on pickles. You know what I mean, Harley?"

Moon looked at me and laughed. "That story was pretty bad, Mark. Did that really happen?"

"Yeah, it really did. Go figure this out, the guy was the valedictorian of our class and went on to become a well-known politician."

"Did you notice a small red x on the side of the jug?" Randall asked Harley.

"No, but I didn't look for one either." Harley sounded as if he were building up to having another fit.

"That's how the janitor kept the doped-up container separated from the rest of the milk," Randall responded quickly, sounding much more confidant and convincing than when he'd begun his fabricated story.

Moon jumped into the conversation again. "That wiry little janitor sounds like he was pretty damn smart, doesn't he, Harley?"

Before Harley could answer him, Randall said, "Anyway, after you passed out, the janitor and two of his buddies burst into the morgue and took the three of us back to the cafeteria. We had only drunk a little of our milk. You guzzled down a big glass—that's why you were dead to the world. The janitor filled us with coffee and kept us moving around until we felt well enough to leave the hospital."

"So then what happened to me?" Harley asked, sounding like a little kid who had been deserted by his friends.

"The janitor and his buddies said they'd take care of you. So we figured you'd be okay and we left," I said. "We were afraid to wait around any longer. We figured someone might find the dead guy in the parking lot ditch and try to pin a murder on us. So we got in the big rig and drove away as fast as we could."

"Think about it, Harley," Moon said. "You would have done the same thing. Wouldn't you?"

Harley sat motionless for a long time and looked straight down the road. "You must be telling the truth," he finally said as he looked over at Randall. "From what I've seen of you so far, you're too much of a wimp to make up something that wild."

"A lot of engineers are that way, Harley," Randall said. "Smart and talented." He picked up speed and we rolled on down the road.

Moon had not had enough; he decided he should try to explain even more about what had happened. "So here's what we're telling you, Harley. It was the janitor, not us, that set you up to be the victim of an autopsy." Unable to leave well enough alone, he went one step further and added, "Maybe this will be a lesson to you, man. Maybe you'll treat people with proper respect in the future."

I glanced back at Harley, expecting to see him red-faced and ready to go into one of his volatile outbursts. Instead, he was sitting down on the couch, calmly stroking Long Dog's hairless back. With fur flying and fleas jumping, the little fella' leaped up and gave Harley a quick lick on the lips.

"Look at all that red rock and rough country out there, Moon," Harley said, as he stared out the window at the barren landscape. "We should have driven over to the Grand Canyon while we were so close. What the hell were we thinking about, boys?"

Harley sounded so friendly that I glanced over my shoulder to see what he was up to and he smiled.

"My hand's throbbing like crazy, Mark. Let me have one of your Percodans, please," Moon said.

"That sounds like a good idea. I've got some pain myself." All of a sudden my back hurt again and my eyes filled with tears. I unscrewed the cap and popped a Perc into my mouth. I handed the bottle to Moon and he gulped down a couple.

"Do you mind if I play the radio, Harley?" Moon asked.

"Go ahead. Play anything you want to, Moon Baby, except opera. My cellmate loved opera and I got damned sick and tired of it. You know what I mean? Sick and tired of being sick and tired." Harley sounded distant and depressed, which was not a good sign.

Chapter Fifteen

We listened to the radio and motored along with little being said for the next thirty minutes until we were about twenty-five miles outside of Gallup, New Mexico. "Here's an old favorite I haven't played for a long time," the DJ on Rock 99 announced. "Takes me back to a great time in my life: l968. It was the year I got divorced from my third wife."

I pointed up ahead at a couple of bikers as the "Ballad of Easy Rider" floated out of the speakers.

"Isn't that a couple of your biker buddies, Harley? I thought there was a helmet law in this state. You'd think those guys would be afraid of smashing their heads in," Randall said, sounding more like his good old sane and conservative self.

"I bet that trucker is upset with them. Truckers don't like it when bikers follow so close," Moon said, as he stared at the road warriors. "It makes them uneasy when they can't see anything in their rearview mirrors."

With their feet propped up on road pegs, their long hair whipping in the wind, a couple of free spirits cruised along in the truck's draft without a care in the world.

"The guy on the right keeps weaving back and forth a lot," I said. "He's getting awfully close to his buddy. I think he may be dozing off."

"Dozing off? Are you serious? Why would someone doze off riding a motorcycle?" Harley said.

"That happens sometimes on a long haul, Harley. I did a couple of cross-country bike trips and believe me, it's easy to become hypnotized by the rumble of the engine. More than once I caught myself jerking my head back just in time to keep from running off the road. The scary thing was, I didn't remember a thing about the last few miles I had covered. I'm surprised more people don't crash. I'll tell you something else about riding a motorcycle cross-country, you find yourself...."

Before I could finish the sentence, Moon grabbed me by the arm and yelled, "Oh my God!"

The cycle on the right had drifted over and clipped the back tire of the cycle on the left. The biker who was at fault overcorrected for the problem and his big black machine shot across the road, headed toward a ditch. The biker on the left managed to skillfully lay his Harley down on the pavement when it turned sideways after being hit. He pulled himself up on top of it and hunkered down like a big bear, riding the chopper down the middle of the road with sparks flying as it turned around and around, scraping against the concrete. A red plastic taillight cover snapped off and bounced high into the air.

The biker on the right, who had caused the accident, sailed off the road. He was thrown off when the front tire of his machine hit the ground. As it crashed down beside him, the end of a handlebar caught him squarely in the neck. His head jerked back as if it was attached to his shoulders with a rubber band and his tongue flopped out the side of his mouth.

Randall slammed on the brakes. We jumped out of the big rig and ran toward the poor guy so fast that Moon and I got tangled up in each other's feet and we both fell down.

"Is my brother bad hurt?" the biker, who had managed to stay on top of his big metal hog until it came to a rest, yelled as he limped down the center of the road towards us. The right leg of his leather trousers was ripped open and his kneecap was covered with blood. "How bad is he?" he shouted when no one answered him.

"He's in bad shape," Randall said, as he bent down on one knee and tilted the guy's head back. He was gasping for air and his lips were bluish gray. A look of panic was frozen on his face.

Without saying a word, Randall reached into his pocket, pulled out a knife, opened the blade and cut a hole in the guy's windpipe.

His brother lunged forward and grabbed Randall's arm when he saw the blood rush from the injured man's neck. "What the hell did you do that for? Are you crazy or what? Stop, you bastard!"

I grabbed the guy by the arm and pulled him away. "Your brother couldn't breathe. He was about to die. Randall's a paramedic. He just saved your brother's life. Do you understand what I'm saying?" I shouted at him, as I kept a tight grip on his arm.

The biker hunkered down beside his brother and with tear-filled eyes; he put his mouth close to his ear. "You'll be okay, Billy Boy. I'll make sure you'll be okay." Billy Boy coughed violently and a shower of blood caused his brother to jump away so quickly that he fell over backwards. He wiped his face with the back of his hand and smeared blood from ear to ear.

After a few deep breaths, Billy Boy's color improved considerably and he gave Randall a pitiful smile.

"Just lay still, my friend. You'll be okay. You can't talk because I had to cut a hole in your trachea so you could breathe," Randall said. He patted Billy Boy on the shoulder.

"My God, look at all the blood. He needs help. What are we going to do now?" his brother asked, as he jumped to his feet and limped around in a circle, moaning.

"I figured that the trucker probably called for an ambulance on his CB. Then again, I also figured he would have stopped to help, but he didn't. Maybe we'd better just get Billy Boy into the big rig and take him to the hospital ourselves. Gallup isn't that far away. I know he looks like a mess right now, but he'll be all right," Randall said to Billy Boy's brother. "What about you? Are you okay?"

"I thought I broke my foot, but now I think it's only sprained. My knee's cut up a little, but not bad. The leather pants saved me."

"You're right, Randall. Let's take Billy Boy to the hospital ourselves," Moon said. "I can have someone look at my gunshot-wounded hand while we're in the emergency room."

Harley grabbed Moon by the arm. "Hold it one damn minute! Hospitals have to report gunshot wounds. I'm not having any of that crap where we toss caution to the wind just because you've got a little scrape on your hand. You know what the hell I mean, Moon Baby?"

"We'll tell them Moon accidentally shot himself during target practice. A bullet bounced off a rock and nailed him in the hand. He really should have someone look at the wound, Harley," Randall said.

Harley's eye twitched the way it always did when he studied really hard on a complex situation. "You're right, Randall. Now that I've thought about it, I remember that Moon really did accidentally shoot himself. That's what you did all right, didn't you, Moon?"

"Yeah, that's what I did all right, Harley. That's exactly what I did," Moon said disgustedly.

I walked around behind the injured biker's head and dropped to my knees. Randall took charge and said, "Let's load him into the big rig and get to the hospital. We're wasting time. Be careful, Mark. Keep his head tilted back and don't make any sudden moves."

Twenty minutes later we pulled into the emergency entrance at Gallup Memorial Hospital and it looked like a Fourth of July picnic. Hundreds of people were milling around in the parking lot. I realized it was not anything that resembled a good time when I looked up on the roof and saw two uniformed men with sharpshooter rifles.

"What's going on?" I asked an elderly gentleman standing beside an ambulance when we got outside.

He squinted his eyes and backed up a couple of steps without saying a word. I must have looked a little scary with Billy Boy's blood all over me. A nurse overheard me and said, "There's a man inside the hospital with a bomb."

"We've got a motorcycle wreck victim in our motor home," Randall barked, running toward the back of the big rig. "I had to do a tracheotomy, and he's got some bleeders that need to be clamped off. He's lost a lot of blood."

The nurse waved at an orderly. "Get a stretcher over here, STAT." She turned to Randall and said, "We're taking everyone who needs serious attention to the operating room until the situation in the ER is clear."

"There's someone inside the hospital ER with a bomb. Can you believe that, Harley?" I said.

"Can I believe that there's someone in the hospital with a bomb?" Harley repeated. "Hell, Son, after all I've been through, I would believe damned near anything—especially if it came from the mouth of a pretty little thing like this cute girlie here." Harley squinted his eyes and smiled at the nurse, showing his widely gapped yellow teeth.

A frightened look came over the nurse's face and she backed up as if she were trying to escape from a vicious dog.

"You heard it right, Harley. There's a crazy old man inside the hospital with a bomb. A crazy old man," I repeated, raising my voice when Harley gave me a stupid look. As I was standing there staring back at him, I thought that if I were to write down all the weird stuff that has happened during the past couple of days and put it in a book, no one would ever believe me that it had actually happened.

Harley's smile widened, "A man with a bomb, you say? It's hard to imagine some of the strange things people will do in this crazy-assed world. You know what I mean, boys?"

Randall looked at Harley and pointed at the hospital door. "Are you sure your brother's still in Chicago?" he asked with a smile. "It sounds like there's a good chance he may be waiting for you right inside."

"Hell, Randall, you might be right. Why don't I just go in there and get the damn fool out for these nice people?

How much more firepower can he have than my two sticks of TNT and a Colt 45 revolver?"

I looked at Randall and Moon and our eyes lit up. "Go for it, big guy," I said. "We're behind you all the way."

Harley scratched his head and grunted like a hog. "I could take the old bastard. He can't be any tougher than me."

An orderly pushed a stretcher up to the back door of the big rig and we loaded Billy Boy on it. The orderly wheeled the poor guy toward the side door of the hospital and his brother limped along beside him, still moaning.

As if a switch inside Harley's head had been triggered to push him over the edge into another one of his insane personalities, he yelled, "I've got to save my brother!"

"You do what you have to do, Harley," Randall said with a big grin. "Save your brother."

Harley grabbed my arm and squeezed down so hard that I bit my lip to keep from yelling. I tried to pull away, but he jerked me back.

With a gleam in his eye and a twisted grin that raised the corners of his mouth, he eased the grip. "Remember the display in the desert when I set off the dynamite and shot at Moon and Randall?"

"Remember? Yeah, I remember. What about it?"

"That was kindergarten compared to what might happen here today." Harley began to sing. "The guy inside's got a bomb. I've got a bomb. Lots of God's children have a bomb."

Taking a good long look at Randall, Moon and me, Harley said, "You boys best be coming along with me. I don't want to be a hero all by myself."

I swallowed deeply and my mouth fell open, but I could not speak.

"You're crazy if you think I'm going in there," Moon said.

"Oh really! I'm not about to leave you sneaky little pricks out here so you can team up with the cops. They would shoot me when I walked back out the ER door. No, I don't think you're going in with me. I know you're going! What the hell do you think I am, crazy?"

"This is a bunch of crap," I heard someone say to his officers as he stepped out in front of a patrol car. He raised a bullhorn to his lips and blasted out a loud warning to the man inside. "This is Captain Lewis speaking. Come out right now with your hands in the air or we'll come in after you. My men have instructions to shoot to kill if you don't comply with my orders."

When there was no response from the bomber inside the ER, Harley shouted, "Would you come over here for a minute, Mr. Patrolman?" Harley motioned the captain toward us by snapping his finger and waving his arm in the air. "Watch me pull the wool over this tinhorn's eyes," Harley whispered as he winked at me.

My heart fluttered and my spirit sank to an all-time low.

"You've gone around the bend, Harley," Randall said, taking a couple of steps backward.

"He's got a death wish all right," Moon muttered. "Maybe this time it will come true."

I knew the captain figured he had gotten hold of a real doozy when he looked at one of his officers and nodded. The patrolman unsnapped the leather tab on his hip holster and rested his hand on the handle of a large revolver.

"I think I can get the guy out for you, Mr. Patrolman. I can get the mad bomber out of the hospital," Harley said in a calm, but firm and confident voice.

The captain laid his bullhorn on the roof of a patrol car. He slid his hand under his coat and walked toward us, not losing eye contact with Harley for an instant. "All right, Mister. What's your hair-brained scheme, anyway?" the captain asked, as he stopped well short of us by about fifteen feet.

Harley squinted his eyes and shook his head. "I don't like it when people call me, 'Mister'. Neither does my brother."

"What the hell are you talking about, old man?" the captain asked, sounding disgusted with himself for wasting his time talking to Harley. "You just show me some identification before you do anything else. I want to see it right now."

"Hey, that's my crazy brother in there, and I'm the only one who can talk him into coming out. Unless you want him to blow up the hospital, you'll let me go do my deal and get him out."

The captain glared at Harley, challenging him with a cold hard stare. "Let's say the man with the bomb really is your brother. How the hell do you propose to get him out of the hospital without him blowing the place up?"

"Well, you see these three boys standing here with me, Mister Patrolman?" Harley asked, pointing to each of us in turn. "These are my brother Willie's grandsons, and he thinks the world of them. That's how I plan to get the poor deranged man outside safely."

There was a note of sarcasm in Harley's voice that bothered me some, and I could tell by the way the captain jerked his head to one side quickly and squinted his eyes that it bothered him even more.

"Is that right, boys? Are you the man's grandsons?" the captain asked while giving Moon a serious law-enforcement-officer once-over.

Without hesitation, Randall took over the conversation and did what he had been doing best for the past couple of days, which was telling lies about anything that needed to be lied about, doing it on a moment's notice and convincing people it was the truth too. "Harley's telling the truth, Captain, sir. That's our grandpa in there all right. They thought he was well enough to come home, but it looks like they were wrong, doesn't it, Harley?" Randall gave Harley a look of grave concern.

The captain stared at Randall with a look of disbelief as he slowly nodded his head up and down. "So you think the four of you can go in there and talk that crazy old man into giving up his bomb and coming outside?"

Harley smiled and shuffled his feet a little. "Well shucks, Mister Patrolman, let me ask you this question, do you have a better plan?"

The captain batted his eyes as if he had been slapped in the face with a wet rag. "I'll be right back." With a grim face he turned away and walked over to discuss the situation with the other officers.

"We're dead now, for sure," Moon said. "We're going into a building with a mad bomber to meet up with another mad bomber. That doubles our chances of being bombed. That's really far out, man. I mean really, really far out. It's been nice knowing you two guys." Moon shook our hands. "For a couple of straight dudes, you've been damned decent to be around." Moon patted me on the shoulder and he looked as if he might cry.

The captain walked up to Harley. "All right, old man. If you're sure you want to try this, you can." He handed Harley the bullhorn and stepped back. He crossed his arms and stared at the hospital entrance while he waited for Harley's message.

"Why are you giving me this thing?"

"So you can tell your crazy brother you're coming in. You can't just walk up on someone with a bomb. You'll scare the hell out of him. He may set the damn thing off before he realizes it's you and blow up the place."

"Good idea, Mister Patrolman." Harley stood there with the bullhorn up to his lips for a long time. He finally dropped it to his side and said, "What the hell am I supposed to say?"

"Tell him who you are and that you're coming in and bringing his grandsons with you. What the hell do you think you're supposed to say?" the captain smart-mouthed Harley and looked up at the sky.

Harley put the bullhorn up to his lips again and stared at the ER door. "Willie, this is your brother Harley. I'm bringing your grandsons, Randall, Mark and Moon, inside with me. All we want to do is talk to you, Willie."

"Tell him we all love him," Randall said.

"Your grandson Randall said to say we all love you, Willie," Harley blared at his pretend brother.

Crash! The window in a room next to the hospital entrance shattered and a man with a high-pitched voice that sounded like the blade of a circular saw cutting through a railroad tie shrieked, "Come on in, Harley. Come on in and bring the boys. It will be good to see everyone again."

We anxiously stared at the broken window in dismay.

The captain looked completely surprised. "I'll be damned," he said. "I just thought you were a crazy old man." He threw his hands in the air when Harley just stood there looking dumb as a fence post. "Well, go on in there and get this mad bomber guy out so I can get on with my life." The captain walked over and patted Harley on the back. "Good luck."

"Well, let's go see your grandpa, boys," Harley looked at us with a grin that ran from ear to ear.

I looked back over my shoulder at the pretty nurse and frowned. She smiled back at me and walked away.

"I can't believe you're going to do this, Harley," Moon said. "Just because you have a death wish doesn't mean you have to take us with you."

"Get your ass up in front, Moon. You know your grandpa's dying to see you first. Randall, you stay on my left and Mark will be on my right. I don't have to tell you how important it is that we maintain our formation."

"I think Grandpa always liked Mark the best," Moon said. The gutsy little guy was making a joke in our darkest hour.

Harley slid his hand under his coat and stepped up behind Moon, touching his back. I looked over at the captain when I heard the click of the hammer on his revolver.

I thought he might get suspicious, but he was busy signaling to the sniper on the roof to move away from the ER in case Harley's plan did not work and the bomb went off. His fellow officers moved the crowd further back.

"I know you've always thought that Grandpa Willie liked Mark the best, Moon," Harley said, playing along with Moon's game. "My guess is it's because you're a damn freak. So let's go inside and you can ask him face-to-face." Harley nudged Moon in the back with the nose of his revolver, and like a pack of blithering idiots on a fool's mission we started toward the ER entrance.

Except for some wild-eyed woman wearing white hospital garb with Psych Unit stamped across the front, who was clapping her hands, and the wail of a siren in the distance, a cast of hundreds watched in silence as we walked up to the door.

We moved a dozen wheelchairs and a couple of stretchers that blocked the door inside the hospital entrance, walked over to the emergency room nurses' station and stopped to check out the scene. Randall pointed at the narcotics cabinet with the door standing open and a key hanging from the lock. "That's just great! Our grandpa's been helping himself to the drugs."

He said it as a joke, but I just could not find it in me to laugh.

From down the hallway came loud, high-pitched laughter that sounded like the voice of Donald Duck.

We looked at one another and Harley had his revolver ready. We slowly walked in the direction of the laughter as we hugged the walls.

The emergency room was laid out with a half dozen treatment rooms surrounding an enclosed island on the right. On the left of the hall, there was a supply closet, an X-ray room, a couple of restrooms and a waiting area. The television was tuned to a local station, which was broadcasting the action outside in the parking lot. They were interviewing the captain and he seemed to love every second of it. The lights in the hallway burned brightly, but the treatment rooms were dark.

"Willie, this is Harley. I talked to you from outside on the bullhorn and told you we was comin' inside. Do you remember me talking to you, Willie? Do you remember me sayin' I was bringing in your grandsons?" After not getting a response, Harley yelled, "I called you, Willie, because I had to call you something to throw the police off the track. What's your real name?" He reached up and turned off the TV.

After a long silence, someone with a hysterical, high-pitched voice called out from one of the darkened treatment rooms at the end of the hallway. "What the hell are you trying to pull anyway? My name really is Willie. In fact, people who know me well call me Willie Goat. Another thing, you don't have to yell. I'm not deaf. Why the hell wouldn't I remember what you said five minutes ago? I'm not stupid either. You know what the hell I mean?"

"Hey man, don't get huffy with me. I was just trying to save you before the cops rushed in and shot you full of holes. I'll have you know that I've got a bomb too. I've got dynamite and a Colt 45 revolver. We explosive experts need to stick together. You know what the hell I mean, Willie? What kind of bomb have you got, Mister?"

"Don't call me 'Mister'! That's what the prison guards made me call them and I don't like it one little bit. You call me that one more time and I'll blow this place to smithereens."

Harley slapped himself upside the head with the flat of his hand. With a quiver in his voice, he said, "I understand and I won't do it again. I was in the joint myself. I don't like to be called 'Mister' either. I don't know what the hell I was thinking about."

"That's all right. Just don't do it again."

"Why don't you step out into the light so we can talk. We need to figure a way out of this mess, okay, Willie?"

"Look out!" Willie called, as a cart with a large, brown cylinder on it rolled out of the treatment room and made a loud, clanking sound as it hit the wall. "I will after you breathe some of that helium, Harley," Willie said, sounding like Donald Duck again.

Harley looked at Randall and shrugged his shoulders. "What kind of crazy stuff is this anyway?"

"Helium. He's been breathing helium and he wants you to breathe it so you'll sound like Donald Duck too. Go ahead, Harley. It won't hurt you. Humor your brother a little bit, man," Randall said.

"Is everyone okay in there?" the captain yelled on the bullhorn.

"Run to the door and tell him we're okay, Mark. Don't try anything funny, like making a break for it."

I hurried to the hospital entrance and waved at the captain. "Grandpa's going to be fine. He's really glad to see us. We'll all be out in a few minutes." I ran back to where the big helium party was about to begin and got in line for my treatment.

"What did the captain say?" Harley asked.

"He just waved his bullhorn and smiled. I think he really likes you, Harley."

"Step out into the light, Willie. I'll breathe the helium and we can talk," Harley said.

"No way, man. Not until you breathe the helium first. I don't trust people anymore who haven't breathed helium. I'm not going to tell you again," Willie shouted, as he threw a pair of scissors out the door. They sounded like the ring of a dinner bell when they bounced off the side of the steel cylinder and fell onto the white tile floor.

"Okay, man. It's okay," Harley said calmly, as he walked up to the brown helium cylinder and stared at the regulator.

Randall walked up to the doorway of the darkened room. "Is it okay if I do it first, Grandpa Willie?"

"I don't care who does it first, but the only one I want to talk to, after they've done it, is Harley." Willie sounded as if he had moved closer to the open door.

Randall opened the valve, turned on the flow meter and handed Harley the mask. "Here you are, Harley. Take in some nice deep breaths."

Harley put the mask up to his face, sucked in all the helium his lungs could hold and in a high-pitched voice, which caused all of us to explode with laughter, he said, "What am I supposed to do now fella's?"

That was all it took to satisfy Mad Bomber Willie, who ran out of the treatment room into the hallway waving what looked like a stick of dynamite. He was laughing so hard he could barely stand up. "Don't screw with me, boys," he giggled. "I'm armed to the teeth and I'll light the fuse on this TNT in a flat-runnin' second." He struck a kitchen match and held it above his head.

"That's nothing but a red candle," Randall said.

"What the hell are you talking about, Son?" Willie threw the match down and stared at it until the flame burned out.

"Randall's right, Willie. You don't have dynamite, you've just got a red candle." I felt sorry for the poor old guy standing there looking so sad and pathetic.

With that bit of unexpected information, Willie broke down and began to cry.

"Oh come on, Willie. Don't cry, damn it." Harley walked over and put his arm around his brother's shoulders and all of us headed back to the parking lot.

When we stepped outside, the crowd cheered and the captain and his officers hurried toward us. A TV cameraman was close behind.

"All right, old man, you're under arrest," the captain said, as one of the other officers read the Mad Bomber his rights.

I couldn't believe my ears when I heard Harley asked the captain if he thought Willie was in pretty bad trouble.

The captain got a little wild-eyed, turned to Harley and said, "What the hell do you think? You're damned right he's in bad trouble. I want you to come down to the station so we can talk and get this all sorted out."

"What happened in there, boys?" the TV man butted in and headed toward Harley with the camera rolling.

"Absolutely nothing happened," Harley said. "Come on, you guys. Let's get the hell out of here." We walked away from the TV man and jumped inside the big rig as fast as we could.

"What's wrong with that old guy? What's going on?" the TV man yelled. "All I wanted to do was interview him for a story."

I rolled the window down partially and said, "He's really shy and he's upset about his brother. You can understand that, can't you, Mister?"

Captain Lewis walked up behind the TV cameraman and said, "I'll see you boys at the station. Thanks for all your help, Harley." The captain waved, then turned around and walked back to the patrol car where one of the officers was putting Willie Goat into the backseat.

"Let's go, man. Let's get the hell out of this place," Harley said, as Randall started the engine.

I hung my head outside as we pulled away and Willie was frantically waving at me out the back window.

Randall looked back over his shoulder and grinned. "Are you going to the station to try to rescue your brother, Harley?"

Harley picked up Long Dog as we pulled out of the hospital parking lot, sat on the couch and said with grin, "Hell no."

We were on the road again, headed toward Albuquerque, New Mexico.

"Well, we lucked out once more," I said to Randall and rolled my eyes.

"I'd say so. I'd say we lucked out big time. Wouldn't you, Harley?" Harley did not answer.

"I heard the ER doc congratulate you, Randall, on your skill with a pocketknife and say that you saved Billy Boy's life," Moon said. "Did you see the way he looked at me when I told him I was a passenger on the back of Billy Boy's motorcycle and that my hand got hurt during the wreck?"

"I thought he was going to call you on it for a second," I said. "You tell a pretty convincing story."

Moon looked at Harley. "I told you I wouldn't cause you any trouble over the gunshot wound, Harley. I did good, don't you think?"

Harley gave Moon a grumpy-looking little smile, but he didn't have anything to say.

Randall looked back at Harley. "That was a brave thing you did, going into the hospital after that old man, Harley. What the hell were you thinking about? It couldn't have been for the glory. You ran from the TV cameraman like a scared rabbit."

Harley gave Randall a cold, hard look. "I didn't want anyone to recognize me, why the hell do you think? If you must know, I went inside the hospital because I thought it really might be my brother. Chicago's not that far away from here, you know what I mean?"

Randall looked at Harley in the rearview mirror. "Chicago is way the hell away from here, Harley. Do you know what I mean? Do you know what I mean? I'm so sick of hearing you say that all the time I can hardly stand it. Do you know what the hell I mean?"

"Well, I'm sick of a lot of the stuff you say too, Randall Rat Face."

"Really, Harley, think about it. If you've said that once, you've said it a hundred times. I guess when you've got a limited vocabulary you don't have a whole lot of choice in the words you can use. What you should do is try to improve yourself, Harley."

Woof! A ball of fire engulfed the back of Randall's head, setting his hair ablaze. He slammed on the brakes and pulled the big rig off the road using one hand, while beating the flames out with the other. Randall screamed as the fire grew hotter and Harley laughed. The flare-up only lasted about 20 seconds, but it was some show to see.

Harley had squirted lighter fluid in his mouth, struck a match and blew it out across the open flame. The fine spray of highly flammable fluid created a fireball that was more bark than bite, but it was hot enough to burn like hell. The smell of Randall's smoldering hair made me sick to my stomach and I gagged. I rolled down the window and the fresh air saved me from throwing up.

I looked at Harley. "That was not very nice, Harley. What kind of person would set another person on fire?"

Harley looked back at me with expressionless eyes. "That's a lesson to all of you boys. Never again push me over the line."

Moon put a damp cloth on the back of Randall's neck, then bowed his head as if he had lapsed into saying a long prayer. Randall pulled back onto the highway and stared straight down the road, living in his mind and plotting Harley's death once again, I was sure.

Harley sat on the couch, petted Long Dog and hummed "Amazing Grace". He hummed it over and over and over, while mile after mile clicked away.

Harley was the first to break the spell of silence. "I hope you've learned your lesson, Randall. I don't want to have to do anything like that again." There was a slight tinge of remorse in his voice, but with Harley, a person never really knew for sure.

I looked at Harley and said, "He's learned his lesson, Harley. We all have. Okay?"

There was another long period of silence, during which Moon studied a road map. "We are three hours from Albuquerque, another eleven to Oklahoma City, six more to Springfield, then only one more hour to Deer Run and I'll be home with my honey babe," he said. "That's if I can get a ride from Oklahoma City to Springfield after you guys cut off and head for Kansas City." Moon added up the total and began to sing. "Twenty-one hours. Only twenty-one hours away from home and no more will I roam, because I'm only twenty-one hours away from home."

"You won't have to worry about a ride to Deer Run, Moon," Harley said. "We'll take you, won't we, boys? Hell, man, I wouldn't miss out on a chance to check out your Dead Head girlfriend and your buddy, Wolff, and his cave."

"You would like them a lot, that's for sure," Moon said, being a lot friendlier to Harley than he deserved.

"Grandpa Wolfgang sounds like a real hoot too, doesn't he, Randall?" Randall didn't answer. Harley tapped me on the shoulder. "Doesn't Grandpa Wolfgang sound like a hoot to you, Mark?"

I nodded my head. "He really does, Harley. He sounds like a real big hoot to me."

Randall looked back at Harley and snarled, "I'm sure they'll really be glad to see you, man. Someone coming into their nice, peaceful place with a gun and dynamite. Instead of saying hello, maybe you can blow fire at them."

"I'll tell you what, Randall. I...."

Moon interrupted saying, "I'm sure they wouldn't mind you coming Harley, if you would get rid of the gun and the dynamite. When you want to, you can be a real likable guy."

A dumbstruck look covered Harley's face. "I'll make you a promise, Moon. I won't wave the gun around or drag out the dynamite unless I'm provoked. That's the best thing I can promise you right now. Okay, Moon Baby?"

Chapter Sixteen

As we passed a mileage sign, Harley said, "Albuquerque's only thirty more miles, boys. I've got big plans for us when we get to Albuquerque."

"What kind of plans, Harley?" I asked anxiously, knowing from past experience that any plans Harley came up with would most probably be detrimental to my health.

"Don't worry your pretty head about it none, Mark. You'll see soon enough, my friend." Harley winked at me and smiled.

Randall looked over his shoulder and frowned. "How do you know it's only thirty more miles? I thought you couldn't read."

"You just can't stop jackin' me, can you, Randall?" He picked up Long Dog and shoved the mutt's nose in Randall's ear. "Arf! Arf!" Harley barked and laughed ridiculously loud.

Randall wiped the residue from Long Dog's wet nose out of his ear, giving Harley a disgusted look. "You're real cute, Harley. Real, real cute. That's the kind of immature stuff that a thirteen-year-old kid would do."

Harley reached up and flipped Randall on the ear. "You think that was cute, do you, Randall? I know something that's going to be a lot cuter and a whole bunch more fun." Harley sat back with a crooked smile on his devious-looking face and slowly nodded his head up and down. I knew what he was up to; he had come up with something he thought was really cool, and he wanted someone to ask him about it.

"All right, Harley. What are you talking about that will be cute and a whole bunch more fun?" I finally broke down and asked.

"I want you to pull this big beast into the first place where we can buy a CB radio. We'll get ourselves set up to do some talkin' to the folks out there in mainstream America," Harley said with a big grin. "I'm starting to sound just like you college boys now, ain't I, Mark? Me talking about things like mainstream America?"

Randall glanced over his shoulder at Harley and frowned. Then with a tongue that was sharper than it needed to be, he said, "There won't be any place to buy a CB radio on Sunday, Harley. Everybody knows that."

Harley reached up and tapped Randall on the shoulder. When Randall didn't respond, Harley said, "Maybe you didn't hear what I said, Mr. Know-It-All. I said there will be a CB installed in this rig before we leave Albuquerque. Either that, or you will be dead from suffocation." Harley waited a good long while for one us to ask him what he was talking about again, but no one did. So he laid it on us, extra loud. "Having your head crammed up your ass is a piss-poor way to go, Randall my boy." Harley laughed at himself as usual.

Randall looked at Harley in the rearview mirror and calmly said, "We've only got a short time left on the road together, and a CB is a pretty expensive toy to be used only for a few hours. Besides, I hate everything about the screeching, squawking damned things, including the stupid conversations. You know what the hell I mean, Good Buddy? Breaker. Breaker. 10-4 and all that bull."

"That's just the point, man. Time's passing us by and I'm not going to miss out. Hell, we've only got a few more hours, and whether you like it or not, I'm going to talk to the truckers. I've got a bunch of important stuff to say. Stuff they need to hear. Do you hear me loud and clear, Good Buddy?" Then Harley stomped the floor and the loud noise scared Long Dog, causing him to bark. "Now look what you've gone and made me do, Randall. You've made me scare Long Dog. You can be such a bastard sometimes."

Harley and Randall pouted the rest of the way to Albuquerque. Neither of them said a word. When we entered the city limits, Randall was the first to speak. "How are you going to pay for a CB, Harley?"

Harley jumped on him quickly. "Where have you been, Randall? Living in your mind? Mark and me talked about who would pay for a CB earlier, and he said we could put it on your credit card. What the hell, man! This is your rig, why shouldn't you pay for the damned thing? Lordy Randall, you sound more like a banker than an engineer smart enough to design a steam engine."

"We'll pay for it, Harley. We'll pay for the damn thing," I shrieked. My nerves were so frayed from listening to them bitch at each other, I would have agreed to almost anything. "Pull in the next place you see that sells CBs. I'll put it on my Master Charge. I don't care what the hell it costs."

We passed a half dozen service stations, a couple of fast-food restaurants and a grocery store. Then I pointed up ahead at a Western Auto store. "There's a place we can buy a CB and get it installed too," I said, happy that the search was over.

"It looks closed to me," Randall grumbled.

"What the hell are you talking about? That big door on the end is open, so someone's in the damn place," Harley said.

Randall pulled the big rig up in front of the empty repair bay. A stocky, older man with bright red hair was sweeping the floor. He danced back and forth to the loud pounding beat of chichi music and didn't notice us until Harley reached over Randall's shoulder and laid on the horn. The man glanced up and smiled, then lowered his head and continued to shuffle around, performing his custodial chore.

"Oh no," I said when I thought about the janitor in the hospital cafeteria and what Harley might do.

"I think they're closed, Harley. This guy's just cleans up, man. You know what I mean?" Randall said.

Harley grabbed Randall's shoulder. "Hold it right there, Son. That store's full of CBs. All we have to do is get one and you boys can install the damn thing, isn't that right?"

"Sure we can, but we don't have a CB and the store's closed, so let's move on to the next place." Randall started to pull away again.

"Stop, damn it!" Harley yelled. Then he opened the door and shouted, "Everybody out, right now."

Long Dog was the first to hit the parking lot, and what did the mangy little dog do? He ran over and bit the janitor on the ankle!

The janitor whirled around with a powerful swing of his push broom. The heavy wooden end caught Long Dog square in the ear. Long Dog rolled over and over until he hit a red metal tool chest, which caused him to come to a sudden halt, and he didn't move.

Harley rushed over to Long Dog's side and screamed, "Randall, come here quick. I think my little dog's dead."

On his way to examine Long Dog, Randall walked up to the janitor and read his nametag. "Way to go, John," Randall said with a smile.

"What are you doing?" Harley yelled at Randall because he was just standing there patting the janitor on the shoulder.

Randall pulled back Long Dog's eyelid and the mutt whimpered and jerked his foot. "He was only knocked out, Harley." Then he looked back over his shoulder and yelled at Moon and me. "Lucky for us, boys, Long Dog was only knocked out."

"I sure thought he was bad hurt," Harley said. "Thanks for looking him over, Randall. I owe you one for that, man."

"Maybe this will teach him the lesson he needed and he'll quit biting people. I mean what the hell, man, can you imagine how scary it would be to see a nasty-looking little mole-faced bastard like that attacking you?" Randall asked, staring at Long Dog and shaking his head.

Harley gave Long Dog a pat on the head, then reached down and kissed him on the nose. "Poor baby. Poor little boy." Long Dog's quick little tongue lapped out and caught Harley on the lips. He smiled and patted him on the head again and Long Dog got in a couple more slurps.

With that disgusting display of affection, the janitor dropped his broom and hurried toward the back door.

"Where are you going?" Harley yelled. "You don't even care about my dog, do you, you crazy old man?"

"Sure I do. Is he okay? I didn't mean to hurt him, Mister. I wouldn't have hit him, but he looked like he may have rabies, and after he bit me I just...."

"You better shut the hell up, Mister, yourself," Harley screeched. "We'll just take a CB radio as payment for what you've done to my dog."

"A CB radio for what I've done to your dog? What are you talking about? I can't give you a CB radio. The store's locked up and I don't have a key."

Harley jumped up and rushed across the floor so fast the guy didn't even have time to blink before Harley shoved the revolver in his face and yelled, "Bang!" There was no doubt that the poor old guy messed his pants. To top that off, Long Dog dashed over and grabbed hold of his pant leg, growling and jerking on the cuff as if he were going to tear the man apart.

Harley got right up in John's face and bellowed, "I want a CB radio, Mister. We've got a credit card to pay for the damned thing, if that's what's bothering you."

Harley cocked the revolver.

"No need to trouble yourself with using the credit card, sir. I've got a CB in my car that you can have. It will only take a couple of minutes to rip it out."

Ten minutes later, we had John's portable CB radio installed in the big rig. When we started to crawl back inside the big rig, I handed John a $100 bill that I had stashed in my billfold for an emergency. It made me feel like an upstanding citizen and separated me from being the sidekick of a psychotic bully and a CB-stealing crook.

Screech. Screech. Squawk.

"Turn the damned squelch control down, Harley!" Randall yelled.

Harley turned it off completely, and then eased the volume back up to the critical point where he would be able to hold a conversation without the irritating noise.

"10-4, Good Buddy. I be sleepin' while you be creepin'."

The trucker lingo went right over Harley's head and with a start, he said, "What the hell did that mean?"

"A trucker told his buddy that he was going to crash in the sleeper cab while the other eighteen-wheeler rolled on down the road. Can you dig what the hell I mean, Harley?" Moon asked. Then he held out his hand and I gave him a big high-five.

"You must be a real CB freak, Moon," I said.

"I had a CB in the VW for a couple of years until somebody like Harley ripped it off. That was back when I was on the move a lot, following The Dead around the country. I listened to the truckers talk a lot, but I never talked back to them."

"Why not?" Randall asked.

"I don't talk to rednecks unless I have to, man. They're too prejudiced and caustic for a longhair like me. Listening to a bunch of them as a steady diet is like trying to stop a toothache by beating yourself in the head with a hammer. The real pain will take your mind off the toothache for a little while, but when that's gone, the throbbing will still be there, and it may even be worse."

"What should I say?" Harley asked. "I sure don't want these good old boys to think I'm stupid."

"You don't want the truckers to think you're stupid? Is that what you just said, Harley?" Randall looked over at me and rolled his eyes.

"You need a handle before you say anything, Harley. What do you want to call yourself?" Moon asked.

"How about Willie Goat, in remembrance of your mad bomber brother back at the hospital?" Randall asked.

Harley laid his head back and began to chant, "Willie Goat, Willie Goat, my brother and my friend. Willie Goat, Willie Goat when will I ever see you again?" He pushed down the button on the microphone and said, "Willie Goat right here. 10-4. Over."

I snickered and Moon laughed. Randall capitalized on the opportunity to verbally abuse Harley. "You just logged on and signed right back off. You know what that means, don't you, man?"

Harley glared at Randall and finally said, "No, what does it mean?"

"Now everyone listening to Channel 19 realizes that you don't know anything about talking on a CB radio. The truckers are all laughing their asses off at you right now, Harley. They probably think you've been locked up someplace for the last twenty years and you're out of touch," Randall said cruelly, pushing his luck.

"What the hell am I suppose to say then, Randall? You smart-aleck asshole jerk."

"Your finger's still on the button, Harley," Moon said. "Everyone heard you say asshole. You're in big trouble now for cussin' over the CB radio. The federal government has people monitoring CB radio channels, listening for people like you. Don't they, Randall?"

"Cussin' while using a citizens band radio is against federal regulations and is punishable by a fine and imprisonment," an anonymous caller advised.

"Do-gooder jack-off," Harley mumbled.

"Try again in a few minutes, Harley. The same people won't be listening in after we get a few miles down the road. You'll be okay now that you've got a better idea of what to do," I said, actually feeling sorry for the miserable-looking old bastard.

A female voice broke came on the air. "Willie Boy. Willie Boy. Where have you been? Your hot-blooded mama's waitin' for you right around the bend."

Harley's face froze. His eyes were as big as quarters. He giggled, slapped his hand over his mouth and sat back in the seat.

"You're hot, Harley. You're hot, man," Moon said. "Say something cool back to her. Go ahead. Say something that will let her know you've really got yourself together."

A pained expression covered Harley's face and he looked as if he were going to cry. "Like what, Moon? What am I supposed to say? I'm not really hot. Hell, I don't even know what that means. Tell me what to say."

"Here, give me that." Moon grabbed the microphone out of Harley's hand. "You've got the Willie Goat right here, girl. I've got ya' talkin' on my line and you're soundin' fine. What be your handle? Over."

"You got Little B commin' back at ya'. Over." The CB lady giggled loudly before she signed off.

"The woman's a prostitute, Harley. She makes a livin' off of truckers and horny bastard like you that drive up and down the highway," Randall said, shaking his head.

Harley grabbed Randall by the arm and yelled, "She's not either, damn you! I don't want you saying that about my new girl."

"Your girl?" I blurted out with a stinging laugh. "My God, Harley. How can you think that she's your girl? You just...."

"Just shut up, all of you!" Harley bellowed, as he grabbed the microphone out of Moon's hand and pushed down the talk button. "This is Willie Goat, Little B You sound like a really fine person to me, Mama. I sure would like to talk to you for a while, if you've got time. Can you just give me a couple of minutes? Over an out. 10-4."

Harley laid the microphone in his lap and waited for Little B to come back on the air, but she did not answer.

"The woman's a whore, man," Randall told Harley once again. "She's going to want money before you can spend any time doing anything. You know what the hell I mean?" After a long pause, Randall said, "Needless to say, you don't have any money."

Before Harley could say anything Little B's gravelly voice came back loud and clear. "Willie, Willie, where have you been? Your Mama's been waitin' for you since way back when."

"Oh Lord, she's a poet, too. There's nothing worse than a whore that's a friggin' poet," Randall said in disgust, as if he knew what he was talking about. "You'd better just zip up your mouth and keep your pecker in your pants, Harley."

"You'd better shut your trap up, Randall," Harley screamed and poked Randall in the ribs. He keyed the microphone up again and fired a message right back. "I've been waitin' for you since way back when, too, Little B When can we get together? Can it be real soon?"

When she did not answer right away, Moon said, "Ask Little B why her friends call her by that name. Go on, Harley. Ask her about that one."

With a voice that cracked as badly as the snap of a dead twig, Harley said, "This is Willie again, over. You don't have to tell me, but I was wondering why your friends call you Little B? It's a name I sure do like."

After a long period of silence, Harley's new girl came back on the air, and I could tell by the sound of her voice that she had been laughing. "It would be best if I tell you about it when we meet up. By the way, Willie, what do you look like?"

I figured that question would scare Harley half to death, but he responded quickly with a big lie. "I look older than I am because I've had a lot of experience. I used to be taller, until I had my knees operated on, which took away about one inch. One of the best things about me is that I've got a lot of money and...."

"That's enough. You sound perfectly lovely to me, Willie," she said cheerfully.

Harley looked at me and whispered, "I'm really going to like this woman a lot. I can just tell, man. You know what I mean, Mark?"

"Hell, boys, this could be a match made in heaven," Randall said. "I can just see Harley and Little B walking down the aisle together, the three of us standing up with Harley, acting as his Best Men. Crazier things have happened. There's someone for everyone, somewhere. That's what they say, don't they?"

"Where are you right now, Ms. B.?" Harley asked, politely with a long slow drawl that sounded as sweet as honey. The switch to Harley using the more formal name of Ms. B. caused Moon and me to raise our eyebrows and Randall groaned.

"I'm parked in the rest area at the eighty mile marker. You can't miss me, I'm the only one in the whole damned place painting a car."

"You're in the rest area at the eighty mile marker and you're painting your car. Hold on for a minute, Ms. B. 10-4. Over." Harley gave me a puzzled look and shook his head. "How far is it to the rest area from here?"

Harley was so anxious to make the contact that was squirming in his seat.

"We just passed the seventy mile marker, so it's about ten miles. In less than ten minutes, you'll be face to face with your new girl. If you play your cards right, you'll be able to find out why all her friends call her Little B." Randall laughed.

"I'm less than ten minutes away, Ms. B.," Harley said, wiping the spittle off the microphone onto the front of his shirt.

"10-4 Willie. You picked a perfect time. I'm almost finished painting my car. It's really pretty. I think you'll like it a bunch. By the way, I like it that you switched from calling me Little B to calling me Ms. B. That shows a lot of respect. I like that in a man."

"What's she doing painting a car in the rest area?" Randall asked curtly. "You'd think there would be some kind of law against painting a car in a rest area. What if the paint were to blow onto other people's cars. What if somebody was walking their dog and they...."

"Who the hell cares?" Harley shouted. "I'm so sick of your critical attitude I could just shove you out the door." Harley jumped up and hurried toward the bathroom. "I'm going to wash up and comb my hair—if that's okay with you, Randall. " Harley yelled back over his shoulder and mumbled something about Randall being a big fat phony as he hurried back to get himself all spiffed up to meet Ms. B.

"I really liked Harley's description of himself—especially where he used to be taller and that he's rich. I wonder what Harley would do when he has to borrow money from one of us to pay Ms. B. for her time.

"What about safe sex?" Moon asked. "Do you think we should say anything to Harley about using protection if he and Ms. B should get romantically involved?"

Randall thought about it for a second and smiled. "I figure about the only disease those two haven't had is leprosy." He winked at me and smiled. "I wouldn't be real sure they haven't had that either." He snickered and we all laughed.

Harley walked out of the bathroom wearing a smile that left no doubt he was excited about meeting Ms. B. At first glance, he did look a lot better with his hair pulled back in a ponytail. Then I noticed the bushy patches of gray stubble growing out of his ears that looked like silk on an ear of corn which detracted from his appearance considerably.

"What do you think Ms. B. will think about the way I look?" Harley asked anxiously.

I looked him up and down while I studied on the question and finally said, "I'd say that she will think you're a handsome, older gentleman. Now that you're cleaned up, you look a lot like Sean Connery."

Harley smiled and nodded his head, as if he knew who I was talking about. "She sounds pretty smart too, don't you think, Mark?"

I looked him straight in the eye. "Harley," I said. "It seems to me like she's got just about the right amount of smarts to be a perfect match for a down to earth guy like you."

Chapter Seventeen

Harley traded places with Moon and scooted the director's chair up between the front seats so he could get a better view. He fired up a Camel and the cigarette dangled from his lips. A trail of light gray smoke formed a heavy cloud that hugged the ceiling of the cab above our heads.

"Don't worry, Harley, you won't miss her," Randall said. "She wants to meet up with you as badly as you do with her. Trust me when I tell you it's from people like you that Ms. B makes her living." Randall looked at me and smiled. "Well, not quite like you, Harley. You are special."

"I know I'm not going to miss her," Harley snapped. "I just want to get the first look at her, that's all—if that's okay with you, Mr. Know-It-All." Harley glared at Randall apprehensively, took a deep drag off the cigarette and slowly exhaled through his nose. "It's been a long time since I've touched a woman, and I'm a little uptight about the meeting, that's all."

"I don't blame you, man. I would be too," Randall said tonelessly.

Harley leaned forward, jammed the cigarette down into the ashtray and recklessly tamped it up and down a half dozen more times than were necessary to put out the fire. Then he slapped his pant leg back and forth to beat out the stray sparks. He looked over at me with basset-hound eyes and humbly said, "I'd sure be beholden to you, Mark, if you could tell me something that would help me to settle down. I'm as nervous as a whore in church."

Randall looked at Harley and laughed. "Hell, man, after twenty years, I doubt if you'll even remember where to poke your thing."

"Oh, I remember all right." Harley grinned sheepishly. "I just don't know how to make my first move. I sure as hell don't want to say something stupid that might scare her away."

"You might not have to worry about that, Harley. You probably won't be able to get it up anyway. That happens to guys like you after they've been locked up in prison, messing around with a bunch of other hairy-legged criminal types. You know what I mean, man?" Randall said cruelly with a big smile.

Harley clenched his fist and squinted his eyes. I thought for sure that he would smack Randall upside the head. Then he scooted the chair back a couple of inches and stared down the road without saying another word.

As we started down a long incline to the rest stop, Harley looked over at me. "The rest area's only a little way up ahead." He pointed out the window at a big, green road sign with an arrow directing us to stay in the right lane.

Moon tapped Harley on the shoulder. "How did you know it's only one mile? I thought you couldn't read." When Harley didn't say anything, Moon pressed him on another issue. "You haven't mentioned anything about going to Chicago to kill your brother for a long time either. What have you been doing, Harley—playing a trick on us all along?"

Harley looked over his shoulder and winked at Moon. Then he turned around and stared down the road again with a distant smile.

And then it hit me! Maybe Harley really was putting us on for some reason. Why shouldn't he? He's psychotic, and that's the kind of stuff psychotics do—that, and things like get upset enough to kill people. I turned my head to one side as if I was looking out the window, but I could still see Harley out of the corner of my eye. I hoped to get a clue as to whether he could read or not when we passed the next road sign I figured he would move his lips or blink when he saw the sign. Sure enough, he followed the sign with his eyes as if he were reading it when we passed by. I turned quickly like a cat about to spring on a mouse and asked, "What did that sign say, Harley?"

He raised his eyebrows and gave me a blank look. "It was a deer crossing sign. Why are you asking me about the sign?"

"How did you know it was a deer crossing?" I asked, smiling smugly.

He looked at me shrewdly. "Because it had a picture of a deer on it."

"There she blows, Harley," Randall yelled extra loud, mocking a sea captain spotting a whale.

"Where?" Harley asked, straightening up in his chair and craning his neck. "What the hell are you talking about, Randall? I don't see anything."

"Sorry Harley, I made a mistake. What I thought was the rest area is only a truck parked alongside the road." Randall pointed up ahead at the broken-down vehicle. "Aww... shucks."

Harley glared at Randall and through gritted teeth said, "For someone who started out to be a decent guy, you've turned into the biggest prick I've ever met, Randall." Harley banged his fist down on the dash so hard that it cracked the vinyl covering.

"I'll be a nice guy again, Harley, when you're out of my life," Randall smarted off and chuckled.

"There she is for real, Harley," I said when I caught a glimpse of a big, tall woman with bright red hair and shoulders that looked as if they belonged on a football player. She was standing beside a rusted-out, green and yellow Edsel parked at the far end of the rest area.

Harley looked in the rearview mirror, licked his finger a couple of times and tried to plaster down an unruly lock of hair, but it popped back up.

"She looks a little bit big, but she's still beautiful. Don't you think, Mark?" Harley purred.

"Big, you say? Are you talking about Little B or the car?" Randall asked. "I will admit that she looks a lot better than I figured she would, Harley. Of course, my biggest question about someone who's built like that would be, is it really a woman, or is it a man that's dressed up like a woman, or is it actually a full-blown transvestite?"

Harley jerked his head around and met Randall with an eye-to-eye glare. "What the hell are you talking about, man? Are you saying that my girl is some kind of sideshow freak? I've about had all the crap I'm going to take from you."

"I'm serious, Harley. There are lots of people running around these days who have had sex change operations. You can't be too careful about who you get hooked up with. Mark and I know a guy who went so far as to get married before he found out that his girl was actually an 'it'. I've just got your best interests at heart. That's all, man."

"The hell you do. You're an ass, Randall. You're a smart-mouthed pig." Harley gave Randall a stiff jab in the ribs with his elbow and slapped him upside the head with the flat of his hand.

The blow to Randall's ear had to hurt like hell, but he didn't even flinch. Red ear and all, he just went right on with the sarcasm. "I'm serious, Harley. All you've got to do is take a good look and you can see that something could be wrong with Ms. B Lordy; she's built like a professional wrestler. I'm not trying to be a smart-ass. I'm just telling you to be careful. That's all I've got to say about it."

"Be careful about what?" Harley barked. He looked in the rearview mirror again and rubbed another wad of spit on his patch of unruly hair.

I looked at Randall and frowned. I could tell by the tone of Harley's voice that he had been pushed to the limit. I could not believe Randall was being so stupid. It was as if he had a death wish.

So what does Randall do, he comes right back with more of his Harley-bashing rhetoric. "Now Harley, let's just say I'm right. Let's just say that what we're dealing with here is a full-blown, hard-core transvestite, someone who is really special. Someone...."

"What do you mean 'someone who's special'?" Harley interrupted.

"By 'special', I mean someone who has pumped iron and gobbled steroids steadily for the past five years. Well, by now, that would make your precious Little B strong enough to squeeze your skinny ass to death with her powerful legs. I can just see you laying out in the parking lot, limp as a wet rag. Do you know what I mean? Harley?" Randall smiled grimly. "Another scenario would be that Little B marries you and takes out a big life insurance policy on you and...."

Harley slammed his fist down on the dash and yelled, "Just shut the hell up, man!" Then he backhanded Randall across the face and blood gushed from Randall's nose. "Ms. B's not any of those things, and you know damned well she's not."

Harley paused for a second and looked at himself in the mirror again. "But if it turns out that I'm wrong, guess who'll be keeping her company when the rest of us pull out of the parking lot and head for Springfield?" Harley twisted his face when he pulled a long gray hair out of his nose and his eyes teared. He looked at Randall. "Think about that for awhile, Mr. Smart-Mouth and see what else you've got to add."

"Are you okay?" Moon asked Randall as he handed him a wet washcloth. "Do you want me to get you an aspirin or anything?"

Randall nodded and wiped the blood off his mouth. He held the cloth up under his nose to stop the flow.

"Did you have to do that, Harley?" I asked. "What's Little B going to think about you hitting people?"

"I had to do it, Mark. Randall's just lucky I haven't blown his ass away before now, the way he's talked back to me. I don't have to take that from a prick like him. I'm the bad guy. I've got the gun and the TNT. Remember?"

I glanced over at Randall and he was wild-eyed. His face was red and he looked as if he were about ready to explode. I smiled and tried to lighten up the situation by saying,

"Being left in the parking lot with a big transvestite could turn out to be one of the most interesting experiences of your life, Randall." I smiled again and winked at him, but he was not in the mood to smile back.

Little B set her can of spray paint down on the pavement and walked toward us when Randall pulled the big rig into a parking spot a couple of spaces away from her car. Harley reached over and pulled the key out of the ignition. "I'll just keep an eye on this for you, Mister Randall," Harley said in a rough voice. Then he issued a stern warning. "I suggest that when you get out of the big rig, you act right in front of Ms. B. Because the next time I draw blood, it will be a large amount."

We hopped out of the big rig and stared at Little B like four monkeys watching a visitor walk up to our cage. Long Dog contributed to the idiocy of our act by circling her and barking at the top of his yapper while Harley screamed at the top of his voice at Long Dog to shut up until it became embarrassing. The stupid mutt finally calmed down after he ran into the back tire of Little B's car and knocked himself even sillier than he already was, but at least he broke the tension and everyone laughed.

Loaded down with gaudy dime-store jewelry and painted with heavy cosmetics, there was a certain vulgarity about Little B that spelled out what she did best.

I stared at the shiny gold snaps that lined the front of Little B's black vinyl jumpsuit and expected them to pop open at any second. It fit like a second skin. "I sure like that outfit," I mumbled under my breath.

Randall shook his head and turned the bloody washrag inside out as we continued to stare.

Harley looked at me and grinned like a kid about to walk into a candy store. Then he hurried toward Ms. B. with his arm straight out as if he were about to greet the President.

"Are you going to be okay, man?" I asked Randall. "It looks like your nose has stopped bleeding."

Randall looked down and tried to wipe a spot of blood off the front of his T-shirt with the wet washcloth. He frowned when it left a big red smear.

"I'm okay now. If I had it to do over, though, I would have used the bone saw on Harley myself back in the morgue."

"I'm Willie Goat, Ms. B. It's very, very nice to meet you, ma'am." Harley's face beamed. They locked smiles. She cradled his hand in hers and held on as if she had captured a wild bird. Chained together, without moving, they stared into one another's eyes. They were truly spellbound. We stared at them as if we had discovered a new spectator sport.

"What's going on?" Randall whispered.

I grinned and shook my head. "It looks to me like love is in the air. Can you smell something sweet? Something with an aroma like honey?"

Harley was the first to break the spell. "My real name's Harley Jackson. Willie Goat is just my CB handle. I didn't want you to think it was my real name. I'm a lot smarter than to have a name like that, you know."

"Nice to meet you, Harley," Little B said with a booming voice that caused Randall and me to look at one another and raise our eyebrows suspiciously. "Who are those fella's—your employees?" she asked with a friendly smile directed toward us.

Harley looked over his shoulder at us. "Why would you think they're my employees?"

"Well, you said you were rich when we talked on the CB. I thought maybe they traveled with you to take care of your things."

"Oh, I'm rich all right, my dear. But all my employees are back at the factory working, making things for me to sell. Then I go out on the road and sell the things that my people make back at the factory. I've got hundreds of people making things for me every day. These boys here, they're just some friends of mine."

"And what about this cute little dog, Harley? Does he belong to you?" she asked, looking down at Long Dog as his busy little tongue licked her painted red toenails, which were sticking out of bright green sandals.

"Yes ma'am, that's my dog all right. I named him Long Dog because he's so long and skinny. I picked him up beside the road. He was starving and about half-dead when I found him, but I'm doctoring him back to health. As you can see, he acts up sometimes, but for the most part, he's a pretty doggone good dog. As you can also see, he's got some skin trouble, but as soon as I get some medicine, I'm going to cure that. I think once he's treated, he'll heal up okay, don't you, ma'am?" Harley asked Ms. B. with a seemingly endless explanation to her simple question.

I wanted to walk up behind Harley and shout in his ear, "How in the hell would she know anything about treating a dog with skin trouble, you rambling-mouthed old fool?" But as usual, I chickened out.

"He's got the mange, Harley. But as luck would have it, I've got some mange medicine in the trunk of my car," Little B said. When we looked at her as if she must be making a joke, she threw her hands in the air. "I know it sounds crazy, but I really do."

Harley leaned down close to Long Dog's ear and in a joyful voice, he said, "You're in luck, baby boy. The nice lady has some treatment medicine that will make your skin better."

Long Dog jerked his head around and licked Harley a half dozen times in the face before he could get out of the way. We laughed when Harley jumped up, spitting out dog saliva and wiping his mouth on the sleeve of his shirt.

I started to ask Little B what she was doing with mange medicine in her car, but decided to let sleeping dogs lie.

Little B batted her pale blue eyes at Harley and smiled. "Are you going to introduce me to your friends?"

"Sure I am, Ms. B. Sure I am." There was a long pause, as if he either couldn't think of our names, or he had lapsed into another trance. Finally, he pointed at me and said,

"That tall, nice-looking guy is my friend Mark." He pointed at Randall and said, "The heavyset fella with the puffy red cheeks is Randall. They're both engineers and really smart guys."

I nodded at Ms. B. and smiled. Randall unconsciously waved the bloody washcloth. "Howdy, ma'am."

"What's the matter with Randall?" Little B asked Harley. "Why has he got blood all over the front of his shirt?"

Harley and Randall's eyes met with a glare that lasted for all of a minute. Finally, Randall looked at Little B and said, "I stopped quickly to avoid hitting a deer and banged my nose into the steering wheel. Thank you for your concern."

Harley took a deep breath and looked at me with a distant smile. "Yeah, that's what he did all right. He almost hit a deer back there close to that deer crossing sign. If I hadn't seen it in time and yelled, he would have hit it for sure. Isn't that right, Mark?"

I nodded soberly and gave Harley a half-assed smile. "Yeah, that's right, Harley. You saved us again."

"My goodness. Are you going to be okay, Randall?" Little B asked.

"I think so. I didn't really...."

"Hell yes, he's going to be okay," Harley hissed, taking a couple of steps forward to reinforce that everything was under control. "Randall is one of the toughest guys you've ever seen. Isn't he, Mark?"

I looked at Randall, then back at Harley and moaned. "Anybody that hangs around with you, Harley, has got to be tough."

Moving along, Harley introduced Moon. "And the other guy calls himself Moon Love, if you can believe that for a name. It's pretty strange, I know, but he's a hippie. He's not really a friend. He's just a guy we picked up alongside the road after his VW bus broke down. He and his friends are called Dead Heads, because they follow a rock-n-roll band around the country. He's a groupie. You know what I mean, Ms. B.?"

"Sure I know what a Dead Head is, Harley. I spent the better part of...."

As if Harley wasn't even aware that Little B was talking, he began to ramble again. "Moon's going to meet up with his girl and a friend named Wolff. They live in a cave on his grandpa's farm near Deer Run, a little town located south of Springfield, Missouri. There are lots of caves down in the Ozarks. Have you ever been to the Ozarks, Ms. B.?" By the time Harley finished his long-winded, exhausting tirade, he had nervously rolled a cigarette back and forth between his forefinger and his thumb until half the tobacco had spilled out the end and onto the pavement.

Ms. B. smiled at Moon and he smiled back. "Moon Love, what a really cool name. Some of my favorite people in the whole world are Dead Heads, and my most favorite group ever is the Grateful Dead. I was a Dead Head myself for a while after Woodstock. My boyfriend and I were caught up in the peace movement big-time back in the sixties. We followed the Dead around the country for almost two years. That was the most laid-back time of my life."

Harley did an about-face so quickly I could hardly believe it was the same person talking. "Well, you're sure going to like Moon Love a lot, Ms. B. He's such an easy guy to get along with and has so many good qualities." Harley sounded fatherly and proud all of a sudden. It was as if Moon was a favorite son.

"You're probably right about that, Harley. I'm sure I'll like him a lot. My boyfriend Billy and I lived out of a VW bus too, Moon." Little B said with a smile that never reached her eyes. Then she looked down and shook her head. "But when it ended, it came down like Humpty-Dumpty falling off the wall."

Harley tilted his head to one side and gave Little B a disconcerting look. "What happened? Why did it end?"

Little B nervously twirled a lock of red hair around her finger, then she set the curl free and it sprang back tight against her head. She coughed and cleared her throat. She stammered, trying to get out the first words. "We were... We were in Boulder, Colorado, at a Dead concert. Dylan was there and so was Pete Seeger. It was a benefit to raise money to support a major protest against the Vietnam War. The idea was to hire hundreds and hundreds of buses to haul thousands of people to Washington, D.C. to stage a protest so massive that even pitiful old Richard Nixon would get wind of our message—for what little that was worth."

"What's the matter, ma'am?" Moon asked after Little B stopped talking and lowered her head. She shook her head and continued. "When the Dead, Dylan and Pete walked out on the stage to do a warm-up number, my boyfriend Billy and a guy who was running with us at the time that we called Whippoorwill Joe dropped a couple of blotters of LSD. As it turned out, the coroner said that what they thought were tabs of acid were actually poison." Little B's eyes filled with tears and she looked away.

"Sorry to hear about that, ma'am," Moon said, grim-faced.

After a moment of silence, Little B said, "But I'll tell you what, Moon. All I have to do is close my eyes and the sweet sound of that band and the good times we had during those days drifts through my head like it was only yesterday."

"I'm really sorry to hear about what happened to your friends, ma'am," Moon said again, and we nodded our heads in agreement.

Harley gave me a sheepish grin, turned to Ms. B. and said, "You and I have really got a lot in common, too, my dear. I was at Woodstock myself. I'm surprised I didn't see you there."

Randall and I looked at Moon and the three of us smiled. I pressed my hand against my mouth to keep from laughing.

Little B threw her arms around Harley and gave him a hug. "We really do have a lot in common, Harley. We really, really do."

As Harley and Ms. B. stared into each other's eyes, the sweetness of love filled the air. It was like sugar candy cooking on a kitchen stove.

I turned my back to them and whispered, "I thought she'd take one look at Harley and run like a rabbit. I guess I was wrong."

"I've read about it in magazines and watched it happen on TV and in movies. I even had a touch of it myself once, but I've never seen it this strong before, and it happened so quickly," Moon said.

"What in the world are you talking about, Moon?" I asked.

"Infatuation, man. What we're witnesses to right here before God and everybody is a hard-core case of infatuation. It's a genuine textbook example. Look at them, they're cooing at one another like a couple of doves during mating season." When we didn't say anything, Moon turned to Randall and softly said, "Doves mate for life, you know."

We walked right past the lovers on our way to inspect the newly painted car and their sparkling eyes remained locked on each other. It was as if they didn't even realize we were passing by.

"Why would anyone in their right mind want to paint a car like this?" I asked, as I stared at the bumper sticker on the rusty, beat-up old 1958 Edsel that read, "If You Don't Like Hank Williams Jr. You Can Kiss My Ass".

Moon pointed at a rainbow that Little B had painted over the wheel weld on the front fender and said, "I sure like the way this part of the car looks, though. I like rainbows about as much as anything."

I nudged Randall when I walked around to the front of the car and saw the outdated license plate. It hung precariously from the bumper, flapping in the breeze, and was secured only by a frayed, brown shoestring.

"Ms. B's from Springfield, Missouri," I said, pointing at the city sticker in the right-hand corner of the windshield.

"She may be a blessing in disguise. Who knows—Harley might decide to stay here with her."

"I bet this thing's got one hog of an engine. Most of these old cruisers had at least four-hundred-horsepower engines, four-barrel carbs, and would run like crazy," Moon said.

Moon stuck his head through the open window and checked out the dash. "I bet it doesn't get ten miles to the gallon." He looked over the top of the car. "Do you mind if I look under the hood, Little B?" She was too wrapped up in one of Harley's stories to hear what Moon said. He looked at me and winked. "I assume her silence means it's okay." He walked around to the front of the car and raised the hood.

"Holly moley! There's no motor," Randall said. "This is going to be nothing but trouble. You just wait and see if I'm not right."

"What kind of trouble?" I asked, as I looked into the open hole at the only thing left under the hood—a grease-covered battery.

Randall pointed at the lovebirds as they walked toward a bench beside the drinking fountain. We stared after them as they sat down and scooted up close to one another. Randall looked down into the greasy hole again and shook his head. "I'll bet you anything Ms. B. will be in the big rig when we leave the parking lot."

"No way, man!" I said.

Randall looked at me and frowned. "What else is she going to do? She's sure as hell not going anywhere in this rig."

Randall hit the nail right on the head when he said that Harley's dick would end up doing the thinking for all of us. I was cursing myself for not having the guts to pick up the bone saw and use it when I had the chance.

Harley stood up and walked toward us when Moon slammed the hood shut. I could tell from the big, rotten-toothed grin that he was about to explode with delight.

"Ms. Canada and me have made some exciting plans that involves all of us, and I want to make the announcement right now." There was a twinkle in Harley' in eye as he paused to wait for our reaction.

"What do you mean 'Ms. Canada?" Randall said with a clenched jaw.

"I want you fella's to listen closely. I need to make sure you understand what I'm about to say because it's very important and I know sometimes you all are preoccupied and miss some stuff."

"What now, Harley?" Randall said. "Is this where you reveal that you're from another planet?"

Harley looked disgusted and shook his head at Randall. "Little B's real name is Alberta Canada. So from now on, out of respect for the woman she really is, we'll all be calling her Ms. Canada. You know what I mean, Randall?"

"Why in the hell wouldn't I know what you mean, Harley?" Randall smarted off and kicked an empty beer can into the gutter.

Harley ignored him and went on with his happy announcement. "It wasn't easy, but I've talked Ms. Canada into going along with us in the big rig."

Randall looked at me and we rolled our eyes. "What did I tell you?" he said. "Didn't I say she would pull it off?"

"She's from Springfield! Isn't that something, boys? This could be the luckiest damn day ever in my whole screwed up, miserable life—me finding Ms. Canada like this and her being on the road to the same place I'm going to. It's fate, fella's. It's fate, that's what it is." Harley's face was lit up like a light bulb.

"I bet it was really hard talking her into going with us wasn't it, Harley?" Randall said sarcastically. "You're some talker all right."

Harley gave the three of us a solemn look to set the stage for what Ms. Canada had said to him during their kissy-faced conversation on the bench. I knew from the way they were giggling that she had told him something real cute. I could also tell by how nervous he acted that he felt like a big pussy with what he was about to say. But Harley was in love and love is blind, so sounding stupid or not making sense did not matter.

"As crazy at it sounds, Ms. Canada said I'm her Honey Bee and she's my Momma Bear." Harley grinned and waited for one of us to comment on his profound statement, but none of us said a word. "You've heard of love at first sight? Well, you're seeing it in action today, Randall, my boy and Mark, my boy and Moon, my boy." Harley was so excited he was squirming around and hopping from one foot to the other as if he were about to wet his pants.

"I'm happy for both of you," I said.

"You know what else she said that's excited me more than just a little? She's been waiting for Mr. Right to come along ever since the untimely death of her last boyfriend, and I've got no reason to believe she's not telling me the truth either, Randall. So that proves she's not some misguided woman like you said and I want a damned apology."

Randall looked up at the sky and yawned. "No problem there, Harley. I apologize for saying anything that may have been offensive in any way. This much I do know though, she thinks you're rich. I doubt that she gives a tinker's damn about you personally. All she wants is your money."

Harley's face turned red, he squinted his eyes and he said, "You just wait and see, Randall, you smart-mouthed little bastard."

"I believe you, Harley," I said, hoping to calm him down. "I think it's you she wants, not just your money."

"Is everything all right, hon'?" Ms. Canada called to Harley as she stood up and hurried toward us when he did not answer right away.

"I'm fine, sugar. I told the boys the good news about you going with us to Springfield. They're excited as all get out." Harley squinted his eyes and glared at Randall. "Isn't that right, my friend?"

Randall glared back at him without saying a word. Moon finally cleared the air. "We sure are, Ms. Canada. We're as excited as can be. I want to talk to you some more about Woodstock. I wish I could have been around in the sixties, following the Grateful Dead." Moon looked back over his shoulder. "What happened to the motor in your Edsel?"

Ms. Canada frowned and shook her head. "It was stolen by a man driving a tow truck. He backed right up to the car, cut a few things loose, then wrapped a chain around the motor and jerked it out from under the hood. The crazy thing is, I was asleep in the backseat at the time and it scared me half to death. I thought it was an earthquake, me having just come from California. I was in San Francisco when that last big one hit and...."

"Didn't anyone try to stop him?" Randall cut in before Ms. Canada could finish the whole story.

"He was too mean for me to mess with, and there was no one else around to stop him." When she stretched her arms to measure the width of the big man's shoulders, three gold snaps popped open on her black vinyl jumpsuit and exposed her braless flesh. Harley's face turned red instantly. He gasped for breath, fumbled with the lighter and lit up a Camel as Ms. Canada closed up the front of her jumpsuit.

Like they say, a picture is worth a thousand words. It only took a few seconds of close observation to decide that Ms. Canada was for sure a full-blown woman and nothing in between. I discounted the statuesque frame and wide shoulders to her just being a big girl. The rugged looks I chalked up to a hard life on the road.

I wished I had a video camera to film our little group of social rejects. I thought Randall and I had reached the pinnacle of weirdness in traveling companions with the trio of Harley, Moon Love and Long Dog. But I was wrong. Anyone who looked like Ms. Canada, lived out of a 1958 Edsel parked in a rest area, fell in love at first sight with a snaggle-toothed, scraggly-looking escaped convict and agreed to climb onboard a big rig with a bunch of strangers and a disease-ridden dog definitely won the contest.

I could only come to one conclusion about Ms. Canada. Like Harley, she was a textbook example of an exotic personality and they could be perfect soul mates. If I were right, they would probably want to go off and do their own thing as soon as possible. This meant that we would drop them off somewhere along the way where they could spend the rest of their lives searching for missing pieces to their fractured minds.

"So you talked her into going with us, did you, Harley?" Randall's laugh held a bitter edge. "You're a really persuasive guy."

"You certainly are, Harley," I agreed quickly, sounding as sincere as I possibly could.

"Like I said, Ms. Canada's from Springfield and since someone stole her engine and she can't get back there on her own, she's agreed to go with us." Harley had a hysterical screech to his laugh; he was obviously so proud of himself that he could barely keep his feet on the ground.

Ms. Canada looked at Moon and smiled. "I think we'll all get along just swell. Like I told Harley, with Woodstock and the Grateful Dead, you and he have a lot in common."

Moon's face lit up and he grinned. "That really must have been something, being at Woodstock. I'm really glad you're here, ma'am."

"Me too, Moon. Harley told me about your bus breaking down and how you're headed to meet up with a buddy and your girlfriend in Deer Run." Ms. Canada sounded enthusiastic about making the trip with Moon.

"This is really something, isn't it, boys?" Harley said with a big smile. "This is going to be a great trip."

Randall shook his head scornfully. "It's really something all right, Harley. Not counting the diseased dog, now it's you three social rejects against the two of us." With that observation, Randall turned around quickly and walked briskly toward the big rig.

"What did he mean by that, I wonder?" Harley said, scratching his head.

Moon looked at me and winked. "Some of us will probably never know." Moon turned to Ms. Canada and said, "Do you have some things you need to get out of the car? I'll help carry your stuff to the big rig, if you do."

"I'll help you too, hon'." Harley rushed to Ms. Canada's side and nudged up against her like a jealous teenager.

"This is really great, Mark. Now both Harley and Moon are sniffing after Ms. Canada like a couple of horny dogs," Randall said. He opened the door of the big rig and settled in behind the steering wheel. I climbed in on the passenger side. "You probably think I'm saying this because I'm jealous, don't you?" He looked at me and smiled. Then he chuckled and we burst out laughing.

We watched as Harley pulled a ragged blanket and a big plastic bag filled with something from the backseat of the multicolored car. Moon jerked a beat-up, black suitcase from the trunk and that made up the sum total of Ms. Canada's worldly possessions.

Ms. Canada put her arms around Harley and Moon's waists and they walked toward the big rig, with Long Dog barking and jumping up in the air in front of them.

Everyone settled down in the big rig, with Harley and Ms. Canada huddled up on the couch behind the passenger seat and Moon sitting in the director's chair. Randall fired up the engine, pulled the big beast out onto the interstate and we headed for Tucumcari, New Mexico.

Much to Harley's dismay, the conversation for the next couple of hours hung mainly between Ms. Canada and Moon Love and centered on Woodstock and the hippie movement of the sixties, the Grateful Dead and the miracle of good old rock-n-roll. Occasionally, Harley would inject a questionable story about something that happened to him at Woodstock or a concert he had gone to with a hippie friend, trying to make himself seem in vogue, after which Randall and I would glance at one another and roll our eyes—a silent form of communication we had used about a hundred times since Harley came onboard.

Harley nodded when I asked permission to use the bathroom and I headed toward the back with a quick step.

I stopped at the doorway when I heard Ms. Canada ask Harley why I needed his approval to take a leak. "There are some things I don't quite understand around here that concern me, Harley," she hissed.

Harley glared at me and stammered. I glared back and smiled, barely able to keep from laughing.

"Mark," he said sternly, after he regained his composure.

"Yes, Harley?" I said, as I took a couple of steps forward and cocked my head to one side so as to offer him my best ear.

"You were only kidding, weren't you, Mark? You don't need my permission to go to the bathroom, do you, Son?" When I didn't answer, he eased up off of the couch and said, "Tell her you were only kidding, Mark. Do it right now. I'm tired of you fooling around."

I winked at him. "Harley's right. I was only kidding, ma'am. Harley and I kid around a lot, don't we, Harley?" I walked into the bathroom and closed the door. I did my business and zipped up my pants. When I stepped through the doorway, I heard the distant wail of a siren behind us and I froze.

"What the hell's going on?" Harley yelled, as he ran toward the back of the big rig, knocking me against the wall.

"What's the matter, Harley?" Ms. Canada asked, making an effort to mask her concern as she hurried to the back and knelt on the bed beside Harley. "Why are you getting so excited?" she asked with a panic-stricken look. "Is there something wrong you haven't told me about, hon'?"

Harley shot her a wilted grin. "Don't worry about it, hon'. Everything will be all right." He turned to me and said, "It will be, won't it, Mark?"

"It sure will," I blurted out.

Harley grabbed me by the arm. "I'll tell you one thing for damned sure, Mark. They'll never take me alive." Much to Ms. Canada's amazement, I'm sure; Harley abandoned his mindless chatter in midstream and pulled out the Colt 45.

So much for keeping Ms. Canada in the dark about the kind of guy you really are, Harley, I thought to myself, as I watched the patrol car bearing down on us at a high rate of speed.

Chapter Eighteen

Harley wiped the sheen of sweat from his forehead and rubbed the back of his hand on the front of his shirt. The nervous tick was back, causing his right eye to twitch. His face was cranberry-red.

"Are you okay, hon'?" Ms. Canada asked, as she pulled a bandanna from around her neck and dabbed a pool of sweat from Harley's chin.

Harley gave her a halfhearted pat on the arm and growled, "Trust me, hon', I'll explain everything later. You've just got to trust me for now, okay?" Harley looked over his shoulder at me and mumbled out the corner of his mouth. "I wonder who tipped those crazy bastards off, huh Mark?"

"Turn on the CB," I yelled at Randall. "See if you can get some news." I looked at Harley. "There's probably something going on down in front of us, maybe a car wreck. I'm sure these guys aren't coming after you."

"What's he talking about, hon'? Why would the police be chasing you?" Ms. Canada asked, as she stared down at the revolver with a wide-eyed, worried look.

Harley forced a smile, then pressed his nose against the back window and watched the patrol car as it moved up quickly. It was close enough that I could see two officers in the front seat and what looked like a German Shepherd in the back.

When Ms. Canada got no satisfaction from Harley, she turned to me for the answer. "Why would the law come after my Harley, Mark? I can't imagine anyone as nice as him being some kind of fugitive."

After an infinitesimal pause, at which point I shouted inside my head, *My God, love is blind*, I calmly said, "I agree with you, ma'am. I can't imagine anything like that myself. Even if they were after Harley, it would probably be a case of mistaken identity." I smiled really big, figuring Harley would be doubly proud of me for defending him so boldly to Ms. Canada, but I was wrong.

He jerked his head around and glared at me as if I had committed a crime. With his right eye fluttering like a wounded butterfly, he said, "What do you mean using that tone of voice with Ms. Canada, Mark? You'll have her believing no telling what about me, you little fart. Friends don't do stuff like that to one another and you know it."

"What an inconsiderate bastard," I said to myself, as I bit my lip to keep from barking back at him. I shook my head and thought that I've got to stop letting him get to me so badly. I glared at Harley and tried to imagine how much fun it would be to stick a hotdog fork into his twitching eye.

"I was just trying to help, Harley. That's all I was doing." I pointed my thumb at the patrol car and said, "I'm a lot closer friend to you than those guys right there, man. I'll tell you that much for sure."

Harley whirled around and glued his face to the back window, which really didn't seem like a very smart thing to do, but I knew better than to try to tell him how to act.

Randall picked up the microphone and tried to find someone to talk to. "Break for a west bounder. Over."

He turned down the squelch control and waited. "You got a west bounder, Good Buddy. Over." The raspy voice of a CB'er came over the airwaves loud and clear.

"A highway patrol car's screamin' up behind us. Is there trouble back behind you? Over."

"Go lick yourself somewhere else. Get away from me, damn it!" Harley yelled, as he shoved Long Dog off the bed with the flat of his foot. Within seconds after the mangy creature hit the floor, he was back whimpering and licking himself again.

"Are you okay, baby?" Ms. Canada asked, as she reached down and picked him up. Before she could pull away, Long Dog licked her under the chin, worked his way around her jaw and reamed out her ear—all in less than ten seconds. Then he wiggled free and the fastest tongue in the west went back to work on himself again, licking loud.

When the highway patrol was within a hundred yards of the big rig, Harley flipped the cylinder open and checked to make sure the revolver was loaded. He wrapped his finger around the trigger, backed away from the window and sat on the edge of the bed with the Colt 45 lying in his lap.

Randall looked around and yelled, "I better pull over, Harley. I better pull to the side of the road right now, okay? It's the law, man. You have to pull over for emergency vehicles. If I don't pull over, they'll stop us for sure." Randall was frantic. His face was bloodless and his eyes were wild looking, as if he had overdosed on fright.

Harley looked at me with disgust and yelled at Randall. "Go ahead and do it, man. Why do you have to ask me about every little thing? Try using your head for a change." Harley gave Ms. Canada a little peck on the cheek. "People are always bothering me when I'm trying to think."

As Randall pulled off onto the shoulder of the road, his CB buddy came back. "I got you some news for that east bounder. Some kind of battle has broken out at the Arrow Head Cafe up in front of you between a bunch of Hell's Angels and some cowboys. A couple of cars are on fire and all kinds of crazy things are going on."

"Turn up the damn radio," Harley yelled, as he turned around and faced the front of the big rig.

After a long pause, the CB'er said, "There's also been a bad wreck behind you at the eighty mile marker. A wrecker, towin' an old car, pulled out in front of an eighteen-wheeler and got his ass greased. Bad stuff happening whichever way you go. Over."

When the highway patrol car screamed past, Harley ran up front and grabbed the microphone out of Randall's hand. "You've put a song in my heart today, Good Buddy. Thanks for all the good news. Over and out."

Ms. Canada walked to the front of the big rig and sat down on the couch. "That was my old rainbow car. The man driving the wrecker had to be the one who stole my motor," Ms. Canada said with a bitter-edged laugh. She laid her hand on Harley's forearm and said, "It was—wasn't it, Harley?"

Harley sat down and put his arm around Ms. Canada's shoulder. He patted her gently. "It sure sounds like it was, hon'." Then he looked at Randall and smiled. "But what it sounds like more than anything else is that the prick got paid back for what he did to you, hon'. That's exactly what it sounds like to me, and that makes me rip-roarin' happy as hell!" Harley yelled at the top of his lungs and slapped his leg.

After everyone nodded in agreement, Moon said, "I can't believe anyone would ever harm you, ma'am. I agree with Harley. It sounds as if the guy got paid back and that's cool."

Harley slipped the revolver back inside his belt and leaned against the wall. He was so nervous that his hands were shaking and his face was chalk-white. He sucked in a long breath of air and exhaled forcefully. Again and again he filled his lungs with deep breaths until he hyperventilated and stopped breathing completely. His lips turned ashen, then he began to breathe again. His color improved and his eyes showed signs of life.

He's too much like a carp to be killed off by anything so simple as a lack of oxygen, I thought to myself and shuddered.

Harley looked at Ms. Canada with a sparkle in his teary, brown eyes. "I've got something... I've got something.... " He paused to catch his breath. "I've got something important to tell you, hon'. But I need to do it in private. That's why I did that thing with the breathing. It's the only way I could get relaxed enough to talk to you about this thing."

"My God, what is it, Harley? With my luck, I bet you're going to tell me you have some incurable disease. It's not leprosy, is it? Lordy, I hope it's not leprosy."

Harley gave Ms. Canada a peck on the cheek. "It's nothing like that, hon'. It's something we both will enjoy."

"Well, okay. Let's do it then, Papa Bear." Ms. Canada laughed and bounced up off the couch.

"You better be good boys while I'm gone, you hear? I'll peek out at you from time to time to make sure you're not doing anything crazy."

After we reassured him that we would be good boys and not cause trouble, he and Ms. Canada strolled to the back of the big rig hand in hand. Harley winked at us and waved when he pulled the privacy curtain.

We looked at one another, snickered and whispered about trying to overpower Harley for a couple of minutes, then put the plan on hold because we would be rid of him soon, and there was no reason to take risks so late in the game.

"That's pathetic," Randall said, as he looked over his shoulder at Long Dog licking himself again. "Do you know why men don't lick their balls and dogs do? Because they can." We laughed quietly.

"I can see why they say you can't teach an old dog new tricks," Moon said. "Why would they want to learn?"

When the lovebirds reappeared, almost two hours later, it was as if Harley had been sprinkled with stardust and Ms. Canada was in charge of the magic wand. I watched Harley and Ms. Canada snuggle up on the couch like a couple of newborn kittens.

The love bug seemed to have rendered Harley harmless, and for the remainder of the trip from New Mexico to just outside of Springfield, Missouri. There was nothing but an endless array of vehicles, road signs and mindless miles.

Randall pointed to the Conoco service station sign twenty-five miles outside of Springfield, Missouri. "I better pull in for some gas."

"I'll call Wolff and get directions to his grandpa's farm while we're there," Moon said, as we pulled off the interstate onto the exit ramp and followed the frontage road to the service station.

Harley seemed overly disturbed by Moon's announcement about calling Wolff and eyed him suspiciously. "You mean you've never been to the farm before? You seemed to know so much about the place that I figured you'd been there a dozen times."

"No, I've never been there before and I didn't tell you I had either. Everything I know about the place, either Wolff or my girlfriend told me. But if you're worried about me calling someone to try to cause you trouble, you can listen in on the conversation.

"Hell, Harley, you can even talk to Wolff on the phone yourself, if you want to," Moon snapped back and shook his head disgustedly.

Harley threw his hands in the air. "Don't worry your furry head about it none, Moon. I planned on talking to him all along. Another thing I'm sick and tired of is having to remind you every time we get out of the big rig that we don't go anywhere unless we're in our V-formation. Hell, man, you're the damned leader. Try to assume a little more responsibility for such an important post, all right?"

Moon batted his eyes and acted as if Harley had caused him to be bum-fuzzled. "I remember, Harley. I remember. How could I possibly forget?"

In a voice that sounded as grumpy as an old dog, Harley said, "All right, everybody out and I mean everybody, except that nasty dog. I don't want him outside biting people and drawing attention to us. We do enough of that ourselves without any help."

"What's the matter, Harley? I thought Long Dog was your best friend," I said.

"Apparently, you didn't see the little weenie hike his leg and wet on my shoe when we stopped at that last rest area."

I exploded with a convulsive laugh. Then I clapped my hand over my mouth and looked away. "Sorry I didn't get to see it happen."

"You saw it, didn't you, hon'?" Harley said to Ms. Canada. "You saw him do that to me, didn't you?"

Ms. Canada gave Harley a clench-jawed smile. "It doesn't matter none, Harley. You're making a big deal out of nothing and you do that a lot. But you've got to stop, or we won't be able to stay together." She reached down and patted Long Dog on the head. "I can forgive you for almost anything, except attacking this poor little dog. Is that the way you're going to treat me after we've been together for awhile?"

Harley hung his head and in a high-pitched nasal tone he whimpered, "No."

We huddled around Moon while he pumped the gas. Then we got some snacks and sodas for the road and maneuvered ourselves away from the cash register, out the door and around the corner to a pay phone mounted on the outside wall so Moon could make the call.

They talked for a couple of minutes. Moon hung up the phone and made a surprise announcement.

"There's been a change of plans. Wolff wants us to meet up with him and my girlfriend at the front entrance to the Bass Pro Shops in Springfield at high noon."

"What for?" Harley blurted out. "Why not go to the farm from here? I don't want to go where there are a lot of people. I bet there's a bunch of them at the Bass Pro Shops. There will be, won't there, Mark?"

"Well, I think that there...."

Harley grabbed Moon by the arm and hissed, "Why didn't you let me talk to Wolff? Call him back right now and put me on the line."

Moon dialed the number, but there was no answer. "He's already headed for the Bass Pro Shops, Harley. He said he was leaving as soon as he hung up the phone. I don't know why you're so worried after all we've been through." Moon smiled and patted Harley on the shoulder. It seemed as if he sincerely cared about the old man.

Harley grumbled to himself about people always trying to pull a fast one on him. We headed back to the big rig for what I hoped would be the final leg of our journey. I looked around when I started to close the door and saw a dozen people positioned so they could peer inside the big rig.

I waved at the curious crowd and smiled as we pulled away from the pumps. "People seemed to think that our V-formation was a little strange, Harley."

Harley shrugged his shoulders. "Who cares?" Then he went on to tell us his plans once we arrived. "When we get to Deer Run, Ms. Canada and I are going to stay on the farm and live in one of the caves along the river for awhile." He looked at Ms. Canada and she rubbed his hand. "That's if Wolff's grandpa doesn't mind. Moon seemed to think that he wouldn't see anything wrong with it."

I looked at Randall, and we frowned at one another.

I breathed a sigh of relief. Even though I knew we were not out of the woods completely, I was no longer worried about the revolver, the dynamite, or violence in general. The threat of such weapons seemed to have been neutralized when Ms. Canada took the lead out of Harley's pencil. What did concern me, however, even though such an instance would be rare, was the possibility of Harley having a complete mental breakdown because of something unexpected happening, like the death of Ms. Canada, or Long Dog.

I played out a worst-case scenario in my mind, as much for my own entertainment as anything else. I knew the odds were that it wouldn't happen, but knowing Harley, it never hurt to anticipate the bizarre. Let's say that Ms. Canada and Randall jump up and head to the bathroom at the same time and they collide with each other. Ms. Canada grabs her chest, falls to the floor and suffers a fatal heart attack. The incident sends a signal to the darkest corner of Harley's mind and activates one of his far-out, warped personalities, who think Randall plotted the demise of Ms. Canada. From that point on, it would be a situation of move over Jack the Ripper—bad-assed Harley's coming through.

As we pulled off Campbell Avenue into the main Bass Pro Shops parking lot, half dozen people, who had been shopping at the Catalog Returns Outlet Store, defied a large warning sign and ran across the busy thoroughfare.

The parking lot was a full-blown vehicles galore, circle jerk, minivans, motor homes twice the size of our big rig, trucks, SUVs and pop-up campers and boats by the score. Not to mention a swarm of cars and six couples up in front of us riding big Honda Interstates and Harley Davidson motorcycles, each one of them pulling a trailer. I looked at their license plates. "Those bikers have made a long haul. They're from Canada."

A sales representative for a roller blade manufacturer was holding a demonstration clinic in a roped-off area close to the log cabin display in the southwest corner of the parking lot. About fifty people were skating around in a circle. Another dozen or so had fallen down.

We got to see the roller blade display three times as we circled around looking for a place to park.

"I'll tell you what I think!" Harley cried out, jerking his head from side to side as he watched all the confusion. He seemed more than just a little bit nervous about the crowded situation, and I was beginning to feel the same way. "I think we'd better get the hell out of here and do it right now, Randall. This is crazy, man. We're going to get run over or something."

"Just let me park in this spot for a couple of minutes and we'll talk it over, okay, Harley?" Randall said, as he pulled the big rig into a space vacated by another thirty-five-foot motor home beside the rod-and-reel repair building located next to the taxidermy shop.

"Oh, this is really nice, Randall," Harley said, as he pointed at a big red and white sign that read, No Parking, Fire Zone. "Not only do you want me to go into a place where there's so damn many people I won't even be able to breathe, now you've set me up as a subject to be arrested because we're illegally parked." Harley gave Ms. Canada a crooked-faced smile and screeched, "I'm never going to win, am I, hon'?"

Ms. Canada cupped Harley's face in her hands and looked deep into his eyes. "Nothing's going to happen to you, hon'. We're in my hometown now, remember? All I have to do is say the word and people I know will see to it that whoever bothers you will be taken care of. So just calm down, okay?"

Randall's mouth dropped open. "Holy smoke, I didn't know there was an Ozark mafia."

Ms. Canada grabbed Harley's hand and grinned. "You just hold on to me, Baby Boy, and everything will be all right."

As I stepped out of the big rig, a young man walking across the parking lot yelled to his buddy, "I'll pick you up at five o'clock in the morning and we'll float the upper part of the Finley River. Be sure you remember to bring a cooler." They waved good-bye, got into their respective 4 X 4 trucks and joined the motorized maze that was circling the building.

"People come to the Bass Pro Shops from all over the world," Ms. Canada said, sounding like a tour guide. "It's a popular stop for a lot of folks on vacation. Look at all the different license plates." Ms. Canada pointed at one from Maine, then double-stepped to catch up with the rest of us traveling in the V-formation.

As we approached the main building, Moon jumped up in the air and waved. "There they are!" he shouted. Then he jumped up in the air again and pointed at two of the most unlikely looking people I would ever have imagined living in or around a place as conservative as Springfield, Missouri.

"I wonder what all the good old boys think, brushing elbows with the likes of those two," Randall said. I smiled.

"That's quite a pair of running mates you got there, my man," I said to Moon, and everyone but Harley chuckled.

Moon's friend, Wolfgang, whom he called Wolff for short, was a nice-looking, tall, thin black man. The presence of such a stunning specimen in the sea of average white faces would have been enough to set him apart, but the bright red poncho and Abraham Lincoln top hat he was wearing assured him a lone spot in the center of attention.

When he got closer, I realized that he was a well-preserved older man, someone at least fifty, maybe more. It was a big shock. I expected a man more Moon's age, someone in his mid-twenties. I stared at him in amazement; his tie-in with Moon just did not make any sense.

Moon's girlfriend was a breathtakingly beautiful Asian woman, with long black hair that glistened in the sunlight. She had a laughing face and light tan skin the color of a golden sunset. My opinion of Moon went up ten times or more.

After hugs and kisses and introductions all around, Wolff said, "Let's go inside the store and I'll show you why I wanted you to come here instead of going directly to the farm. I don't mind telling you, I have something to show you that I'm very proud of."

"How long have you lived in Deer Run?" Ms. Canada asked, as she stepped out of her assigned place in the V-formation behind Harley and stood beside Wolff.

"I moved there from Berkeley about two years ago to take care of my grandfather after he fell off a horse and broke his hip."

"That's too bad," Ms. Canada said, sympathetically. "How's he getting along?"

"He's doing okay now and could probably get along fine without me, but I've grown really fond of being around the old guy. I've gotten really attached to the area. So I plan to hang around for some time. There's no comparison to the quality of my life since I moved to the Ozarks. You can't get much further away from the fast lane than living in a cave on the backside of a farm where the nearest road is a mile away," Wolff laughed.

As we walked toward the front door and passed a life-sized statue of Uncle Buck, who was a relative of the real-life founder of the Bass Pro Shops, I saw Harley and Wolff shoot a quick glance at one another that seemed strange. Harley had a lingering smile that made me suspicious.

Once inside the front door of the Bass Pro Shops, we walked under a flock of stuffed white doves that were headed south as fast as their stationary wings would allow them to fly. Off to the left was an out door scene that featured a mounted quail, a couple of turkeys and a cock pheasant poised as if he were about to fly. A raccoon, a badger, a red fox and a black bear flanked a big bull elk, with his head held high. At the end of the panoramic taxidermy display were two baby deer. A plaque in front of the darling little Bambis read: These fawns died at birth.

"Look at all the stuffed animals in this place, and we're not even inside the store yet," Randall said, as he gawked around.

"Specimens of taxidermy are referred to as something that has been mounted rather than something that has been stuffed," Harley said to Randall, trying to impress Wolff with his vast array of outdoor knowledge, I was sure.

Wolff gave Moon a thumbs-up and smiled. "I'm glad you're back, my friend. We've missed you a bunch. Grandpa even fixed up the little cabin out back by the spring branch so you and Blossom can hang out with us for as long as you want." He winked at Moon's girlfriend. "How does that sound to you, babe?"

She smiled at Wolff and snuggled up to Moon like a purring kitten.

"Blossom just finished her degree in elementary education from SMS College," Wolff said. "Fact is, we've been waiting for your arrival Moon, so we can have a big celebration."

"I plan to start teaching in the fall," Blossom said. "I got a job at a school close to the farm."

"Blossom," I repeated the name to myself. I was saved from drowning in her big, brown eyes by the giggles of two teenage girls behind us. I knew they were poking fun at us. I could not help imagining how quickly their attitude would change if I introduced them to our group's cast of characters.

I could have Harley twirl the bloodstained revolver around on his finger like a gunfighter in an old-time western movie. The infamous Ms. Canada could dazzle the impressionable young ladies with a couple of her daring road stories. Wolff could whirl his red cape around like a bullfighter while Randall charged him like a raging bull. Moon Love and the beautiful Ms. Blossom could stand on the sidelines and cuddle and coo. For the climax, we could station the girls up front at the head of Harley's V-formation and march to the big rig. Our mascot, Long Dog, would leap out and send people scurrying across the parking lot as he nipped at their heels.

The girls must have sensed that my mind had run amuck because they hurried away quickly when I turned around.

I've been exposed to Harley's insanity too long, I though. I smiled at the thought of us getting rid of him in the next few hours—maybe.

We walked past the information booth and ambled over to check out another nature display across from the footwear department. Wolff grabbed Moon by the arm and stopped us. "What I want you to see is over here. Follow me."

We trailed along behind Wolff to a huge freshwater aquarium the size of a swimming pool that contained numerous jumbo-sized largemouth bass and other species of fish native to inland lakes and streams.

"Is this it, man?" Harley asked. "Is this all the hell you wanted to show us?" Harley sounded disgusted.

The two of them threw me for a loop when I saw Wolff glare at Harley. "Come on, old man. Have I ever steered you wrong about anything in the past?" Randall and I gave each other a wide-eyed look. It was crazy to even think such a thing, but there sure seemed to be a connection.

How in the world could two people who seemed so completely different possibly know each other?

"Wolff, do you and Harley...?"

"You see that big fish in the corner of the aquarium?" Wolff interrupted me and pointed at a huge specimen that hugged the backside of the tank. We stepped up to the guardrail that protected the thick glass wall to get a better view. "Grandpa and I floated the James River two weeks ago and on the last cast, I...."

"Where the hell's the flathead? I don't see no flathead." A man wearing faded bib overalls and a ball cap asked a shy-looking young boy standing beside him.

We glared at him for intruding, but the guy was too obsessed with finding a flathead catfish in the tank to notice even an offbeat group of freaks like us.

When he stood on his tiptoes and craned his neck, another fish caught his eye. "There's an albino cat right there. Do you see 'em, Son?" the loudmouthed fella yelled. "That's an albino cat all right." Before the kid could say anything, the guy bellowed out again. "But where the hell's the damned flathead?"

I looked down at a muskrat mounted on a piece of sun-bleached driftwood and noticed that his shiny glass eyes were perfectly focused on the gaunt-looking guy's face. I pulled from my vast amount of experience in high school as an amateur ventriloquist and conjured up my best muskrat voice. "You're the one that's a flathead, Mister. Any muskrat can see you're nothing but an inconsiderate old man."

The guy's jaw fell open as he stared at the muskrat and the muskrat stared back. When he realized that he was the butt of a joke, his face tightened and turned red. He jerked his head around and gave each of us a careful once-over. But we maintained a sober facade and played like we were preoccupied with watching the fish swim around in the tank. When he turned around, I tapped him on the shoulder. "Excuse me, Mister. I believe that's a flathead catfish right there." I pointed at a spoonbill catfish, which looked a world apart from a flathead.

Before the guy could say anything, Randall jumped into the conversation. "It's either a flathead or a sturgeon. I have a hard time telling the two of them apart, but I know for sure it's not a shark."

The flathead man smirked at Randall, grabbed the boy by the arm and tromped off through the crowd. "Why in the world wouldn't they have a flathead catfish in the tank? They've got every other kind of damned fish except a damned flathead," he mumbled to himself as he stepped lively though the crowd.

"I caught that fish right there on the float trip and grandpa scooped it up in a net," Wolff blurted out, pointing at the big fish again.

"I didn't know you were a fisherman, Wolff," Moon said, stepping to his right for a better look at the prize specimen that hung suspended in the water under a floating log, which had been placed in the tank to provide structure for the fish.

"What kind of bait did you use?" I asked.

"I was using...."

"What the hell kind of fish is it anyway?" Harley butted in, squatting down to get an under the belly view of the prehistoric-looking thing.

"I believe that's a long-nose gar, Harley," Ms. Canada said casually. "Am I right?" she asked Wolff, and he gave her a surprised look. "From its size, I would think it might go better than twenty five pounds, which could be a record for the species—at least in Missouri."

Wolff raised his eyebrows and titled his head to one side. "You sure do know your rough fish, ma'am, because that fish right there weighed twenty-five pounds, ten ounces, and it is a Missouri record."

We stared at the prehistoric-looking creature for some time. Then everyone shook Wolff's hand, and there was a round of clapping and congratulations. The dead give away was when Harley patted Wolff on the back and said, "You always were one hell of a fisherman, Doc."

Moon's mouth dropped open, when I gave Randall a look of astonishment, he said, "What the hell's going on? Do you two guys know each other or something?"

Wolff looked at Harley and smiled. "Let's go upstairs to Hemingway's Restaurant and I'll buy us all some lunch. I've got a story to tell that I think everyone will find interesting as about anything can be."

Chapter Nineteen

The hostess seated us at a table for six across from the gigantic saltwater aquarium, which served as the backdrop for a highly polished mahogany bar. We watched the aquatic activity in the impressive enclosure and marveled at a sea turtle that cruised the full length of the thirty-foot tank, then doubled back again. It was as if he were a sentry keeping watch over the other sea creatures all trapped in the same little world. At the same time the waitress walked up to take our order, a big moray eel slithered out from behind a big rock and nabbed a bait fish that swam too close.

"Pretty classy restaurant for a fishing tackle store," Randall said to the waitress, as he looked around at the artwork and stuffed fish hung on the walls.

"Thank you," she said. "It's become quite a tourist attraction. People come here from all over the world. Are you ready to place your order?"

"Give us a few minutes, please," Wolff said, as he looked at Harley and his eyes filled with tears. "It's good to see you again, Doctor Simpson. What's it been now, my friend, fifteen years since we last talked?"

"It's been at least fifteen or maybe a little more," Harley said, his voice cracking as he wiped his eyes with the back of his hand and looked away to regain his composure. "Fifteen long and lonesome ones for me, that's what it has been for me. But it looks as if you've done okay, Dr. Pollen."

"I see you're going by a different name these days, Dr. Simpson. Let me see if I can guess why," Wolff said. "Have you named yourself Harley after the Harley Davidson motorcycle?"

Harley cleared his throat and started to say something, but Wolff motioned for him to stop so he could continue with his story.

"When I taught psychology at Berkeley from 1963 to 1968, that man right there was one of my dearest friends." Everyone gasped at the surprising news.

"What did you say?" I asked. I was watching the moray eel finish off another baitfish and thought I had surely misunderstood.

"You heard me right, Mark," Wolff said, smiling at Harley and nodding his head. "Dr. Simpson, who now calls himself Harley, was a professor of English literature at Berkeley. On top of all that, he is also a Rhodes Scholar." Wolff smiled again and looked at each of us in turn while he waited for a response.

The shock of such bizarre news stunned everyone. We just sat there stone cold sober and looked at Wolff.

Finally, Randall jumped up from the table, turning over his chair in the process. "Dr. Simpson! My God Wolff, you can't be serious. This is a joke you guys have made up to try to drive me even crazier than I already am."

"Oh, I'm serious all right," Wolff said. "Dr. Simpson and I lived in the same house across from the Berkeley campus, and we were the best of friends." Wolff winked at Harley. "I've still got the diagram of that last chess game we never finished, if you ever want to sit down and try to beat me again."

I looked at Harley as a tear slid down his cheek and he turned away.

"Good Lord, Wolff. What happened?" Ms. Canada asked. "What caused him to go from being a professor at a prestigious school like The University of California to the common criminal he is today?" She patted Harley on the arm. "No offense meant by that, hon'." Before Wolff could say anything, Ms. Canada looked away, buried her face in Harley's shoulder and began to cry.

Wolff cleared his throat and solemnly said, "Have you ever known anyone struck by lightning?" We looked at one another, shaking our heads, and no one said a word.

Harley dried his eyes with the tail of his shirt. "If I had it to do over, I wouldn't be sitting at this table right now. Because once you've been struck by a bolt of lightning heavy enough to do the kind of damage that fireball did to me, you're a whole lot better off dead."

Within seconds, there was not a dry eye to be found around the table. Even Wolff, who seemed to have everything under control better than anyone else, could not fight back the gush of tears.

The waitress walked up to the table again, then raised her eyebrows and backed away, startled. When she saw the motley-looking crew sobbing in unison she said, "I'll come back for your order later." She looked over her shoulder when she turned around and said, "I'm sorry about whoever died." Everyone nodded their head.

Wolff peered over the top of gold-wire-rimmed; glasses and gave each of us a silly grin. "She probably figured it was not a good idea to serve us food while we were crying. We might choke to death and what a mess that would be."

"All right, Harold. You either stop talking about that stupid flathead catfish not being in the tank and do it right now, or me and the kids are going straight home," a wiry-looking woman with bright red hair jumped up from a table and yelled at her husband.

"Okay, I'm sorry, Eleanor. I won't bring it up again," Harold whimpered and ducked his head.

"Lordy, Wolff. What in the world happened to my poor, unfortunate Harley anyway?" Ms. Canada asked, looking at Harley and shaking her head.

"Dr. Simpson and I were walking across the Berkeley campus one afternoon in the spring of 1968 when a bolt of lightning struck a tree about thirty feet in front of us. The good doctor here took a glancing high-voltage jolt. Lucky for him, it wasn't a direct hit."

"I beg to differ with you on that one, Dr. Pollen," Harley said. "It wasn't lucky for me at all. I would have been better off to have been put out of my misery right there on the spot." In a bitter tone of voice.

Everyone looked at Harley with unspoken sympathy. Ms. Canada stared deep into his misty, red eyes. "That's the saddest story I've ever heard. I'll do anything in the world to help make you feel better for the rest of your life, Dr. Simpson. You don't mind if I call you Dr. Simpson from now on, do you?"

Harley gave her a quick little smile that never quite reached his eyes. "That would be real sweet of you, hon'. A real sweet thing indeed."

Ms. Canada looked at each and every one of us to make sure she had our complete attention. "How about the rest of you calling Harley Dr. Simpson too from now on? As far as I'm concerned, Harley was the name of a person who has got himself up from the table and is now gone."

"I would be honored if everyone called me Dr. Simpson, sweet lady," Harley said, as he cleared his throat, wiped his eyes with the table napkin, and we nodded in agreement.

"Sorry to say, Ms. Canada, I'm not the saddest part of the story yet, ma'am." Wolff reached across the table and patted his long lost friend on the back of his hand.

Dr. Simpson smiled. "You were a good friend to me all those years before I got into bad trouble, Dr. Pollen, and my only friend after I got turned into a crispy critter. I don't know how I would have …"

Dr. Simpson got so caught up in a wave of emotion that his right eye began to twitch, and he could not finish the sentence.

The waitress walked up to our table again. "Are you ready to...?"

She stopped in mid-sentence when Dr. Simpson glanced up at her with his twitching eye, and she saw the tears streaming down his puffy red cheeks.

"Give me a sign when you want me to come back and take your order," she said. "You might keep in mind we stop serving food at 10:00 p.m." She walked away mumbling something about a man obsessed with flathead catfish and the guy with a twitching eye.

Randall looked at Wolff intently like someone who might be studying a statue of a man with a half dozen heads. "So what happened to Dr. Simpson after the lightning strike, Wolff?"

"Well, the next thing I knew, Dr. Simpson...."

"It was as if I walked into the middle of a big ball of cotton," Dr. Simpson said, interrupting Dr. Pollen. "I was surrounded by white light and my whole body felt numb. I thought I had been injected all over with a local anesthetic. Either that or I had drunk a pint of moonshine whiskey, all in one big long gulp. I'm so afraid of storms now when I hear the sound of thunder, I get really nervous. Sometimes I even throw up. Just talking about it is making me have goose bumps." Dr. Simpson held his arms out and goose bumps covered his forearms. "You boys remember how upset I got during the storm in the desert, don't you?"

I assured him we remembered how nervous he was. It was obvious why Dr. Simpson freaked out during the storm. "Is there anything that can be done to help you get over being so afraid?" I asked.

He closed his eyes as if he were saying a prayer, looked over at Ms. Canada and smiled. "The only thing I can think of that can help me I already have. It's the love of this sweet lady right here. She has given me more to live for than anything I've run across in the last twenty years." Dr. Simpson patted Ms. Canada on the arm and they looked at one another like a couple of love-struck teenagers.

Randall and I looked at one another and rolled our eyes. Dr. Pollen gave Dr. Simpson a nod and carried on with the story. "The next thing I knew, Dr. Simpson was lying on the ground. His earth shoes had been blown off and the bottoms of his feet were charred as if he had walked across a bed of hot coals."

"The rush of it all might have been an interesting experience, if it hadn't been for all of the horrible side effects," Dr. Simpson said grimly.

"What were the side effects?" I asked Dr. Pollen. Periods of insanity had to be one for sure, I was curious about some of the others, I was a lightening victim some day myself.

"Confusion, depression, memory lapse and in Dr. Simpson's case, psychosis to the extent that he would sometimes exhibit a half dozen different personalities all in one day. That's what caused him to get on the wrong side of the law. While some of the personalities were as kind and loving as anyone could be, others were quite violent in nature."

Randall and Moon looked at me, and we frowned at one another. "Yeah, we've seen a little sample of the best and the worst of Dr. Simpson's personalities during the past couple of days. Haven't we, boys?" I said.

Randall shook his head and gave Dr. Pollen a bewildered look. "What did Dr. Simpson do that caused him to be sent to prison?" He asked.

Dr. Pollen looked at Dr. Simpson for sometime without saying a word before he finally said, "He was sent to prison because he...."

"That's okay, Wolffgang," Dr. Simpson interrupted. "I'll tell them what happened the way I told it at my trial." He looked at Ms. Canada with sad eyes and started to say something a couple of times, but he could not get the words to come.

"It's okay, hon'," Ms. Canada said. "Whatever you did doesn't make one bit of difference to me, one way or the other. I'm sure you've heard the old saying 'except for the grace of God, there go I.' You're with me now, Babe, and that's the only thing in this big, cruel world that counts."

Dr. Simpson leaned over and laid his head on her shoulder for a moment before he began the heartrending story. "I was sitting in my car in front of the Berkeley student union about two months after the big lightning strike destroyed my life. I was trying to remember what it was I started out to do. I knew when I left the house, but by the time I got...."

Dr. Pollen interrupted after Dr. Simpson paused for sometime and seemed to be bogging down. "For the first couple of months after the lightening strike, Dr. Simpson's lapse in memory was so bad that he needed to reason out the procedure each time before he did something even so simple as starting the car or going for a walk around the block.

Randall giggled. "Maybe he shouldn't have been driving." Everyone in the group stared Randall down and he looked away.

Dr. Pollen started to tell his story again. "So like I was saying, even though he may have been someplace a hundred times before, Dr. Simpson had to use a road map to find out how to get there again. His memory improved considerably after the first sixty days or so, but his psychosis got progressively worse." Dr. Pollen gave Dr. Simpson a sympathetic smile. "I'm sorry, my friend. I didn't mean to interrupt, go ahead with your story."

Dr. Simpson nodded. "Anyway, I was sitting in my car and when I looked out the window, I saw a punk skin head kid trying to steal a young girls purse. I jumped out and rushed over to help her. The kid took a swing at me. I shoved him down. His head hit a rock, and he was dead instantly."

"Oh my God!" Ms. Canada moaned, almost tipping the chair over when she scooted it back from the table. She looked as if she was about to faint.

I looked around the room and everyone in the restaurant was staring at us. I reached down and picked up the Abe Lincoln hat, put it on my head and stood up. "We were having a heated political discussion, talking about the horror of prejudice and what Dr. Martin Luther King did for segregation. You all are free to join us if you want." I sat back down, removed the tall, black hat and winked at Dr. Simpson. "Please continue with your story, Professor."

"Thank you, Mark. That was a lovely speech about a topic of injustice that's near and dear to my heart. Anyway, in my mental state, I didn't realize that I had shoved the mugger down ten minutes after it happened."

"Oh my God," Ms. Canada said. "What in the world happened next?"

Dr. Simpson put his hand on her arm and squeezed it gently. "To make a long story short, hon', I was put away for killing the guy while trying to save the girl's life."

"Why didn't you claim self-defense?" Randall

"He did," Dr. Pollen said. " I retained one of the finest attorneys in San Francisco for his defense, and I even produced a half dozen character witnesses, but we lost."

"How? How could he lose?" Ms. Canada cried out, causing the people at neighboring tables to gawk at us again. I picked up the Abe Lincoln hat and held it above my head until they went back to the business of eating.

Dr. Pollen smiled at Ms. Canada. "The jury appreciated that Dr. Simpson had performed an act of valor. The attorney for the defense painted a convincing picture of Dr. Simpson's mental illness. Which he said caused a potential threat to society. They committed him to the state mental institution."

"Oh my God," Ms. Canada shouted again and her eyes filled with tears.

"The old Harley, before he became the new Dr. Simpson, told us he was framed by his brother for a murder he didn't commit and he was sent to prison for twenty years. He said that he escaped from prison and was headed for Chicago to kill his brother so he could square the rotten deal," Randall said, looking at Dr. Simpson with raised eyebrows.

"Well, I don't know about ...."

"This much I do know, Dr. Pollen. He's sitting there right now with a revolver stuffed down his pants. That's what he's been using to hold us hostage. He also had TNT strapped to his leg for the first part of our journey together. I don't mind telling you, he scared the living hell out of us.

Isn't that right, Mark?" Randall looked at me and I nodded my head.

When I did not answer Randall right away, he looked at Moon and asked him to verify his story. "Isn't that right, Moon?"

Moon nodded his head. "I'm afraid he's right about that, Wolff."

"I know I haven't been a very good boy lately," Dr. Simpson said as he turned away and stared at the sea turtle in the aquarium.

Dr. Pollen looked at Dr. Simpson and he sounded like a father scolding one of his kids. "When we leave the store, you'll have to give me the revolver. Promise me that you will."

Dr. Simpson looked at Dr. Pollen with a twinkle in his eye and smiled. "I will, old friend. I really will. You know that I never harmed anyone in my whole life on purpose, and I'm not about to start now."

"I know you never have, old friend," Dr. Pollen said, "and with everyone's help, I don't think you ever will." He winked at Ms. Canada and she smiled. "I started a lightning strike support group after your terrible tragedy and I correspond with a number of victims frequently on the internet. We even hold an annual meeting where members can get together and talk to one another about their condition; this helps them feel like they are not being looked upon as a bunch of freaks. If you got involved with a bunch of fellow lightening strike victims would help you an awful lot."

"What do we do now?" I asked Dr. Pollen,

"Well, I guess the next move is that Moon, my daughter, Blossom and I will head back to the farm. Ms. Canada and Dr. Simpson, can come along and stay with us as long as they like, and you boys are free to go on with your lives."

"Dr. Simpson and I have a nice little dog out in the big rig that we need to take along to the farm too," Ms. Canada said, and Randall laughed. "We also have some gear out there that we need to take with us as well."

The waitress attempted one more time to take our order. walked up to our table and asked if we were ready to order our food. We all decided that after our emotionally draining conversation, nobody was hungry anymore.

When we stepped outside the building into the parking lot, Dr Simpson raised his arms above his head and looked up at the wide-blue sky. "What a beautiful day to be enjoyed by all of God's creatures." He looked down at Ms. Canada and took hold of her hand. "If the Bass Pro Shops people will go along with my plan, would you consider getting married to me in front of the big fish tank sometime soon? We can take pictures with Wolff's Missouri record Gar swimming in the background."

Ms. Canada gave Dr. Simpson a kiss on the cheek and whispered something in his ear that made him blush and duck his head. We all smiled at their happiness and Moon even danced a little jig.

When we walked up to the big rig and Ms. Canada opened the door, Long Dog jumped out into her arms and gave her a tongue-licking kiss.

Ms. Canada, Long Dog, Blossom, Moon Love and Dr. Simpson got into Wolff's green and white VW bus with the red peace symbol painted on the front. We laughed when Wolff cranked open the sunroof. We heard everyone start to sing along when the sound of Sugar Magnolia drifted out of the bus. We waved goodbye to the motley crew as Randall drove us out of the Bass Pro Shops parking lot. We headed for Kansas City.

I was overcome by a rush of relief. I became keenly aware of everything around me. The sunshine was brighter and the air smelled fresher than ever before. When I glanced over at Randall and he smiled, I forgave him for all the irritating things he had done during our trip. I looked out the window and waved at a kid riding his bike. For the first time in my life, I truly appreciated the fact I was still among the living on God's green earth.

Author's Bio:

It was in the solitude of the Ozark streams, deep hollows and blue-hazed vistas that Rolland Love first became interested in writing. He grew up in the Ozark Mountains, a rugged section of the country that extends from mid-Missouri into northern Arkansas. As a boy, he lived on a spring-fed river and spent his summers helping an uncle run a float camp. Swimming, fishing and guiding fishermen down the river, he paddled wooden jon-boats that his uncle made by hand. His love for the country and people, as well as this special environment, ultimately motivated him to share his experiences with others through his writing.

Although the characters and stories are drawn from a myriad of people, tall tales and experiences Rolland has had, they could have happened anywhere in America. Much of the content of his books are based on components of a real life adventure. Rolland is the author of three novels, The Blue Hole, River's Edge and Toe Tags and TNT. He has published fictional short stories, co-written a best-selling computer resource directory, co-founded an educational software development company and is a registered respiratory therapist.